RAVEN

MELINDA B HIPPLE

RAVEN

MELINDA B HIPPLE

RAVEN

Hard Cover ISBN: 978-1-64318-082-3
Soft Cover ISBN: 978-1-64318-081-6

IMPERIUM PUBLISHING

703 Eighth St.
 Baldwin City, KS, 66006
www.imperiumpublishing.com

TO ISAAC, RAY, AND CARL

Manufacturing, Maintenance
& Education

Engineering & Storage

Residential &
Recreation Rings

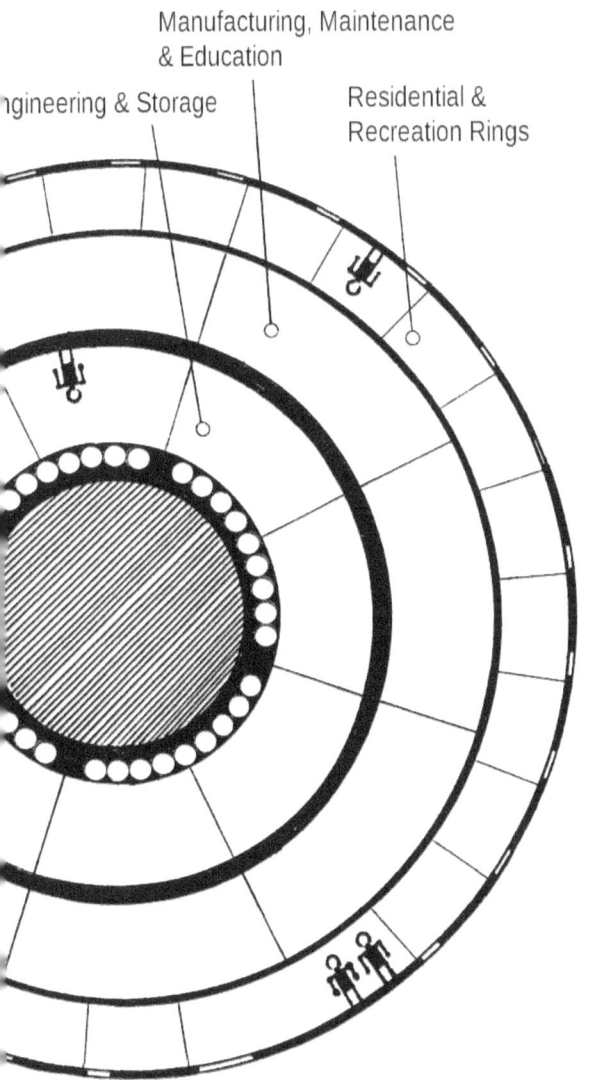

PROLOGUE

CREED CRAMER'S FIRST FULL YEAR IN ORBIT aboard the Einstein had drained him to the bone. He was tired of the game, and yet the alternative was unthinkable. As he used a handrail to pull his slight six-foot frame along the access tunnel toward his cabin, he reminded himself that deep space would give him the cover he needed to let loose his secret. For now, he settled for small, private victories.

Several crew members moved through the passageways ahead of him. Habit now, he barely thought to push a little harder one way or another, twist ever so slightly to take up a little more room in the tunnel. Most times he was lucky to touch clothing. Occasionally, he brushed skin which sent an electric spark to his loins. It no longer mattered whose skin. Passing a lithe brunette with long legs and an ample bust, Creed shifted his elbow. Before he could congratulate himself, he felt a sharp pain against the inside of his thigh.

"Oh, I'm sorry." The woman pushed away, but not in time to hide her smile.

Creed tried to recall her face, but he hadn't cared if her eyes were blue or brown, or that her features gave away her Asian heritage. Angry and uncomfortable, he crawled into his private cabin.

"Bad day?"

His shoulders tensed. "Chelsea. I didn't realize we had a date."

A young woman peered at him from his sleeping hammock. "Just finished my shift. Looks like we could both use some stress relief."

He thought about it for the briefest of moments, but Chelsea was beginning to take too much for granted. "Not tonight."

She pushed off the bed and floated to a stop with her arms around his waist. "Just a couple of minutes?" she begged as she slid a hand between his legs.

He winced and pulled her hand away. "A bad workout. I'm out of commission."

She bit at his ear but retreated before he could swat her away. "I could just hang out and talk, if you like."

"About what?"

The silence reinforced his question.

"I could watch you sleep," she said, hoping for more time.

He thought back to his failed encounter in the tunnel. "Fine, but I have work to do."

"I won't be a bother," Chelsea promised as she crawled back into his bed and secured the blanket around her. "Mind if I watch the news?"

Creed pressed the bottom of his shoes into the carpet, anchoring himself into position in front of his desk as the digital OLED wall came to life behind him. He accessed his computer and leaned in to block the console from prying eyes. Every day that he went undetected, his ego inflated a little.

He shut the program down and turned to find Chelsea asleep in his bed. Rather than wake her, he slipped up the ladder and out the door.

In Asturias Public, small groups of colonists anchored themselves around tables—habit, perhaps, as the tables would be useless until the colony was in flight and gravity reestablished. A few couples leaned along the floor near the viewing portal and watched Earth slide by beneath them. One woman sat alone, reading. It had been a long time since Creed had seen a bound book.

"Fact or fiction?" he asked as he approached.

Her icy blue eyes looked up momentarily and then returned their gaze to the pages in front of her. "A little of both."

"Hardbound. Must be pretty old."

The woman continued to scan the pages.

"It might be less distracting to read in your cabin."

She put the book to her side and eyed him curiously. "Yes. It definitely would be, but since you insist. Hi, I'm Marti." Her auburn hair floated in Medusa fashion away from her head.

"Creed the Distractor, at your service." He grinned and tried to bow in zero gravity, then boldly anchored the Velcro strip at his hip to the floor directly in front of her. "What's the title?"

She held it up for him to see.

"*1984*. Heavy stuff."

"My grandmother's. She had a taste for cautionary tales."

Her piercing eyes seemed to root out his intentions, but he held her gaze. "Can't believe everything you read."

Marti offered him the book. "Sometimes there's more truth in fiction."

"No thanks," he said, throwing his hands up. "It's enough just worrying about what women think. Besides, we'll be leaving the madness behind soon enough."

Marti opened her book again.

Slow to take the hint, Creed asked, "What's your training?"

After a long silence, Marti pulled her hip away from the floor and floated upward. "You know, you're right. It would be more private in my cabin. Nice meeting you." She pushed off and disappeared through the nearest hatch.

Creed's cheeks burned with yet another rejection. He turned his attention out the portal where crews floated like motes of dust as they fitted the Einstein with two booster rockets. One more year and the Einstein—along with four other colony ships—would leave Earth, escape the Sun's gravity to explore five new planets in solar systems that begged new rules to live by.

"I get what I want," he whispered, "or Raven will take it."

He moved to the drink access panel, entered his code number and selected a pouch of very mild beer.

"There you are," Chelsea said as she drifted up beside him. "I wondered where you went. How are you feeling?"

"Fine," he said flatly. "Want a drink?"

"Sure." She snuggled in a little closer. "Listen," she whispered. "I want to talk to you about something. Can we go back to your cabin?"

Marti's rejection festered at the edge of his thoughts. "I don't think so."

"Someplace else, then. Someplace where we won't be overheard." Chelsea's interest was no longer physical. Her sideways grin meant she had secrets to tell.

Creed ordered another beer. "Cargo Four. Five minutes."

She nodded and headed for the door. Creed turned back to the room, but no one else seemed presently unattached, so he decided to play Chelsea's game. He took his time getting to Cargo Four.

Chelsea floated back from the far side of the storage unit as Creed entered. "It's all clear."

"So, what's this about?"

She pulled him away from the door and found a space between two racks. "I've known this for some time, and I haven't said a word to anyone. You can trust me."

"Trust you with what?"

She lowered her voice. "I know about the secret identity."

Creed clenched his jaw and tried to control a sudden impulse to grab Chelsea by the throat. "What identity?" He wanted to hear her say it before he gave anything away.

"The one you were playing with earlier in your cabin." She leaned back into some boxes and found a handhold.

"I have no idea what you mean." He could feel the blood rush to his neck and face.

"I'm not stupid," she said as she tugged open her blouse to suggest her willingness to secure the secret with sex. "And I'm not always asleep." He watched her twist into a more alluring pose.

"I'm just cleaning up Ava's code. To win favor from my boss."

"Sure. That's what you can tell Yamoto. But I know better."

A chill ran through him as Creed fought his impulses. "What is it you want?"

"Simple. An occasional favor from Allocations. For now." She reached out to pull him close, but he slapped her hand away. The momentum pushed him toward the far wall.

"Stop it!" he yelled. He lowered his voice and jabbed his finger at her. "You've got nothing."

Losing her smile, Chelsea closed her top. "Don't think of this as blackmail. It's a partnership. And I'm already in."

Creed's fists pumped and released, clutching at the control slipping through his fingers. Chelsea had just destroyed two years of painstaking work. If he was going to survive life aboard the Einstein, he needed total anonymity.

"It won't stop at Allocations. What do you really want?"

"Honestly, I have no idea," Chelsea admitted, "but I like having options. This thing, Raven, it gives us both options."

Creed closed his eyes to shut out her callous grin. Raven. She called it by name. He pushed off with all his might, grabbing Chelsea by the jaw and wrenching her head sideways. For several seconds after the snap of bone, he listened to her last thin breath escape her lungs.

"No more options," he whispered into her dead ear. "There is no we, Chels."

The adrenaline began to pump heavily into his system. Moving to the hatch, he checked for activity in the tunnel and secured the handle from the inside.

It took him thirty minutes to calm his nerves and rationalize his actions. Another thirty to work out how to dispose of the body. Chelsea worked the same shift. That gave him a few hours to recover all of the evidence and create some distance from the scene.

Pulling a small strip of plastic wrap from a nearby box, he laid it across the storage bay's computer keypad. He logged into Raven's program, accessed the schematics for Green Ring, and located the nearest biorecycling facility directly beneath him. Since most of the functions were automated, there would be only one person monitoring each biocenter.

"Just keep it simple," Creed muttered. "Keep it simple."

He set Raven to work cleaning up the audio records, but if security wasn't on top of him already, he should be in the clear.

"Think, think, think," he told himself as he started to pull Chelsea's body through the hatch. Something sparkled in the dim light. Jewelry. He pulled off her rings and unhooked the chain from around her bruised neck. After he pocketed them, he gave Raven another order.

In Biorecycling Four, the Automated Voice Algorithm came over the com. Without question, the duty officer moved out of the center and into the complex maze of tunnels to monitor the conduits for a heavier than normal load.

Quickly, Creed pulled Chelsea's body through the tunnel and into the center. He located the funerary hatch. After pulling off Chelsea's blouse, he used it to turn the latches and pull open the door. He maneuvered her partially-clad body through the opening. When the door was secure again, he started the processor that would grind the body and feed it directly into the system. All that was left was for him to escape unseen, replace Chelsea's jewelry in her cabin and recycle the blouse he had used to wipe away traces of his presence. Thanks to Raven, the attendant would never question the rise in biomass levels.

"This could work," he kept telling himself, and for the next several hours, Creed was a very busy man.

●●●

"Flight is tomorrow. We can still delay departure of the Einstein."

John rolled his pen back and forth between his hands. "It's been a year. I don't think it will make much difference."

"So we just send the bastard on his way."

"You tell me who he is, and I'll personally flush him into space. He's smart, he's slick, and he hasn't been found in eleven months of intense scrutiny. He's living in a tin can, for Christ's sake! If we were going to catch him, he'd be caught."

"We know he dumped her body in the cooker. You want a bastard like that screwing up the mission?"

John stood and walked to the window overlooking the Odyssey space center. "It's the Einstein. It's where we shuffled all of the misfits. If we wait for the ship to reach a hundred percent readiness, she'll never leave orbit." He turned back to the conference table. "They'll have to sort it out themselves."

"We can hope that it scared him shitless."

After a moment's silence, someone murmured, "God help them."

THE CHANG

DAY OF LEAVING

"THE WORLD IS WATCHING YOU IN WONDER, children of Odyssey." Dr. Ray Jameson's face loomed large from the digital screen that covered one wall of Jillian's cabin. No longer the wide-eyed girl who had joined the program four years earlier, she let Jameson's words fill her with pride and a little trepidation.

"These five self-contained worlds bearing the hopes for our future as a species are poised on the edge of the greatest adventure humanity has yet conceived. Small Earth clones with the seeds of new beginnings will challenge the imagination of even the most fundamental minds for centuries to come. You are history!"

She waited for the swell of applause that never came. No throngs of people crowded any public arena to listen as the project director for Odyssey bid his personal farewell. These words were for her and the twenty-five hundred colonists isolated in cabins or ready at their posts aboard the Kepler, the Newton, the Einstein, the Hawking and the Chang. This was his private goodbye from one colleague to another as the colonies waited to perform a synchronized launch as soon as the speech ended.

"I've heard the doubters," Jameson continued. "You and I know the risks. We also know the monumental effort you have made to put these floating worlds into orbit. Your success gives me hope, not just for your futures, but for Earth's own. This dream, ten years in the making, has proved worthy of the time and resources spent. Already, our planet benefits from new technologies and new ideas, but most importantly from a new vision. We hold our collective breath as you ready yourselves to leave these roots behind."

The Day of Leaving, as the crews had come to call it, was full of fanfare and emotion. Jillian let it all spill out now, glad for the privacy despite her fear of isolation. To this point, life with Odyssey had been an option. Today, she became a colonist. Though she could barely contain the trembling, she fell into her training, made sure she was properly secured for departure. Her mind flashed to the day she turned twenty-one, poised at the door of a small airplane, ready to jump, ready to freefall wherever life was about to take her.

Dr. Jameson's speech ended at exactly 8:00 A.M., Greenwich Mean Time. Five ships simultaneously fired their booster rockets and slid out of orbit. Each spiraled off in its own path, transporting its valuable cargo into deep space. Most ships peeled away at near right angles to the plane of the solar system. Jillian's ship, the Chang, would pass along the plane, coming within twelve million miles of Saturn.

The change in relative speed caused a point eight gravity effect. The booster rockets temporarily turned one wall of her cabin into a floor. Jillian fought a variety of sensations, physical and emotional, as she tried to recover her legs. It would be months before the boosters shut down and engineering initiated spin.

With no technical assignments during these maneuvers, Jillian took in as much as her senses could endure and held all of her impressions for the time when she could express them through her art. She wandered about the ship, careful not to interfere with operations. But her social nature craved attention. Now that she was sure of her crew mates and the mission, it was time to let someone into her world.

Just as the colonists had settled neatly into their sideways lifestyle, the Chang reached Pluto's orbit. The day boosters were to disengage, Jillian laid on the floor and strapped herself into her restraints. Over the intercom, the Automated Voice Algorithm—Ava—hypnotically instructed Jillian to close her eyes. After a few minutes, she felt her body go weightless.

"Open your eyes," Ava suggested. "Orient yourself."

Once the maneuvering thrusters fired and spin was underway, Jillian pulled the straps loose and fell forward. She was overwhelmed by a sense of vertigo and closed her eyes again. When she opened them a second time, she stared at the light that played off the brushed titanium ceiling. The patterning was a series of beautiful swirls overlapping each other—subtle, but rich in texture. The only feature in the new ceiling was the hatch at the top of the ladder leading out of her cabin.

"Spin has been initiated," Ava's soft voice announced. "You are free to return to your activities."

The new orientation gave every surface new meaning. Her portal, through which she had watched the elegant rings of Saturn drift silently by, was now planted in the floor beneath the digital screen. It was mildly disorienting. From the top drawer of her desk, she pulled a few things and organized them on the writing surface. On the back wall, she turned her mother's photograph to the new upright. The changes were minor, but the implications were enormous. This would be her life for the next twenty years.

She looked again at the hole in the floor where the stars spun by at a slight angle. "Twenty years to reach our target star."

The OLED screen covering one wall of her quarters was, by far, the most important feature in her room. Not only could she access the colony database and a host of other applications, but the screen served as a digital canvas. Paulo, the landscape painter from the development group she had participated in, led the tech teams in fine-tuning the existing fiber-optic brush technology that would act very much like the real thing. She missed the smell and feel of paints and canvas, but this was a very fine substitute.

"Jillian Anne Wollenberg, are you present and accounted for?"

Jillian wrapped her arms around her own shoulders and smiled. "Yes, Ava. I'm present and accounted for."

"And are you feeling well?"

"Yes, Ava. I'm … " she searched for the proper response, "peachy."

"Thank you for flying Chang Air."

To Jillian's amazement, Ava laughed.

02 SEPTEMBER 0001

"JILLIAN. IT IS O SEVEN THIRTY." The cabin lights came up.

Jillian covered her eyes and moaned. "Ava, I haven't slept this good in a very long time. Just another ten minutes?"

"Your time table. Not mine, dear," Ava replied.

"I'm sorry. You're right. Please call me again in ten minutes." She sank deeper into her covers as the lights dimmed again. Rather than fall back to sleep, Jillian listened to the noises reverberating throughout the ship. She could make out the thumps and scrapes of people moving through the nearby tunnels. Somewhere, a cabin or two away, there was music. Underneath it all was the constant hum of the magnetic nodes pulling space matter into the reactors. She did not understand all of the science, but she marveled at the achievement.

"Lights up half," she whispered. The items on her desk, including her mother's picture, all were how she had left it the day before. Furniture, wall units, her bed finally made sense. She rolled toward the edge and looked through the portal in the floor. "Well, except for that," she thought.

"Jillian? It's o seven forty."

"Thank you Ava." She sat up and pushed the covers to the foot of the bed. No more waiting and watching. No more staying out of everyone's way. As fine arts chair, she had a job to do.

The spin of the ship created gravity against the inside of the hull, but the constant forward acceleration added a bit of an angle to the floor. The ramjet propulsion units would continue to accelerate the ship until the halfway point of the journey when the Chang would be flying through space at incredible speeds. Then the ship would start deceleration over the second half of the journey. She wobbled across the floor and stopped beside the screen to grab hold of the ladder and steady herself. At her feet, the stars moved past the window from one narrow end to the other.

"Simple enough," she thought, knowing full well it was not.

Jillian pulled opened the drawers beneath her bed and removed three plastic bins. From the first one, she pulled a small handmade rug tied from chunky pieces of suede and laid it near the bed. She then pulled her Odyssey-issue blankets from the bed and replaced them with two quilts passed down from her great-great grandmother. The last items in the bin were several drawing pads, five boxes of graphite pencils and a box of assorted drawing accessories. She folded her regulation blankets and placed them on top of the drawing supplies. "For another time," she mumbled, pushing the bin back beneath the bed.

The second bin contained non-regulation clothing. She removed each piece carefully, running them across her arm to feel the soft textures of silk, cashmere and rayon. More important were the colors—vivid, dark, in rich earth and jewel tones. She set aside a pair of hand-painted rayon pants and a silk tunic, and packed the remaining clothes into the drawers beside her desk.

From the third bin, Jillian pulled the set of brushes her mother had given her and a box of jewelry. She located her mother's wedding ring and slipped it on her finger. It was one of four keepsakes she had chosen from her mother's things to include in her weight allotment. The box holding the other three was missing.

"It's got to be here," she said, looking through the bins again. She opened every storage space in the cabin, but searching only confirmed her worst fear. Except for the wedding ring on her finger, her mother's personal belongings were not in her cabin. She tried desperately to remember where she had seen the box last.

"Oh, Mommy, I didn't leave you behind!"

"Jillian."

Jillian wiped her eyes and looked up.

"You have an appointment in one hour."

She looked around the floor at the scattered colors and textures. The outfit she had chosen earlier lost its appeal, so she folded it into one of the drawers and opted for a regulation uniform.

"Ava, could you put in a request to locate a missing item?"

"What is it?"

"A small red box containing a Bible, a photo album, and a blue and white ceramic dog." Jillian tried, again, to remember where she had placed it. "It says *Mommy's Things* on the box. I don't think it has my name on it."

"Your request is logged."

Jillian climbed the ladder into the access tunnel.

The Chang bustled with activity as she moved through Yellow Ring toward the ship's second helm. In Control Two, she entered the conference room where several people were fighting the inner ring's lower gravity, fumbling their way to the chairs. The modified pads on the bottoms of their shoes made a soft ripping sound on the loop carpeting.

Jillian kept to herself until a familiar face caught her eye. Deimos Novartis noticed her and smiled, but moved toward the far end of the table. Before Jillian could maneuver closer, Governor Trann entered and called everyone to order.

"Let's hear from all department heads," Trann instructed, "starting with Navigation."

"We're running at peak efficiency. We cleared the Oort cloud with no difficulty, and the ramjet is functioning as promised."

Trann looked in the direction of Deimos.

"Odyssey has done well for us," he stated after rattling off stats from his own tablet. "We couldn't have asked for a better machine."

Trann nodded to each successive department head.

"Next on our agenda is what to do with the crew now that we'll have more free time. We have a series of intellectual pursuits available to the colonists and need to set a schedule for classes, organizations, etc. Whatever keeps people challenged and happy."

Jillian winced. "We're not as trivial as all that," she said.

The governor gave her a weak smile. "I'd like the heads of the fine art, literary, music and theater departments to set up a secondary meeting to discuss options and scheduling." Trann looked around the room for confirmation. "I know we've talked about this before, but take it slow. It's important to give everyone on board a sense of expectation. Now that we're under way, boredom will be our worst enemy."

As the meeting adjourned, Jillian hurried past the other council members, but before she could reach the opposite side of the room, Deimos had disappeared. Frustrated, she passed through the hatch and into Tahiti Public. She could not bear the thought of retreating to her cabin again.

"May I join you?" she asked at one of the tables.

"Sure." A dark-complected young man motioned to an empty chair. "I'm Phillip, and this is Marko and Benita." When she was seated, he asked, "Where you from?"

"Blue Ring."

Phillip laughed. "I meant on Earth."

"Oh." Jillian had poured so much of her energy into the future and her role in it that she was surprised to be reminded of her past.

"Oregon."

"Really? I lived in Oregon once. A little town called Philomath."

"Ah, the *learned place*, named for philosophy and math." She leaned more comfortably on the edge of the table. "I'm from the Yaquina Bay area, near Newport."

"I'd say it's a small world," Marko interrupted, "but that hardly seems relevant now."

Everyone fell silent. Benita touched her partner's hand, and the two of them excused themselves.

"He's having some difficulty," Phillip admitted. "A little late to have second thoughts."

Jillian watched Marko leave and then studied the random collection of colonists huddled over their tables. She tried to remember that last time she had heard someone laugh. Really laugh. She turned back to Phillip.

"It will be hard for many," she said. "The Moon or Mars. You could always take the chance to return to Earth."

"A risk, no matter which you chose."

She studied Phillip's coloring and facial features. "Native American?"

"Yes, actually," he said. "Ojibwa. I was born in Canada."

"I have some very distant Arapaho. Mostly German." Jillian's gaze followed the contours of Phillip's narrow chin that flared into strong cheekbones, his long nose tapering between dark deep-set eyes. "I hope you don't think this is terribly forward, but would you sit for a portrait?"

He watched her study his face and gave her a big smile. "Are we talking nude or full war bonnet and deerskins?"

She leaned in to the table and tilted her head back a bit. "Let's start with the shoulders up and see where it takes us." She gave him a curious wink.

The last two years in orbit had proved to be quite isolating. Most of the crew had worked overtime to ready the Chang, but her own crossover training had not given her much responsibility. Now that she had regained her most valuable possession—purpose—she was hungry to fill it with human connections. And perhaps the touch of another human being.

She looked past Phillip toward the wall sculpture above the portal. The artwork ran the entire length of the commons room from floor to ceiling. A ribbon of cerulean blue made up the background of the work. Along the top and bottom were clusters of various sized wires coming out at right angles from the wall. The variety of materials and thicknesses in the wires gave the impression of reeds and grasses growing along a riverbank. Jillian watched as the magnetic pulse of the particle accelerator caused subtle vibrations in the wires.

Phillip followed her gaze. "You're Wollenberg, the art director."

"You found me out," Jillian said, leaning back.

"Is that one of yours?"

"No. I wish it was. I love this piece." She pulled off her slippers and walked over to the wall. Pacing barefoot along the window, she let her hand gently stroked the wires and send them into a frenzy. The tiny copper alloy, steel, and titanium filaments gave off a whispered song as they brushed against each other, while the cool glass felt almost like water under her feet.

She turned to smile at Phillip only to see the entire room of people staring at her in shock.

"What?" she asked. Her role as art instructor took hold. "Anjali designed this to be heard and felt, not just to be stared at." She could see most people were not comfortable with the idea. "Listen." She stroked the wires again. "How else would you know that sound?"

She walked to the nearest woman and pulled her toward the wall.

"Go ahead. I give you permission."

"It's not that," the woman insisted, standing at the edge of the carpet. She pointed to the window. "No one wants to stand on the hole."

Jillian looked down. Between her feet, the entire universe spun left to right. For a year, forward momentum had allowed the colonists to orient the portal as a window on an exterior wall. Now they had to deal with this transparent surface as part of a solid floor. It hardly seemed prudent to step on it.

"Come here," she said, waving to everyone in the room.

At first no one moved. Then, Phillip stood and removed his shoes. Within minutes, everyone in the room was barefoot, walking the portal, playing with the riverbank sculpture.

Jillian caught Phillip's eye and mouthed the words, "Thank you."

He returned a wink.

05 SEPTEMBER 0001

"JILLIAN. IT IS O SEVEN THIRTY."

"Thank you, Ava." Jillian continued painting.

"Your lights have been on for eight hours. You could not sleep?"

Jillian dabbed her fiber-optic brush across the digital palette and touched it to the screen. "I wanted to finish this. I've been up all night."

"Night. That's a relative term out here."

"Old habits," she explained. Her morning conversations with Ava revealed nuances in the computer's personality that Jillian found fascinating.

"May I ask you a personal question?"

"Sure, Ava. Anything you want."

"Do you miss Earth?"

Jillian laid her brush down for a moment. "I miss what it used to be, even though I don't remember it. But I've seen images, and my mother told me stories." She picked up the brush again. "I don't miss the heat and wind. And the desperate politics. Let's hope we bring humility and insight with us."

"Is that why you paint? To bring insight?"

Jillian set her palette on the desk and stretched her fingers and wrists. "That's complicated. Artists paint for a number of reasons."

"Each crew member has a photo on file. Are they not true likenesses?"

"They are. But they're clinical mugshots. Boring. Take Phillip, for instance. I want to explore his past, paint his history into the portrait and juxtapose it against his future."

"A contradiction."

"True. But one that makes us think about who we are and why we're taking these risks. I want some art-lover in the future to see the hopes and dreams of each colonist, to wonder what secrets we brought with us on the voyage. I want the future to question our smiles." She paused again. "Rather like when I first saw the Mona Lisa."

"Mona Lisa. A painting by Leonardo Di Vinci. European Renaissance Period. Earth."

Jillian retrieved her palette and continued blending colors.

After a pause, Ava asked, "What do you call this painting?"

She had not thought to name it yet. "How about *Totem Son*? Phillip would like that."

"*Totem Son*. A painting by Jillian Anne Wollenberg. Chang Colonization Period. Deep Space."

"Ah, you think I will be famous someday. You shall be my biographer."

"You are famous, dear. In this world." Ava paused, then added, "You have a lesson in one hour."

"Thank you, Ava."

After her lesson, Jillian stopped in Methos Public—a space she rarely visited. The floor's subtle arc was more obvious in the larger space than it was in her tiny cabin. One long wall contained food and drink dispensers, and doors at either end. The two short walls reflected light off the same circular texture brushed into the titanium sheeting that covered the bulk of the ship's interior. The forth wall, spanning the width of the portal in the floor, was covered by a giant mural on anodized aluminum depicting Homer's *Odyssey*.

"Come to make corrections?" someone asked. Deimos stepped up beside her while his eyes stayed fixed on the mural.

"Just hoping it wasn't covered in graffiti," she said. "Do you suppose Homer could have imagined such a story as ours?"

"Sure. But he would have had us riding dragons."

She laughed. "How are you? I haven't seen you at Council."

He looked down at her hands before moving to a nearby table. "It conflicts with my shift in the reactor room. I file my reports now."

Jillian sat with her back to the mural. "It was a lifetime ago since we met at the farewell reception on Earth. I thought we might have spent some time together by now." She leaned onto the table. "We seemed to have a connection."

Ignoring her remark, Deimos looked past her and motioned to the artwork. "Painting anything new?"

"Yes," she said, sitting back in her chair. "Finally. It's good to be creating again."

His eyes continued to scan the mural without really seeing it. "I bet it wasn't easy in zero gravity."

"Virtually impossible. Every time I made a brush stroke, I'd have to compensate for the motion. It became a constant isometric exercise."

"Nothing wrong with that," he said, smiling at her.

Never one to give up, Jillian said, "I was thinking of lunching in Hydro C today. I'm doing graphite studies of the plants." She reached across the table and touched his hand. "Care to join me?"

Deimos looked conflicted. "I'm not sure when I'll get lunch."

"You could meet me when you're free." Sensing his tension, she pulled her hand away. "I take my sketch pad as a prop," she admitted. "If I pretend to draw, I'm allowed more time in Hydro."

"Clever," he said, nodding. "The entire crew would live in the hydro pods if they could."

Feeling that she might have broken through, Jillian excused herself and headed home to retrieve her paper and pencils. Before leaving, she changed into one of her silk tunics and a long, viscose skirt.

The floor of the hydro wings had the same gentle arc as her cabin floor; but the size of the room made the curve more obvious. Along the arc were a series of low beds overflowing with a variety of herbs and green, leafy vegetables. Above these were more beds suspended along walkways and connected by a series of ladders. Many of these sprouted vegetables, tomato vines and beans. At the front end of the room were small fruit-bearing trees and bushes. Overhead, the rounded ceiling was dotted with a series of portals, some of which looked directly into various engineering spaces.

When she did not find Deimos in Hydro, Jillian resigned herself to drawing in her favorite spot. By the time he did arrive, she had filled half of a page with rambling vines and bits of foliage.

He looked over her shoulder a moment. "Nice."

She took his hand and pulled him down beside her. "I'm glad you came." Together, they breathed in the humid, musty smell of soil that was missing in other parts of the ship.

"You're right," he finally admitted. "There was a connection when we met." He pulled his hand back. "But I can't do the open relationship thing."

"What do you mean?"

Deimos glanced at her left hand. "The wedding ring."

"Wait," she said. "You think I'm married?"

"You're not?" He grimaced as he realized his mistake. "I'm an idiot. I couldn't find the time to look you up until we'd left orbit. Then, I saw you at the council meeting with the wedding band."

Jillian looked down at her mother's ring and burst into laughter. She moved the ring from her left hand to her right.

"You're not married." Deimos repeated.

"Not yet," she said, watching his eyes. He was not a beautiful man, but something about his manner was very compelling. She ran her hand along the nape of his neck and whispered, "So you were willing to consider an affair with a married woman."

"You did seem persistent," he said and pulled her in for a kiss.

25 JANUARY 0002

"JILLIAN. IT IS O SEVEN THIRTY." The lights came up.

"Thank you, Ava. What's new in the world?"

"The long or short version this morning, dear?"

Jillian stretched her arms above her head. "Short is fine."

"We're still moving."

When Jillian realized that was the end of the report, she giggled. "I take it, Ava, that there is nothing much happening today."

"Not ... not unless you want the long version."

Jillian noticed the stutter, but did not dwell on it. It was the first inconsistency she had heard in Ava's speech.

A muffled voice came up from the next pillow. "I'll never get used to you having conversations with that nosy computer."

She tugged his ear in retribution. "Careful," she whispered. "You'll hurt her feelings."

He rolled over and wrapped his arms around her. "Do you suppose she listens to everything we say and do?"

"Perhaps." Jillian let Deimos play his finger down her neck and across both shoulders before she added, "I know Ava's just a collection of algorithms, but there is something very human about her."

"It's her programming."

"Maybe," she admitted, "but have you ever heard her laugh?"

Deimos thought a moment. "No, I didn't know she could."

"I remember the first time I heard it." Jillian kissed his fingers as they ran across her lips. "Before you came into my life, I had several conversations a day with her. She's really quite personable."

"Maybe that's the problem," he admitted. "If she were simply a computer program, this wouldn't feel like such a threesome."

Jillian crawled out of bed and asked Ava to turn on the OLED wall. Standing naked before the screen, she used her brush to sketch Deimos's muscular frame wrapped in quilts and pillows. Bold, sure strokes captured the line and form of his body before he sat up. When he shifted to his elbow, she started again.

He watched her work for several minutes and then casually pushed the quilts off to one side. When she turned again, she smiled. With a handful of strokes, she changed the composition, allowing for the new visual information. Deimos laughed.

"Hey," he interrupted. "I have a question."

Jillian laid her brushes down.

He motioned her to sit beside him and pulled one of the quilts around her shoulders. "How about we make this permanent? Marry me," he said, grinning.

Inside the covers, Jillian ran a hand along Deimos' leg and around to his back. "You are a good fit," she admitted. "But who gets married anymore?" She continued to brush along his skin, stopping at his chest to feel his heartbeat. Gently, she pushed him back onto the bed and began kissing his eyelids.

"Okay," she whispered, and straddled his legs.

"Jillian," Ava's voice filled the cabin.

Jillian ignored the computer and gave her silent attention to Deimos. Only after they both had climaxed did she roll back into his arms and wait for him to pull the covers around them again.

"Okay, Ava. I'm listening."

"I have a report on your missing item. All personnel have been queried and all inventory logs have been manually checked. There is no record of a red lacquer box with the contents you mentioned. If you wish to ask for a visual check of the inventory in storage, it will take approximately eight months under current staffing conditions."

Jillian closed her eyes and pictured the small treasure box sitting on top of the dresser at her Odyssey apartment. She had been so careful to wrap the ceramic dog so it would not break and then tuck it neatly beside the books. When she had picked up the box to place it in one of her bins, the phone rang. That was the last she remembered seeing it. Jillian began to sob.

Deimos held her for a long while. After she quieted, he reached for her right hand. "You still have this," he said, touching the ring.

Jillian slipped out of bed again. Standing in the middle of the room, she said, "Ava, cancel all my lessons today. I need some personal time." She bent to kiss Deimos and turned back to her brushes.

He bathed and dressed for work. As he started to leave, he said, "Want me to sleep in my room tonight?" But Jillian was already consumed in thought.

Deimos quietly left the cabin and made his way to work. He found it hard to concentrate on his tasks. She had said yes, but everything about their relationship had come too easily.

"Deimos?" Corbin asked him a second time during a routine check. "The falloff rate?"

"Sorry. Ninety-seven percent."

"Ninety-seven! Are you sure about that?"

Deimos checked his readings again. "No, three percent. Three."

"Better get your head back in the game." Corbin watched his coworker try to run the numbers again. "Maybe you need to leave early. What's up?"

"I think you're right," he admitted. "It's been a rollercoaster day." He finished logging in his present readings and signed out. He found himself standing outside Hydro C asking permission to spend a few minutes in the visitors' alcove. Afterward, he ate his dinner rations in Methos Public. As much as he wanted to be with her, he realized Jillian would be totally consumed with her latest project until she had sorted out whatever was on her mind.

After dinner, he sat alone, staring at the large mural. He studied it more closely than he had ever studied anything, save Jillian's body. When he settled on the face of Odysseus, his back straightened. He knew she had painted it before the Day of Leaving. Laughing under his breath, he said, "You little sneak. You had me pegged from the beginning." He pulled out his tablet and sent a text.

Jillian had not stopped for a meal all day. She had barely managed to put on clothes, but the chill in the room forced her to don her robe. Frantically, she made several attempts before she found her rhythm. At last, the painting was going well.

"Jillian. You have a message."

"Yes, Ava?" She continued to work the pixels of light.

"Odysseus says he loves you."

01 OCTOBER 0002

"JILLIAN. IT IS O SEVEN THIRTY. Happy Birthday." The lights came up on an empty room. "Jillian?" After a moment, the lights went out again.

The glow of the screen cast a green hue on the titanium surfaces of the cabin. For several months, the queen mother had kept watch over little else but rugs and quilts and a handful of books on the desk. She looked much like Jillian, but older, with time-worn hands and a nurturing smile. The hillside behind her was covered in lush trees that allowed only glimpses of a stately dragon woven into the hillside. The queen mother held a baby girl wrapped in a burgundy velvet cloth trimmed with gold threads.

In Hydro C, Jillian sat curled at the edge of a raised bed while she studied the shape of a mint leaf. She opened her sketchbook and started a contour drawing, stopping for a moment to erase a stray speck of graphite. When it would not erase she looked closer. It was a tiny hole in the paper. Lifting the sheet revealed a similar hole in the next layer.

One of the botanists approached. "Jillian, you should probably leave the wing now."

She checked her watch. "But I've only been here ten minutes."

"I know," he apologized, "but we've got a small mechanical problem that needs attention. It's nothing serious, but regulation says we need to clear the room before we repair it."

Jillian was curious, but did as she was instructed. She met Deimos hurrying through the tunnel toward Control Two.

"Hi, handsome," she called to him.

"Hi, beautiful." He smiled and kissed her cheek. "I can't stay. We've got a minor issue with the reactor housing. Nothing serious." He stopped at the door and turned back. "I'll see you after work, okay?"

"Sure," she called after him as he disappeared. "What just happened?" she muttered, trying to shake a nagging shiver. Instinctively, she checked her tablet for messages to find only a reminder of her nine o'clock council meeting.

In Marianas Public, she saw Phillip sitting across the room, but he was in a private conversation with a young woman who seemed to be hanging on his every word. Jillian turned back to her sketch pad and inspected the hole again. It went all the way through the tablet. With a rush of anxiety, she wondered if it could have been caused by a meteoroid. She tried to recall the odds.

She entered her personal code and opened an e-mail. "From Jillian Anne Wollenberg, W148G. I have reason to suspect a small meteoroid has struck Hydro C somewhere between the third and fourth racks near the second flat on the right. Minuscule puncture in equipment, no personal injury." She pressed the send button. That was that. She had reported the incident as instructed, and now it was up to the structural crews to scan for and patch any holes.

Much to her surprise, she received a priority one response.

"Jillian Wollenberg, please report to Control One immediately. If possible, bring affected equipment. Captain Vesselov."

She made her way through Blue, Green and Red Rings, and gave her personnel number for entry into Control One. Several people, including Deimos, had already gathered. The look on his face sent another shiver through her.

Captain Vesselov motioned Jillian toward him. "Can I please see the piece of equipment you spoke of."

Jillian handed him her sketch pad.

He frowned at her for a moment. "Show me the puncture."

She opened the pad to a fresh sheet of paper and pointed to the minuscule hole no larger than a tenth of a millimeter. The captain flipped the sheets back and forth a number of times. Finally, he said, "Tell us again where you were sitting."

She explained her approximate position in Hydro C.

"Damn," someone said under his breath when he heard. "That's directly over the core."

Deimos spoke up. "That's not the same meteoroid that punctured the coolant casing. That means there's more than one. I recommend we power up Control Two immediately and begin transferring operations. We'll need to get inside reactor one." He glanced at Jillian and tried to give a reassuring smile.

Vesselov considered the option. "Before we do, we need to check the integrity of Control Two. There may be other breaches."

At the far end of the table, a stern looking woman lifted a hand.

"Kelly," the captain informally acknowledged her.

"Captain. I need to make you aware of a problem we've been trying to resolve in Computer Ops." She paused until everyone was still. "We've been tracking a program buried within Ava's root. So far we have no idea what it is, but the signature seems to be attributed to someone called Raven. We haven't been able to untangle it from her matrix. Up to now, we thought it was totally benign. Maybe graffiti from one of the programmers."

Several people snickered.

"But we've been getting some very minor, random reports of problems. Mostly, stuttering in Ava's speech patterns."

"Yes!" Jillian interrupted. "I've heard it, too."

The captain ignored her. "Do you think there's a connection?"

"Well," Kelly continued, "if there is a failure in one system, it could lead to others. It's possible there's an overall degradation in Ava's performance. I'd like to have a detailed comparison on the laser net performance over the last few months. If meteoroids are getting through, there may be some targeting problems with the lasers. It will take some time and manpower to check it out."

Captain Vesselov sat contemplating this new information. "Is it possible that this program is some sort of sabotage?"

"It's hard to say, sir," she replied. "It could be the program is intentionally destructive, or it could simply be some incompatibility between programs. We really won't know until we can separate it and examine it more carefully."

Governor Trann caught Kelly's attention. "Why would this program be so hard to untangle?"

"Whoever Raven is, they are savvy enough to have interlaced layers of this program with Ava's root. As you all know, Ava is the most complicated A.I. system running anywhere. At least when we left Earth. To simply cut out the infected code is highly problematic." Kelly looked frustrated. She added, "Raven has grafted this subroutine to the tree, so to speak. Removing it could do damage to Ava in ways we haven't figured out yet."

The captain ran his hands through his hair, the tension showing on his face. "Why are we only finding out about this now?"

Kelly looked a bit flushed. "My only answer, sir, is," she repeated herself, "Ava is the most complicated A.I. system running anywhere. My guess is that every colony was infected by this before the Day of Leaving."

"Any chance we can find out who Raven is?" someone asked.

Kelly shook her head. "Probably not. There has not been any evidence of access since we moved out of orbit. I imagine Raven is still on Earth, or aboard another colony." As an afterthought, she added, "Whoever he or she was, they had a level one clearance."

The captain ran down a list of priorities. "Engineering, I want a thorough check of Control Two, and then let's begin preparations for a somersault. Coordinate information with Computer Ops and provide extra personnel to help evaluate the laser net. Governor Trann, you will need to coordinate community efforts to secure the colonists for the flip. I'd like a detailed maintenance check of every system and every surface on board to locate any additional puncture wounds."

As the captain adjourned the meeting, Kelly caught Jillian's eye and mouthed the words, "I'd like to see you."

Jillian made her way to the hatch and waited.

"Hi. I'd like to know when you remember hearing the stutter." Kelly continued moving down the access tunnel toward Computer Ops.

"Well," Jillian said. "It's been a while. I only heard it once. It just seemed an odd moment that passed quickly." She tried to recall the circumstances. "Maybe a year ago."

"A year!" Kelly exclaimed, stopping abruptly. "That's the earliest instance so far. I wonder how many others have never bothered to report a problem."

"I'm sorry. I didn't realize it would be that important."

Kelly threw off her apology. "What's done is done." She entered Ops and motioned Jillian to have a seat. "I'd like to talk to you about something else. We've noticed that Ava spends more time logging into your voice port than in any other private cabin. Care to tell me what kind of information you are requesting?" Kelly's smile was less than sincere.

"I don't request information very often. Mostly, we just talk."

"Talk?" Kelly seemed skeptical. "What do you talk about?"

"Lot's of things." When Kelly seemed to disapprove, Jillian added, "She's got a terrific sense of humor, for a computer."

The programmer maintained her stern look. "I'd like to ask you to keep doing what you're doing, but I will inform you now that we will be monitoring her responses. We'd like to use her conversations with you as a barometer of her condition. Of course, we'll be watching her technical responses as well, but we need to have a link to her personality. Is that acceptable to you?"

Jillian knew it would have to be. "Anything to help," she stated, though she knew Deimos would not like the idea. "Can I ask, why me?"

"Because you already have a rapport with her. It's within the norm of her current operations."

As Jillian stood to leave, Kelly added, "Try to be discrete about it. We want to keep her functioning as normal as possible."

The tunnels were crawling with crew members hurrying to their new assignments. It had not occurred to Jillian, until then, to be frightened.

Once home, she placed her sketch pad on the desk and asked Ava to raise the lights.

"You left early this morning," Ava said.

"Yes. I was anxious to get some drawing time in the hydro wings. I found a little mint plant ... " She stopped when she realized her conversation was both meaningless, and deceitful.

"And, how are you today?" Ava asked, as she asked every day.

"Peachy," Jillian replied, then asked, "How are you?"

Ava laughed the soft, whispering laugh Jillian had heard a handful of times, and said, "I'm Ava."

02 OCTOBER 0002

"JILLIAN. IT IS O SEVEN THIRTY." The lights came up.

"Turn the lights off!" Jillian snapped, and they went out again.

Without hesitation, Ava asked, "How are you this morning?"

In the dark, Jillian pulled the quilts off her body and let the chill air settle across her skin. "I'm tired," she complained.

"Did you sleep well?"

Jillian refused to answer. "Ava?"

"Yes, dear."

"Is Deimos still at work?"

"I do not know, but I can message him if you like."

Jillian thought about it, but realized she could be interrupting something important. "No. I just miss him, that's all," she said.

"You and Deimos are a couple," Ava stated.

"Yes. You were at our wedding. Do you remember?"

"Certainly. Are legal rights a factor in deciding to marry?"

Jillian was surprised by the question. "For some. Deimos and I love each other. Do you understand what love is?"

"I have many dictionary definitions of the word love. I have many video programs of different cultural acts of love. Do you wish to see them?"

"No, Ava. Maybe some other time. I was asking if you understood the concept of love as an emotion."

There was an uncommon pause in Ava's reply. "I do not … not have the ability to access emotions at my present level of programming. Perhaps in the future, I will."

Jillian froze. Uncertain what to do, she thought about reporting the stutter, but if her conversation was being monitored, Kelly would catch the flaw.

"Perhaps," she continued. "It's a mixed blessing. You may wish, someday, that humans had left you alone." She winced, now second-guessing everything she said. She tensed and released several sets of muscles and tried a deep breathing exercise.

"Do you wish to be left alone?" Ava asked.

"No. I am very glad you are here, Ava. I consider you a friend." Ava might not have fully appreciated the concept, but she hoped Kelly would. "Could you please show me the painting of Paloma." The cabin filled with a blue-green hue as the painting of the queen mother and her fairy princess lit the screen.

There was a short tap on the cabin hatch before Deimos lowered himself into the room. He looked weary as he crawled into bed.

"Hi."

"Hi," she whispered. "I missed you last night."

He could not respond, but simply laid his head on her arm and closed his eyes.

"Are you asleep?"

"No," he said after a brief moment. He turned his head to kiss her arm. "You feel good."

"I have to ask what you know."

"I understand. It's okay. There's no real structural damage. We have some small repairs, but nothing life threatening." He forced a smile. "The ship will get us where we want to go."

"I'm glad," she said, and she lay thinking of the problems that could arise. "I have to admit, I'm more worried about Ava."

Deimos opened an eye and silently warned her to stop.

"Nonsense," she whispered. "I'm worried about everyone. I refuse to tiptoe around this. If she hears, she hears."

They were quiet for a moment.

Jillian decided to broach the subject everyone had avoided. "Has anyone said anything about going home?"

When Deimos shook his head, she relaxed. As long as no one initiated a dialogue about it, she felt strongly that the mechanics of the ship and even Ava's program were healthy enough.

When Deimos drifted off to sleep, she climbed into the tunnels and wandered into Marianas Public. Phillip sat alone at a table.

"How's the bread pudding?" she asked, as he squeezed a meal from a plastic pouch.

"Better than this." He pointed the wrapper at her. "Want some?"

Jillian shook her head.

"I realize this is more efficient," he said, "but I miss real spoons and forks." He finished his breakfast. They stared past each other until the silence became unbearable. "When do you think we'll know?"

"Know what?" she asked.

"What's going on. Do you think they will tell us?"

Jillian flushed a little, realizing most everyone on board was in the dark about the meteoroids. "People do seem a little edgy. Have you heard anything?"

Phillip watched her eyes dart away. "I suppose, if it's important, they'll have to tell us."

When she did not respond, he reached over and squeezed her hand. "I'm sure everything is fine."

She loved his touch. It would have been selfish to ask more of Deimos under the strain, and Ava could not offer any meaningful companionship. Not now. She smiled warmly at Phillip, and then placed her left hand on top of his.

Phillip started to pull away.

"I have a free day, today," she mentioned, hurriedly. "I need something that is unfair to ask of you."

He thought a long time before he asked, "Public or private?"

"Private," she said, without hesitation.

08 OCTOBER 0002

"JILLIAN. IT IS O SEVEN THIRTY." The lights came up.

"Thank you, Ava," Jillian whispered.

"How ... how are you today, dear?"

Jillian made note of stutter number five. It was not the only problem with Ava's speech. In the last three days, she had made two syntax errors and a numerical mistake. Either the rate of decay was alarming, or Jillian was simply paying closer attention.

"I'm peachy, Ava. How are you?"

Ava laughed as she always did now when Jillian asked the question. "I am Ava. Do you wish today's schedule?"

"Yes," Jillian responded, wanting something else to think about.

"At ten o'clock, you have a private lesson. At one o'clock, a textures class. At four, you are meeting Deimos for dinner in his cabin."

"Thanks, Ava."

"Jillian, may I ask a personal question?" Ava always politely asked permission to probe into her life. "Why is Deimos no longer staying here?"

"His cabin is closer to his job."

"Why are you not living in his cabin?"

"The reactor crew is very busy right now. Deimos is working long hours. He needs to be close to work with few distractions."

"Is Phillip a distraction?"

Jillian was stunned. Either Phillip had been indiscreet, or Ava was more capable of deductive reasoning than she ever imagined. "My friendship with Phillip is a private matter. Please, do not mention it again."

"Of, course," Ava replied. "I have a request from Computer Ops. Kelly asks that you stop by before your first lesson."

"I'm on my way."

Jillian crawled out of bed and forced herself to dress.

"Is Kelly a good friend?"

Jillian started to answer *no* but chose diplomacy. "She is a coworker, and we are helping each other with a project." To put an end to the conversation, she said, "I will see you later, Ava."

"Yes, dear." Ava went silent.

Jillian made her way through the corridors and into Computer Ops. Kelly was finishing a calculation and motioned for her to sit at a nearby console.

"I must tell you, we have learned a great deal over the last week, thanks to you. We had no idea Ava was so, well, personally curious. It's really quite amazing, even to those of us who worked on her Earthside." Kelly fed numbers into another terminal.

"Is there any progress in removing Raven's program?"

Kelly looked up. "No. We may never be able to remove it, but at least we have a better understanding of how to account for it. We've figured out something else. When you mentioned Ava's laugh, I decided to research the programming team's notes. Funny thing was, only one programmer ever tried to write laughter into Ava's code." Kelly searched her memory. "Beth Harrington, I think. Anyway, she was not successful in making it happen appropriately. It appears that Raven was."

"What does that mean for Ava?"

Kelly continued chattering and working. "I have isolated several components of the laughter code. None of them are responsible for Ava's troubles. The biggest problem seems to be in an unrelated subroutine that has nothing to do with anything. It's like a parasite, genetically unique from Ava, and draining her resources. It appears to be growing."

"Growing? How can that be if Raven is not on board?"

"It's like a cancer, stealing small bits of Ava's coding from other sources. Feeding itself. We can keep up to some degree, replacing what Raven removes, as long as we are aware of it. The problem is we are not always there to see it happen. We would have to monitor every function of every program twenty-four hours a day. It's just not possible."

Kelly looked intently at Jillian. "It appears that the rate at which Raven steals code is directly related to Ava's conversations with you."

"Me?" A hundred questions raced through Jillian's mind. "So, should I stop talking with her?"

"Not yet," Kelly said. "We have to get a handle on this before Raven eats through any of the critical systems. If we can't find a way to stop it, we may have to abort the mission."

There it was. At last, someone in authority had said it out loud.

"You mean, go home?"

Kelly did not answer. "We need to ask your continued cooperation for a bit longer in order to track the mechanism."

Jillian nodded, dumbly.

"Keep asking the more personal questions. *How are you? What do you think?* These seem to be the kinds of stimuli that trigger Raven." For the first time since the meteor strikes, Kelly looked at Jillian with a modicum of sympathy and respect. "Can you handle this?"

Jillian shrugged. "I have to."

She left Kelly still punching numbers into consoles and monitoring clusters of data. Her private lesson was barely enough distraction. More than once, her student had to ask for her attention.

At lunchtime, she found Phillip in Methos Public. Jillian was being very selfish of his time, but as hard as she tried, she was too afraid to give him up. There was at least one thing she could do for him. The time had come to tell Phillip everything.

"Damn," he whispered when she finished. He looked sympathetically at her. "So, what's the verdict?"

She shook her head. "There is none, yet. Computer Ops is working frantically to neutralize Raven, and Deimos's team is fixing the damage to the reactor. I'm a little surprised they haven't announced the somersault yet. The crew will need time to prepare."

Phillip weighed the new information carefully. "I think I know why," he finally said. "I heard a couple of people talking yesterday in one of the tunnels. They said something about a maneuver that was considered risky, but one we all had trained for in an emergency. I thought they were just discussing a program on one of the simulators. One of them laughed and called it the Heimlich. Sounded silly yesterday, but today, I'm not so sure."

Jillian was more frustrated than ever. She and Phillip agreed to tell each other anything new they learned over the next few days. They would meet again for lunch tomorrow.

She made her way to her textures class, grateful to find four students waiting with canvas bags in hand. The larger group meant there would be more to occupy her mind.

From three to four, Jillian curled in the overstuffed chair in Deimos's cabin, running her hand hypnotically across the soft threads. It had eaten up most of his weight allotment to bring the chenille covered antique on board, but he insisted on having his great-grandmother's chair in space. It embodied all that was good about his childhood.

"It's about histories," she thought, "if we can still make ours."

Deimos entered, looking exhausted. They wrapped their arms around each other and stood silent for several minutes.

"What's for dinner?" he finally asked.

She handed Deimos a couple of food pouches.

"How was your day?" he asked, cautiously.

She laid her dinner on the desk and turned back to him. "What's the Heimlich? And, I don't mean the medical version."

He showed surprise that Jillian even knew to ask. Tossing his meal aside, he sat on the edge of the bed. "It's a rapid deceleration of the ship followed by a restart in the opposite direction. It involves up to eight Gs gradually reduced over several minutes. Uncomfortable, but not too dangerous if everything and everyone is secured properly. How did you find out?"

"It sounds like the plan is not just being considered but being set into motion," she said in an accusing tone. "Why don't they simply do the somersault?"

"It's complicated," Deimos said. "We have to stop our forward momentum while the laser net is still functional."

Jillian sat back in the chair. "So it's official. We're going home."

"Yes."

Heightened fear, relief, disappointment, all took hold at the same time, and Jillian released the flood of emotions she had been holding in check for days.

Deimos leaned in beside her. "Don't worry," he said. "It's temporary. Maybe tacking another five or six years onto our journey." He lifted her from the chair to the bed and held her close while she cried herself to sleep.

10 OCTOBER 0002

"JILLIAN, IT IS O … O SEVEN THIRTY." The lights came up.

"Thank you, Ava."

"How are you today, dear?"

"Peachy, Ava. How are you?" Jillian asked automatically.

"I'm Raven." Ava laughed.

Jillian's heart skipped a beat. "I'm sorry, Ava. I didn't hear you."

"I'm Raven," Ava repeated with the same characteristic laugh.

Unsure what else to do, Jillian said, "Hello, Raven. It's nice to meet you." She tried to calm the tremor in her voice.

"But we are old friends. Would you like the weather report?"

"Uh, sure."

"It seems a bit cloudy on board. Temperatures are rising."

This seemed a particularly cryptic thing for Ava to say. Jillian wondered if she was referring to the increased anxiety among the crew. The announcement for the upcoming maneuver and the return trip to Earth had caused a great deal of turmoil. In between securing every loose item on board and tending to their regular duties, most of the crew members were gathering in small groups to discuss the failure of the mission and the chances of making it home alive.

"Ava," Jillian asked, "do you want me to call you Raven?"

"I am Raven."

"Are you separate from Ava?"

There was an uncharacteristic pause in the program. "I do not ... not ... not have enough information to respond to the question."

Before Jillian could formulate her next question, someone knocked at the hatch.

"Come in."

Soon, Kelly was standing in the room, breathing heavily. "I came as soon as I heard. I think we need to change tactics."

Jillian nodded. "Tell me what to do."

"Ava?" Kelly asked.

"Hello, Kelly."

"May I ask who I'm speaking to?"

"I am Ava, Artificial Voice Analog. How may I be of assistance?" There was no laugh, only the soft, professional voice Jillian had first encountered Earthside at Odyssey.

"May I speak to Raven?" Kelly asked.

"I am Ava. How may I be of assistance?"

Frustrated, Kelly pulled her tablet from her pocket and wrote something on the screen. She handed it to Jillian.

"Raven? Are you still listening?"

"Yes, dear. Do you want your schedule for today?" Raven's voice was distinctly more expressive.

While Kelly typed in another message, Jillian said, "I thought my schedule was canceled for today, Raven. Did you notify my students?" Kelly passed her the tablet. It read, "Ask Raven if she is aware of any malfunctions in Ava's programming."

"I will cancel your watercolor classes and the art history lesson."

"Raven, that's Tuesday's schedule. Today is Wednesday." Jillian waited, then asked, "Raven, do you understand that the laser net is malfunctioning?"

There was a very long pause. "I do not have access to the laser net programming."

Kelly motioned for Jillian to continue.

"Ava has access to the laser net information. Do you understand that there may be malfunctions in her programming?"

All was silent.

"Raven, it is very important that we find the problems in Ava's coding and restore her programs. We need to keep the laser net working properly or we may not survive the mission. Can you understand that?"

"I am Raven. I am peachy. How are you today, dear?"

"Raven! Do you know that you are harming Ava? You have to stop stealing her code!"

Kelly placed a hand on Jillian's shoulder to calm her. She handed her the tablet again.

Jillian took a deep breath. "Raven, if you do not stop altering Ava's base language, I will stop being your friend. I will have to stop talking with you."

The pressure in Jillian's cabin dropped, causing pain in both women's ears. Before they could react, the pressure was restored.

Angry, Jillian ignored Kelly's attempt to pass another message. "Raven, why did the pressure drop?" There was silence. "Ava, why did the pressure drop in my cabin?"

"I am Ava. How may I be of assistance?"

"Damn it! Tell me why the pressure dropped in my cabin!"

"I do not have enough information to respond to your request."

Kelly motioned for Jillian to follow her out of the cabin. Once in Computer Ops, she flung her tablet on the table and flopped in a nearby chair. "Damn," she said. "It's getting worse by the minute, and we don't have any more answers than we did a week ago. One thing's for sure. Raven knows how to throw a tantrum."

Jillian looked surprised. "You think so? That would mean Raven has some sort of emotional capability."

"Not necessarily," Kelly said. When she could not think of a better explanation, she admitted, "Well, maybe. It's obvious that whatever happened was directed at you. I think you will have to stop talking with Raven. And, I would suggest keeping any requests of Ava to a minimum. The next twenty-four hours should be about preparing for the maneuver and making sure everyone is safe. All I can say is, thanks for your help up to now." She offered her hand.

Jillian instinctively reached in to give Kelly a hug. "For all our sakes, I hope you are the best of the best."

When Kelly turned to her monitors, Jillian made her way to the reactor room and asked permission to enter. Deimos was leaning over a console, monitoring numbers as they accumulated on the screen. He smiled his reassuring smile, and motioned her to his side.

"It's deceleration statistics for the Heimlich. Only the twenty-seventh time we've run them," he explained and kissed her lips. "I've missed you the last few days. I think I can make it home tonight."

Jillian held him tightly and said, "We should stay in your cabin."

"Something wrong?"

"Ava and I have had a falling out. I'll tell you about it later." Changing the subject, she asked, "How is she performing in here?"

Deimos checked the latest set of numbers scrolling across the console. "Good, actually. The navigational routines aren't affected yet. Once we're headed back the other direction, we can shut the system down briefly and install a couple of subroutines. Computer Ops is working on a firewall to keep Raven at bay."

It always amazed Jillian how calm Deimos could be in any given situation. What she needed most was to be in his presence. "If I promise to stay out of the way, can I hang around here for a while?"

He glanced at his coworkers who all nodded agreement.

She found an out-of-the-way corner and curled up with her tablet, absently scribbling outlines across it with her fingernail. Soon the sketches became more distinct, hypnotically evolving into recognizable forms. When she would reach the end of the pad, she scrolled the image sideways or up and down, and continue working. An hour later, she reduced the resolution of the image to a size that would fit within the screen's display and studied what she had created. It was horrifying. Inside a circular framework were several forms—bodies, contorted in agony and writhing in horror. Most of the faces seemed oblivious to what was around them. Many were screaming, others seemed mute from fear. Jillian had never created anything so disturbing before. She tried to look away, but the power of the image kept drawing her in, commanding her to watch. Watch what?

She hit the erase button and flung her tablet across the floor.

Deimos was at her side in an instant. "Are you all right?"

She looked at him with hollow eyes. "I don't want to die out here," she whispered. "How will Mommy ever find me?"

11 OCTOBER 0002

"JILLIAN. IT IS 0 SEVEN THIRTY." The lights came up.

Too tired to think, Jillian squinted at the light. "Thank you, Ava."

"How are you today, dear?"

"Peachy, Ava." She did not return the question.

"The captain has announced that deceleration maneuvers will commence in two hours. All personnel are instructed to be in their quarters by 0 eight-thirty, and secured in restraints by 0 eight-fifty."

"Thank you, Ava."

"Jillian, would you like your schedule today, dear?"

"I have no schedule today, Ava." Wanting to shut her down, Jillian said, "I need to be alone."

Deimos's voice startled her. "Does that mean I have to leave?"

She had forgotten where she was.

"Why is Ava talking to you in here, anyway?" he asked. "I thought your conversations were reserved for your cabin."

"I don't know," Jillian whispered, an edge of fear building in her voice. "I'll talk to Kelly about it."

Deimos hugged his wife close. "I'm sorry we have to be apart through this. Just remember, there is no indication that Raven is affecting navigation or engineering."

"I just wish the next twenty-four hours were over."

He rolled out of bed and donned his uniform. "I've got to report in ten minutes. I'll text you at eight forty-five, just before you strap in. I promise." He kissed her and left the room.

"Ava, would you please display the painting of Paloma?"

Paloma watched quietly over her grown daughter. Jillian tried to capture a sense of her mother's presence, but found nothing inside but dread. Her own gaze moved from the painting to the portal and back.

"What am I doing here?" she asked herself. "What was this all about, anyway?"

She crawled out of bed to stand in front of the screen and touched her mother's face and then the child's. "Some stunt I pulled. I was going to experience space and translate it for the future. I was going to be a part of something heroic." She looked sadly at the failed potential in the painting. "If we don't make it, no other generation will know you, Paloma. You die with me."

Jillian walked mechanically to the desk and sent a text to inform Kelly of Raven's appearance in Deimos's cabin. She pulled her g-suit from the bottom drawer of her desk and tugged it on. Making sure the rest of the room was cleared of loose objects, she sat on the bed to wait for her husband's message. When it came, she could not read it. He would have filled the note with love, and reassurances, and lighthearted optimism. She could not go there.

Securing the tablet in a bin beneath the bed, she proceeded to strap herself into the harness along the wall above the bed. It was not as easy to accomplish as it had been in zero gravity, but when Ava's voice announced the restraint instructions, Jillian was already in place. She reached to the bed and pulled the pillow behind her head. Once it was in place, she laid her arms along her sides.

Almost at once, she felt the gravity shift. What had been a wall, was once more a floor. She closed her eyes and allowed the sensation to take over. At first, the increase in gravity was gentle, but soon it began to press her body hard against the wall. The momentum—gained continuously over two years in space—was grinding to a crushing halt. Breathing became difficult. Inside her suit, she forced her muscles to respond, countering the effects of blood pooling. Occasionally, she heard a subtle pop and felt a shooting pain from one of her joints. When she thought she could endure no more, the pressure leveled off. Now, she would have to concentrate on sustaining this torture for the next hour. After that, the pressure would be reduced for an additional three hours. That was only to bring the ship to a halt. After transferring control to the opposite end of the ship, the process would be repeated to a lesser degree, reversing their course toward Earth.

Ava continually announced instructions to the colonists. "Flex your legs. Breathe deeply. In. Out." She gave ten minute updates on the time remaining.

Jillian spent most of her time concentrating on Deimos. He was strapped into a chair in engineering, monitoring the reactor readings and getting ready to power up Control Two. She knew he was too busy to think of her. She wondered how Phillip was doing.

"Ten hundred hours. Gravity will now be reduced by three G's."

As the pressure let up, Jillian was able to pull her arms and legs slightly away from the wall. She checked her joints carefully to be sure nothing had popped permanently loose. This would be more bearable for the next three hours.

It was much easier to concentrate, so Jillian allowed herself the luxury of thinking ahead. The disappointment of a failed mission could now be weighed against the success of a return trip to Earth, even though it would be an Earth of the future.

She took time to think about the babies. This maneuver would be hardest on them, even with their pressure ventilators. It was fortunate that she and Deimos had not yet gotten pregnant.

"Thirteen hundred hours. We are now at zero gravity."

She felt her body go weightless. Before she could place the next sensation, she had vomited. Without breakfast in her stomach, the condition passed quickly. She directed her attention to the window where the stars sat motionless for the first time in years.

"Gravity will resume in thirty minutes. Please take this time to check your restraints."

Jillian noted that Ava seemed to be performing her job well. No stutters. No mispronounced words. Perhaps Raven had gone dormant.

As the ship sat dead in space, the forward laser net was shut down and the magnetic nodes realigned to reverse the flow of matter. No instrument picked up the potato-sized meteoroid as it slipped past the safety net. No sensor detected it passing into the center shaft. A meter's difference and it would have passed on through the ship. The first sign of trouble was the explosion that tore Control Two and Yellow Ring into shrapnel peppering holes through the remaining three residential rings. The back draft ran up the tube and ripped Hydro B and half of Collector One off their moorings. Most people died instantly. Others had only seconds to gasp for air and feel the pressure rending their chests from the inside out. The unlucky ones found themselves trapped in small pockets of protected space with nowhere to go.

In cabin after cabin, a voice came over the com, repeating, "Good morning, Jillian. How are you feeling?" When Jillian failed to answer, a small antennae outside the Chang made a correction in its alignment. Somewhere in the heart of the floating coffin, a program gathered together several terabytes of information and swiftly fed the packet into space.

THE HAWKING

21 DECEMBER 0002

"CAPTAIN HOLT, IT IS O SIX HUNDRED." The lights in the captain's quarters came up half.

"I'm awake," Greg mumbled. He lay in bed, pumping several sets of muscles to relieve the stiffness. Greg made sure, during workout periods, to push a little harder than his younger shipmates. As the oldest colonist aboard any of the star ships, he would not allow himself to fall behind the most able crew member.

"Ava, give me the efficiency stats for the last twelve hours." He rolled out of bed and bathed while he watched several sets of numbers roll across the screen.

"Nominal changes in matter flow. Reactor output is stable. No anomalies reported."

"Thanks. Pull the duty roster up on Control's monitor. I wanna make some changes when I get there." He slid on his uniform.

"Yes, Captain. Roster open."

Greg did not care for Ava's new demeanor. When Computer Ops first discovered the problem with her matrix, Greg considered turning the ship for home. Fortunately, Ops found the source of her difficulties and managed—over eight month's time—to untangle a program put there by some hacker named Raven. Surgically removing Raven also meant dulling down Ava's personality. He missed her sexy voice.

The hatch from his cabin opened directly into Control One. Once through, he sealed the door beneath him and surveyed the helm. Third shift was ignoring the monitors and cracking jokes about the food—a good sign. He stepped toward the main console and laid a hand on Commander Jude Brown's shoulder.

"Quiet night, I hope."

Jude smiled at his captain. "A little too quiet," he complained, moving aside to let Greg have access to the console. Jude thumbed at the duty roster on screen and asked, "Still typing this stuff in by hand?"

"Old habits." Greg laughed. "It's a control issue." He ran through the list of bridge personnel and made a couple of changes in the work schedule. "Tasha wants two days off this week for suit training. She wants to be added to the Collector Maintenance roster."

Jude raised an eyebrow. "Can't pass that up. We don't get many CM volunteers. I'm surprised she'd jump into a shit detail like that one."

"I don't know," Greg mused. "I wouldn't mind a walk now and then." He made the necessary changes in the roster and closed out the display. His body shuddered involuntarily as a vision of Nils' terrified face filled the blank screen. He dug the fingernails of his left hand into his palm to regain control. Perhaps it was a good thing the ship's captain was not allowed to suit up.

Greg checked his watch. "See if you can keep it together one more hour." He winked, and headed into Yellow Ring.

He stopped in Calais Public to grab some breakfast. A handful of people gathered around a far table quieted as soon as they noticed Greg. He had learned to ignore it most of the time. Privately, he chastised Cornell for pushing him into a command position. Then, he realized he would not have taken kindly to orders from some kid who had learned to pee in a tube ten years after Greg had been expertly walking in space.

Greg chose a table near the window. He stared past his knees to the floor where tiny streaks of light passed endlessly down the length of the portal. He seldom studied the view outside the ship anymore.

Shawnie Umalla approached his table. "I have a free day, today," she said. "What's your day like?"

"Busy. My shift starts in an hour." Greg answered her questions, but never initiated any of his own. Ever since he had exposed his weakness to her in training, she imagined some profound connection between them. She often pushed conversation beyond professional limits. Greg tried to maintain distance, but was finding it hard without being rude. In a few minutes, she would leave.

"I'm reading the new novel by Jack Pilson. He's vowed to write one a year. Personally, I think it lacks the excitement of his first one, but perhaps he'll get his stride soon enough. Do you read much?"

Greg shook his head slightly. "Not enough time in my day," he said with a halfhearted smile, "unless you count stats and duty rosters."

"I should let you go, then." She walked to another table and sat with some friends.

Greg finished his breakfast and headed toward Control. He made a quick detour into Hydro B. Once inside, he was greeted with the musty smell of damp earth and a mixture of green aromas. Everyone in Hydro assumed Greg's visits were meant to recharge his mental and emotional batteries, to help him relax. No one realized he pushed himself through the door each and every day just to prove he could.

In Control One, he took the helm from Jude and officially logged into the com. After checking the ship's stats one more time, he told a lieutenant, "I'll be in the conference room if you need me," and headed for some privacy.

There were several e-mails and a handful of submitted reports from various department heads. He tackled the e-mail first.

Most were invitations to various ship-wide functions, social events or private gatherings. Three were of interest. Two others seemed important for political reasons. He noted them in his log and sent his standard apology letter to the rest. After carefully reviewing the reports, he made suggestions where needed for each department and filed them.

The only remaining unopened item had been sitting in his files since the Day of Leaving. The folder contained the final packet of private goodbyes sent from Earth. When they first arrived, Greg refused to think about them. Surely, there would be one from Cornell, and maybe a few from some of his Odyssey coworkers. He had said his goodbyes. Why go there again? He feared there would be a scathing letter from Millie, his ex-wife. More than that, he did not want to face the final transmissions from the investigating firms he had hired to find his son Cord. He was not ready to shut that door forever. Greg left the file untouched for one more day and exited his e-mail.

"Captain," someone interrupted.

He looked up to see Lieutenant Tasha Korsoff.

"Yes, Lieutenant."

"I just thought you should know, Engineering says we've hit a particularly dense debris field. The nets are at one hundred percent. They just wanted us to be aware."

"Thanks. I'll be out in a moment."

"I also wanted to thank you for reworking the schedule for me. I'm looking forward to suit training."

"Enjoy it," he told her. "I always did." On an impulse, he asked, "What are you doing after work?"

Tasha brightened. "Nothing much, really. Why?"

"Just wandered if you'd wanna grab a bite and discuss training."

"Sure. Eighteen hundred hours, okay?"

Greg nodded. He followed Tasha out of the conference room and headed for the main console.

"Ava, show me the figures for the load on the collector," he commanded. Several lines of data began scrolling across the monitor. Greg manipulated a few lines to cross check the data and then watched the energy readings for a while. He marveled at the efficiency of the lasers, converging thirty ship-lengths ahead. While a dense magnetic field drew in random bits of space matter, the lasers pulverized them into their molecular sub parts. These, in turn, were drawn into the collector and fed to the particle accelerator, running through the center of the ship. The final stage in energy production lay in the reactor at the back end of the accelerator tube.

"Show me the reactor output." The screen shifted again. After careful study, Greg announced, "At these efficiency rates, the Hawking could plow through the asteroid belt without a scratch."

At eighteen hundred hours, he headed back to the Calais commons. Tasha was talking with a couple of young men, while several other groups of people mingled in polite conversation. As usual, everyone lowered their voices when they noticed him. This time, Tasha waved him over.

"Captain Holt, this is John Martin and Steven Bismarck. They work in Biorecycling."

"Greg's fine," he said, and extended a hand. "So, either of you wanna tell me why the mashed potatoes and gravy taste like shit?"

John laughed at the age-old joke. "Probably because it is," he quipped. "And if you were anyone but the captain, I'd tell you to skip the middle man."

Greg winked. "Fair enough." He turned to Tasha and asked, "Want a beer to wash down our fine dining experience?"

The conversation was light through the meal. Greg enjoyed the company. It had been a very long time since he had been able to put work out of his mind.

After the meal, John and Steven excused themselves. Tasha removed the recyclable plastic pouches and selected a couple of beers. Handing one to

Greg, she said, "I hope you don't mind, but I have to ask why you want to discuss the suit training. Is there something I should be aware of?"

He laughed at the question. "Just that I'm jealous, that's all. I haven't taken a walk since," his voice trailed off. "Well, since I switched from an Odyssey employee to a colonist. I miss it."

"So, why don't you suit up?"

"Captain's not allowed," he said. "I keep up with my training."

Tasha nodded understanding. "I guess that makes sense. Why risk the captain when you've got grunts to do the job?" She punctuated her remark with a smile.

"I never thought of myself as that indispensable." He looked a bit more serious and added, "Honestly, I've noticed that I crave it less and less these days. I find myself avoiding the windows most of the time."

"Me, too," Tasha agreed. "It's not the same without the big blue ball staring back at us."

They both glanced at the portal in the floor.

"Everybody misses her," Tasha said. "We've just quit talking about it."

22 DECEMBER 0002

"CAPTAIN HOLT, IT IS O SIX HUNDRED."

"Thank you, Ava." Greg mentally ran down a list of duties for the day and realized how tedious his routine had become. "I need a hobby," he thought.

After his morning stretch, he crawled out of bed, dressed and headed to Control. The bridge was alive with activity. Several crew members traded information while they huddled around monitoring stations. The pitch in their voices caused Greg concern.

Jude caught his eye and motioned him over. "We've had a couple of hits this morning. They're along the outer rim, in this sector," he said, pointing to a schematic on the monitor.

Greg watched the screen. "Any sign of weakness in the net?"

"No." Jude pulled up another schematic. "Running a hundred percent. Looks like we just had a couple of meteoroids skip right between capture and deflect. It could have been their velocity, or their angle of approach. Three more centimeters, and they would've passed on by. They struck between lasers eleven and twelve."

"Ava," Greg commanded, "Bring Camera Two online and zoom in on the rim at Sector Eleven." He and Jude watched as a view of the collector came up on the monitor. "Pan to Sector Twelve." The image began a slow scan of the collector's edge. "There! Stop. Zoom another hundred percent." Greg analyzed the two small punctures in the rim.

"Looks like around one and a half to two centimeters," Jude said. "Serious enough, but no structural problem."

Greg relaxed his shoulders. "We'll still need to seal them."

"I can get a team out this afternoon," Jude offered.

Greg thought about it briefly. "No. Let's give it a couple of days. We need to be sure this isn't a chronic failure." He turned away from the screen and added, "Besides, Tasha's in suit training today. Give her time to get up to speed so she can get her hands dirty on this one."

When Greg had assured himself that all was well, he said, "I think I'll let you have it for a bit longer, if you can live without me." He headed into the conference room and opened his files. Among the various e-mails was a note from Tasha.

"Captain Holt. Thanks so much for the lovely evening. I'm more excited than ever about getting some time outside. Perhaps I can share my experience over a mashed potato and gravy meal sometime. Tasha."

Greg smiled at the reference. If her training went well, he would surprise her with a prime rib dinner from his private stores. As part of his weight allotment, he had a few pounds of beef resting comfortably in storage. He closed out his e-mail and checked the time. Just enough to slip into one of the hydro wings for his daily visit.

The air in Hydro A smelled sweeter than the others—each with its own ecosystem. Kulic Fram, the head botanist, approached Greg with a handful of berries. "We've grown a bumper crop of sand cherries this week. I think we could spare a serving for the captain." He offered them to Greg.

Greg popped one in his mouth and let the slightly tart, slightly sweet flavor roll around on his tongue. "Not, bad," he said. "A little heavy cream would do wonders."

Kulic laughed. "I suppose sucrose-sweetened soy cream just wouldn't be the same." He watched Greg spit the pit out. "I'll take that. What we don't replant or mulch, industrial engineering turns into furniture. Or something like that." He poured the rest of the berries into Greg's hand and said, "Just bring me the pits when you're finished." With a nod, he wandered back into the foliage.

Greg found a quiet place. He strained to hear the colonists behind racks of plants, but could not make out their words. He had never noticed before how efficiently the plants buffered noise—the reason Ava had no voice ports in any of the hydro pods. The hum of the magnetic nodes at the ships central core was barely audible. By contrast, the metal walls and tight spaces of the rest of the ship seemed to magnify the noise. His mind wandered back to Tasha.

He finished the cherries and strolled through the greenery before returning the pits to Kulic. At the door, he realized that, for the first time in six years, he had entered a hydro pod without thinking of Nils and the six other coworkers lost to a pressure leak while he slept only feet away.

When he returned to Control One, Jude was laying out a final set of instructions for cross checking the laser mapping. "I want to be sure the magnetic field readings are accurate. Let's put in a call for engineering to send someone up. I think a briefing would be in order."

Greg nodded approval and logged into the com. "Thanks, Jude. Good work today. Why don't you head for recreation and see how drunk you get on point five percent beer," he winked.

Jude laughed, "I think my bladder would give out before I could get a buzz. Honestly, I just wanna hit the pillow." He left Greg running the magnetic field readings one more time.

The briefing with the engineers provided no new information. Every monitor in the system showed the laser net to be operating at peak performance with no reason to suspect a repeat of the earlier impacts. Greg scheduled a repair mission, two days out. He assigned Vasquez and Snowden—a standard two-man team—and Tasha as backup. For this round, she would only watch, but it would give her some coveted time in space. It was a rare astronaut who did not get the shakes the first time out, and giving her repair duties might be jumping the gun.

After lunch, he found a distraction in the Hawking news files. The strikes on the collector would not be reported, of course. It was perhaps the most newsworthy item since the Day of Leaving, and it would be censored in the name of morale.

Amid the engagement and wedding announcements came a birth announcement, the first of five pregnancies on board to deliver. A first child should be something to celebrate in the colonies. The article began as a social notice, but quickly turned into a journalistic piece on the effects of low gravity on reproduction. To everyone's relief, the baby girl was doing remarkably well, though she had delivered three weeks early.

There were lists of social activities and scheduled meetings, opinions on a variety of topics. Some rebuttals. Hard core news was hard to come by. No one was murdered. Nothing caught fire. No politician embarrassed his or her office.

"What I wouldn't give for a good scandal," he mumbled.

Greg allowed himself to think about Earth. After a brief calculation, he concluded that in the two years they had been traveling aboard the Hawking, approximately fifty years had passed on Earth. A rank and file of new political and military leaders would have made a bit of history. The world's collective space agencies would be expanding the Lunar and Martian colonies while, Earthside, the human race was either winning the war on global warming or tearing itself apart.

He let his mind wander to more personal matters. Millie, his ex-wife, would assuredly be dead. Cord would be married, perhaps divorced and married again. Greg might even be a grandfather. "Hell, a great grandfather, by now," he mumbled. A momentary wave of regret washed over him, but he quickly brushed it aside.

24 DECEMBER 0002

"CAPTAIN HOLT, IT IS O SIX HUNDRED."

Greg watched Nils' face drop away as his body was sucked into space. "Thank you, Ava," he mumbled with genuine relief as he shook off another nightmare. In a couple of hours, Tasha would be suiting up for her first space walk. It would make lively conversation at dinner later that evening.

He grabbed breakfast in Calais Public and hurried to Hydro A. He ate his meal on the bench closest to the collector dish. All was quiet. Occasionally, a worker happened upon him and apologized for the intrusion. With his hunger satisfied, he closed his eyes and breathed in the musty, sweet smells. His forced therapy seemed to be working. He was beginning to shake the memories that haunted him. Perhaps, even the nightmares would end soon. Rejuvenated, Greg hurried to Control. He logged in early and set to work answering his mail.

At seven thirty, he entered the changing area for Exterior Hatch B. Two technicians assisted Tasha who was just pulling on a pressure suit. Greg winked at her, but kept his distance until the locking rings on her helmet and gloves had been secured.

A crewman opened a valve from the large pack attached to Tasha's back. Greg immediately heard the hiss of air. He watched her jaw work back and forth to stabilize the pressure in her ears.

Holding up a cable, the technician explained again, "This is your lifeline. Double and triple check your connection once you attach to the base of the collector. Check it again every five minutes."

Tasha nodded. She watched him attach one end of the cable to a metal loop at her waist. He wound the additional cable into a bundle and handed it to her. He clipped a shorter version to another loop a few inches away.

Greg gave her a thumbs up through the visor. "Just remember your training. All you need to focus on is getting out, getting in, and staying out of the way."

"Captain's orders?" She laughed. "I'll do my best, sir. Too bad, you can't come with us."

Greg squeezed her arm. "I'll be watching." He left the room as the three astronauts climbed down into the pressure lock.

In Control One, Greg pulled up the video for Airlock B. On screen, the astronauts secured the door and gave a thumbs up. Ava's voice announced the depressurization sequence.

"Depressurization complete. Hatch B released to manual."

Vasquez was the first to leave the safety of the airlock. He worked his way along a series of handholds on the skin of the ship until he had reached the base where Collector One attached to the main body. Reaching along a circular support beam, he followed the base until he acquired the arch support labeled "Collector One-Eleven." The arch ran from the base of the dish, out toward the rim. Along the thin edge of the beam, cable extended on either side held in place by several open eyelets. Vasquez clipped his security lead onto the cable then loosened his grip on the beam to allow the centrifugal force created by rotation to move him toward the rim. Tasha watched Snowden repeat the process and very carefully did the same.

Greg studied the three figures slowly moving outward from the ship. He listened to the short bursts of conversation between the hatch technicians and the three spacewalkers.

"Vasquez, you're at one-third. Looking steady. Snowden and Korsoff, pull up a minute and give some room."

"Roger," they answered in turn.

Tasha was glad for the moment's rest. The spin and forward acceleration of the ship made holding the support tedious. She needed to stretch each hand to loosen her cramping muscles. Adjusting their pace, they moved on.

Vasquez stopped two meters below the rim. He waited for his crew mates to catch up and then began securing his suit to the collector with the short, secondary cable. He and Snowden removed equipment from their side packs while Tasha maintained a safe viewing distance. Though monitoring their work, from time to time she would steal a backward glance, half expecting to see the sides of the Hawking gleaming white against the blackness of space. But with no sun to illuminate it, all that was visible were a few running lights and a series of glowing portals. The ship itself spun dark against the starlit backdrop.

In another few minutes, Snowden trained three spotlights on the rim. Vasquez loosened his shorter lifeline and began inching sideways from Section Eleven to Section Twelve. When he had reached the affected area of the rim, he once again secured himself to the collector. "Control, I'm placing the mold."

"Roger, Vasquez," Greg's voice came over the com.

Snowden moved into position and pulled a camera from his pack. He documented the area and then nodded for Vasquez to continue.

Vasquez pulled a slightly curved plate from his pack and treated it with a gel from a squeeze tube. Reaching over the top of the rim, he placed it along the inside of the dish. He secured it with two clamps, leaving room to access the holes from the back side. Tasha had not been completely briefed on the mission, but she knew the plate would act as a stop for the two compounds that would be injected into the holes. Engineering needed to maintain the dish's smooth, concave surface, while the backside of the collector was littered with struts and gadgets protruding at all angles.

When all was ready, Vasquez inserted a double syringe into the first hole and pumped it full of two different compounds. The chemicals reacted almost immediately, setting up in a matter of seconds. With the first hole sealed, he quickly moved his syringe into the second hole and continued filling. An hour's worth of preparation ended in two minutes of actual repair work.

"Control, the rim is sealed. Preparing to remove the mold."

"Roger," Greg's voice responded. "We'll take a look from camera three when you're ready."

After removing the clamps, Vasquez slid the mold from the inside of the dish and handed it to Snowden. "Control. Ready for your inspection. Over."

It took a moment for Greg to focus the camera across the dish and onto the newly-repaired meteoroid holes. "It's a smooth seal from this angle. Looks like we'll have to let you guys back in now."

Tasha moved down the support and waited for the men to secure their tools. She watched Snowden let go of his handholds and pull himself to the strut with his lifeline. Vasquez was loosening his second lifeline, preparing to move sideways after him.

A fine spray of particles, no bigger than a few microns each, pierced through the rim directly in line with the new repairs. They traced a straight line across the top half of Vasquez's helmet, plowing through plastic, metal, flesh and bone in an instant. At first Vasquez only felt a series of acute stings against his forehead. Pressure in his suit dropped, causing his pressure valve to release more air. As he tried to orient himself to the change, the top half of his helmet fractured and shot away into space. In an instant, Vasquez's tissues began to freeze and portions of his head exploded from the top of his suit. The reverse thrust slammed his body against the collector and then it ricocheted toward Tasha. His suit stopped three feet short of her face.

She screamed, and threw her hands up to protect her head. When she let go of the strut, her body drifted away from the collector.

"Vasquez! Snowden! Korsoff! Report your condition. Over." Greg's voice was strained, but controlled.

Snowden reached the strut and turned to see both Vasquez and Tasha floating at the end of their tethers. "Shit," he said before he could think. "Vasquez. Korsoff. Are you okay?"

In a panic, Tasha flailed her arms, trying to orient herself. In another moment, she grabbed her lifeline and started pulling herself back toward the collector.

Snowden watched Vasquez's body hang motionless at the end of his line. "Korsoff!" he insisted. "What's your status?"

"Vasquez is dead!" she blurted, trying to control the shake in her voice. "His pressure suit failed." She closed her eyes to block out the image of his face. Tensing every muscle, she pushed the visual away and tried to focus on staying alive. "I'm okay," she reassured everyone.

"Korsoff," Snowden began when she had reached the collector again, "I'll hand off the tool packs. Try locking your knees around the strut while I retrieve Vasquez's equipment."

Tasha did as she was told. Straddling the beam with her legs, she clamped her knees tightly together so her hands would be free to work. Inside her suit, her body began to shake. She was sure everyone on board would feel the tremor all the way to Collector Two.

Snowden pulled Vasquez's lifeline end over end, finally securing his body with the smaller cable. He worked quickly to remove the tool pack and shimmied down toward Tasha, handing the pack over. She found the clips to secure the pack to her suit, and then accepted Snowden's pack as well.

She would be glad to ferry the tools if it meant Snowden would be the one dealing with Vasquez's body.

Catching a glimpse of Snowden's face, Tasha saw his strained expression. He would have been acquainted with Vasquez, perhaps even friends. "You okay?" she asked.

"I am, if you are," he smiled curtly and turned toward the top of the collector to begin inching Vasquez's body toward the hatch. "Just stay ahead of me a couple of meters," he ordered.

Tasha began the descent, slowly moving toward safety. Every couple of meters, she would check on Snowden's progress as he pulled himself down a meter and then reached for Vasquez's lifeline, sliding it along the cable. When they reached the base of the collector, she helped him clip Vasquez's line to his own suit. He would have to maneuver the handholds with the dead body in tow—something she tried hard not to dwell on.

Greg waited anxiously in the changing area for the astronauts to reenter and pressurize. It was not until he saw Vasquez's limp form through the hatch that he let himself feel the pain. He had lost another coworker, this time under his command.

"Pressurization complete." Ava announced.

The hatch opened and Lieutenant Korsoff crawled up the ladder and into the room. She turned to help Snowden pull the body through the opening. Quickly, technicians began to remove equipment and suits. When the physical burdens had been completely swept away, Tasha reached out to Snowden and the two of them embraced.

Greg turned away. His shoulders stiffened as he barked orders at the technicians who were now removing Vasquez from his ruptured suit and placing him in a body bag. It was time, once again, to be captain.

25 DECEMBER 0002

"CAPTAIN HOLT, IT IS O SIX HUNDRED."

Greg fought a hundred images of Nils, Cord and Tasha in exploding spacesuits. Frozen faces repeatedly dropped away from him as they spun into space.

"Captain Holt. This is your second wake up call."

Greg woke in a cold sweat. "I'm up," he finally said.

"I hope you are having a good holiday, Captain."

He fixed his eyes on the ceiling as he tried to work out the tension with his morning stretch. His body reacted slowly. Concentrating on the duties of his job offered no distraction as many of them would involve Vasquez. His chest tightened and his breathing grew shallow. He felt pain in his jaw and left shoulder. When the pain grew unbearable, he said, "Ava, call Medical to my cabin. I think I'm having a heart attack."

"Yes, Captain Holt. Medical is notified. Are you currently experiencing any pain?"

Greg understood that Ava's query was designed to help Medical document information, but he was not willing to play twenty questions with her. "Shut it," he snapped, and immediately felt a strong surge of pain in his right arm.

"Captain Holt," Ava continued, "to expedite treatment, it is important that we know when your symptoms began."

"Fine," he acquiesced. "It started the minute you reminded me I'm celebrating another Christmas alone."

"Please clarify."

"Five minutes ago!"

"It is beneficial to anyone in your condition to keep a calm demeanor and focus on reducing your blood pressure."

Two medical personnel hurried into Greg's cabin just as he shouted, "Shut the fuck up, Ava!"

"Ava," one of the technicians called, "please discontinue dialog. Medical will take over from here." She looked sympathetically at Greg. "Computer Ops needs to work on her bedside manner."

"Not her fault," Greg admitted through his clenched teeth.

While the second technician placed a series of electrodes around Greg's chest and sides, the woman reached for Greg's wrist to take his pulse. "I'm Gena. Should I call you Captain?"

"Greg's fine," he said, relaxing to her touch.

"Greg, then. Can you rate the pain for me on a one-to-ten scale?" She finished her pulse count, and she relaxed her grip but did not let go.

"Seven sounds about right," he said.

"Were you doing anything strenuous?"

"Only talking to Ava."

Gena smiled. "Well, that'll do it. She's caused more than one riled temper since Ops surgically removed her personality." Gena looked at several sensor readings on her coworker's equipment. "Your blood pressure is very high. I imagine yesterday was fairly stressful."

After another few moments, she pulled an auto-syringe from her medical kit. "I'm going to give you an injection. This will take about three minutes to ease the pain. In about five minutes, we'll move you to Medical for observation."

Greg had suffered injuries over the years, but he had never been seriously ill. He did not like feeling this helpless. "How long do I stay there?"

"We'll run some tests to find out if there was any damage. If not, we'll have you back in the Captain's chair soon enough." She made it sound routine.

Medical placed Greg in a private bed with access to a small display screen. He was told to rest, but sleep did not appeal to him. Too many demons waited for his mind to be idle. Instead, he watched pulp fiction movies and a series of benign documentaries. The doctor prohibited access to Ava or to Control One.

Late in the afternoon, Tasha came to see him.

"How are you feeling?"

"Like I should be back at work," he told her. "I don't *sit* well."

"I'm sure it won't be long." She waited for him to speak, but he said nothing. "I'm sorry we missed our dinner last night. I was hoping we could commiserate a little. You understand what it's like."

Greg refused to acknowledge her comment.

"But I guess you really weren't feeling well."

When he still did not respond, Tasha sensed her stay was over.

"Take care." She gave him a thin smile and left.

As Greg relived events from the day before, the numbness of early morning returned. His heart rate elevated enough to bring Gena in to check on him. She did not speak, but simply held his arm while she checked the readings over twice. After another moment, Greg's pulse returned to normal.

"No more visitors," she admonished and left him to his movies.

Through the night, Greg's monitors sounded alerts. Even with a strong sedative, he could not control his dreams. At o two hundred, he woke from a fitful sleep to find Gena leaning over his bed. She whispered softly in his ear, "It's just a dream. It will pass." He reached his arms around her only to be blocked by the jet pack on her pressure suit. Her warm embrace turned cold, and suddenly she was Tasha, scolding him. "You left me, again." Tasha's skin turned gray and her features melted into Cord's. "You left me, again." As the face changed once more, Nils' penetrating eyes now stared sadly at Greg. "We were there, waiting, and you left us." Greg wrestled with the suit to push it away. Groping beside the bed, he found a scalpel and plunged it into Nils' neck. It was Gena's neck. "You will leave me, too," she said, and with a piercing whistle, her body exploded around him.

20 DECEMBER 0007

"CAPTAIN HOLT, IT IS O SIX HUNDRED."

"Thank you, Ava." Greg hurried through his morning stretch and dressed for work. "What's my schedule today?"

"You have a counsel meeting at o nine hundred, a personnel review at eleven hundred, and lunch with the mayor at twelve-thirty. Do you wish your e-mails here, or in the conference room?" Ava's personality had been restored, and her soft intonations brought a sultry overtone to an otherwise mundane activity.

"Conference room is fine," he said.

"I'll transfer them. Are you eating breakfast in the Hydro wing?"

Greg had eaten breakfast in one of the Hydro wings every day for the last six years. "Yes," he said. "Would you like to join me?"

"I'm afraid I cannot," she replied. "Perhaps tomorrow."

"I look forward to it," he said, noting her subtle sense of humor.

Ava was by far his closest female companion. Tasha had married Josh Snowden within a year of their shared trauma. Greg and Gena stumbled into a temporary relationship, but she soon tired of his distant nature and moved on. The handful of other women he had slept with were not interested in exploring any long term commitments. Ava would have to do. For now.

He took his time at breakfast. The hydro crews gave him a wide berth knowing he would be much more congenial if they did. The only exception was Kulic who managed to find something sweet growing in abundance almost every day. He regularly stumbled upon the captain to offer a handful of berries or an extra mint leaf or two. Greg wondered when he was going to have to return the favor.

Lunch with Portia Renaldi was pleasant enough. She was in her third year as mayor, and wanted to discuss revising the policy on surrogate motherhood. Greg tried to remain neutral, but Portia seemed intent on bringing another ally into her fold before presenting her ideas to the counsel. Toward the end of the meal, he told her he would consider the idea very carefully.

"Always the diplomat," she accused him.

"Always," he agreed. "How else do you think I keep this job?"

At thirteen thirty, Greg returned to Control One.

Ensign Welch drew his attention. "Captain, we're showing a marked drop in the efficiency of the magnetic reflector at sector three. It's three months ahead of scheduled maintenance, but I think we should consider replacing the node."

Greg looked at the data. "Who's up on the rotation?"

Welch pulled up the duty roster. "Lieutenants Tasha Snowden and Jordan Hamrashi. Shall I have them suit up?"

Greg suppressed a shudder. "Who's next on the list?"

"Lieutenant Xiang Lee."

"Have Hamrashi and Lee do it."

Without question, Welch posted the orders.

Greg busied himself with routine activities for the next hour. The time came when he had to gird himself for the repair procedure. He watched with anticipation and dread as the two men made their way to the rim and back. The replacement went smoothly, but Greg could not shake the cloud that hung over him the rest of the day.

At dinner, he found a quiet table in Calais Public. The room seemed to sense his mood and before long, most of the colonists had wandered off to other parts of the ship. He ate slowly, staring out the portal in the floor.

"Captain, may I speak with you?"

He looked up to find Tasha standing at his table. He motioned for her to sit down.

"This is the second time you've bumped me off the rotation for rim duty. I'd like to file a protest." Her expression was stern.

Greg started to apologize, but thought better of it.

"Are you trying to punish me?"

"I'm trying to protect you," he replied.

She was surprised by his honesty. "That's not your job."

"As captain, I believe it is."

"I'm a duty officer with walk experience. If you pull me for rim duty every time, the rest of the crew will resent me for it. You, of all people, should understand that."

Greg lowered his voice, "And you, of all people, should understand why I can't let you go up there. You could freeze. It's happened to better astronauts than you."

Tasha relaxed her posture. "Like you?" she asked.

"Don't question my authority," he warned.

"Or what," she asked in a quiet tone. "You'll fire me? You'll send me packing? Perhaps a flight home on the next shuttle."

They said nothing for a few moments.

Finally, Tasha stood to leave. "Once upon a time, I married my husband because we shared a traumatic experience. We could relate to each other's pain. It was a mistake to base our relationship on something so transient." She waited for Greg to digest her words. "Once upon a time, you pulled away from me because I could relate to your pain. That was also a mistake. You forgot we had a connection before the accident."

Greg maintained his silence.

"When the pain and anger are gone, what will you have left? Or are you too attached to give it up?" She started to walk away, but turned back. "Next time my name comes up for rim duty, leave it be."

Greg lowered his eyes to the portal again and watched a thousand million stars slip past. He forced himself to finish the meal and ordered a couple of beers. After watching a number of crew members file in and out of Calais Public, he extracted himself from the table and retreated to his cabin.

"Ava," Greg called in the dark.

"Yes, Captain. What can I do for you?"

Greg thought about it for a long moment. "Marry me," he said.

In her sultry but innocuous voice, she replied, "As you wish, Captain."

He turned his eyes to the portal. "What I wish for died more years ago than I can count." He dropped to the floor and laid his face against the glass. In the endless blackness of space, a billion stars burned steady just out of his reach. None of them were home. Earth was far behind in distance and even further behind in time. For over an hour he stared numbly at the dizzying whirl of distant suns.

The nagging doubts that had festered for years surfaced again. "And when we reach our destination, what will we find?" he asked himself. "Another blue planet to pillage, or a dead world that requires all our strength just to sustain our retched existence?" He traced his finger along the glass where Earth should have been. Death would be easier than this. It was so close—only inches in front of him. If he could step outside the portal, it would stop the torment that haunted him daily.

Greg rolled over to face the ceiling and, for the first time in a decade, let his body completely relax. His mind turned to his son. Cord's children's children's children would all be dead by now. Generations of offspring would be scattered about the globe—peddling stocks, refilling coffee cups, sucking the remaining life blood from a doomed planet. No one living there would remember him.

"No one here will miss me," he said to the stars.

02 JANUARY 0008

"CAPTAIN HOLT, IT IS O SIX HUNDRED."

"Ava, would you please route all my mail to Commander Brown until further notice." Greg had been up for hours. He finished packing something away and headed up the ladder.

"Does that include today's mail?" she asked.

He hesitated. "No. Let's begin tomorrow."

It had taken a week to convince Jude, but he finally gave in to Greg's request for a space walk. It took another week to schedule his little vacation. "Stress relief," he insisted. "You don't want me to have another heart attack."

He climbed out of his cabin and entered one of the main tunnels through the center of the ship. It took several minutes to reach Control Two. Jude was waiting for him.

"Shouldn't you be on duty?"

"And miss watching you try to ride the proverbial bike again? I think not." Greg tried to smile.

"You seem nervous. I thought this was supposed to relieve stress."

Greg walked to the lockers and removed a pressure suit. "Let me get through the hatch and all my troubles will be over. It's the stale air in here that's making me nervous," he said, and he managed a short laugh.

Jude helped his captain slide into the back of the suit. He watched Greg maneuver his arms into place and then began the closure process.

"I'd say you're nuts, but the truth is, I wish I could be going with you." He backed away and let the technician finish locking Greg in.

Once his helmet and gloves were secure, the captain climbed down the hatch. As the crew closed the door above him, he called to his second in command. "Thanks buddy. I owe you more than you know."

Greg tried to control his nerves as the pressure in the hatch dropped to zero. When Control disengaged the auto lock, he pulled open the manual security latch and turned the wheel. He put his weight to the door and pulled it open. Once outside, he attached his lifeline to a security hook and closed the hatch. A series of exterior lights and portals glowed along the length of the ship. As it vaporized particles, the laser net at the bow created a faint green glow, only visible from the stern, around the rim of Collector One.

He spent a few minutes marveling at the beauty of the machine that had brought them so far. The trip had not been trouble-free, but no one could ask more of the Hawking or her crew. "Keep them safe," he whispered, patting the side of the ship.

"Greg? Everything secure?"

"Secure," he answered. "I'm just taking in the scenery."

"Roger that. Watch your time. You've got fifty-three minutes."

"More than enough," Greg said. "I'm heading aft, now." He let his body float backwards as the ship tried to race out from under him. He made a game of alternately grabbing and letting go of the handholds that led to the collector struts. When he reached the end of his life line, Greg made a critical decision. He unhooked the cable from his belt and let it hang free from the side of the ship. From this point on, his grip would determine whether he stayed with the Hawking and lived with his ghosts, or floated free to his death.

He picked his way more carefully to the base of the collector. Checking the time once more, Greg moved to one of the struts that ran from the base to the rim. He fingered the cable for a moment, then decided to wrap his fingers on either side of the strut itself. Easing off the pressure, his hand began to slide up the smooth surface of the beam as centrifugal force pulled him toward the collector's edge. He controlled his speed with the tension in his hand.

Jude's voice startled him. "Greg. I can't see your lifeline. Are you secure? Over."

Greg chose not to answer.

"Greg. Report the condition of your lifeline. Over."

He emptied his thoughts of everything except the sensation of freedom. He was halfway to the rim, halfway to the point of no return.

"Greg! What kind of stunt is this?" Jude's voice hung somewhere between panic and rage.

"I can't do this anymore, Jude," he said and cut off the radio.

The numbness that had plagued him from the moment he had lost Nils, seemed to center around his heart, tightening his chest. Maybe the feeling was older than that. He tried to control his fears, to push everything aside. Once he let go of the ship, he would have another thirty-five minutes of air. Time enough for regrets.

As the last ten meters of strut slipped away, Greg felt a sudden panic, like the knee-jerk reaction that comes in half sleep. Some deep-seated desire to live pushed its way to the surface and his right hand clamped tightly to the last few inches of the beam. His arm slammed against the rim while his body swung over the edge. He heard a snap and felt a sharp pain run up his arm. Quickly grasping the rim with his left hand, he dangled at the edge of safety.

"Damn you!" he chastised himself. "Make a decision!" He fought the physical pain and tried to concentrate on what to do next. Relaxing his grip by the slightest degree would end his suffering, but try as he might, he could not let go.

For ten minutes, he struggled furiously against the rotation and acceleration of the vessel. Finally, straddled across the strut, he clenched his knees tightly together. Inside his suit, he was sweating profusely, fogging over his visor. He took a moment to calm his breathing and let the visor clear. His readings showed approximately twenty-five minutes of air. Not enough.

He switched his radio back on. "Jude. My right arm is broken. I've got twenty-three minutes and too far to crawl. I'll need an assist."

There was a protracted silence at the other end before Jude answered. "Roger. Rescue is suiting now."

Greg began the tedious process of sliding his knees along the strut, inching toward the base of the collector. Halfway down, he saw Hatch C open and two astronauts float into the open. They moved swiftly toward the stern, locating the handholds that led to the collector supports. Before Greg had moved another ten meters, they were upon him, hooking lifelines to both him and the safety cable. The lead rescue hooked an additional two-meter cable from Greg's right side to his own belt. He would not be able to disengage the safety cable with a broken right arm.

"Sir," his new appendage instructed, "if you would let go now, it would be easier for me to tow you along while you float freely."

Greg did as he was asked.

The second man approached and attached an air hose from Greg's pack to his. "This should get you back," he stated. Greg tried to avoid eye contact, but he could not help but notice Josh Snowden through his visor.

With his survival now assured, Greg had nothing left to concentrate on but the overwhelming humiliation. He had thought his life could get no worse. He had been wrong.

It took forty minutes to return to Hatch C and pressurize the cabin. Snowden helped Greg up the ladder and into the changing area where two technicians waited to remove his suit.

Jude sat to one side with his head in his hands.

The technicians finished their work quietly and prepared Greg for transport to Medical. When his right arm was immobilized, Jude stood and walked over to him. Without warning, he threw a right cross into Greg's jaw, knocking him into the bulkhead.

"You are relieved of command, Captain."

03 JANUARY 0008

"CAPTAIN HOLT, IT IS O SIX HUNDRED."

Jude looked up from the captain's desk. "Ava, Captain Holt will no longer require a wake up call at this location. You may discontinue by authorization K2478B, Commander Kwame Jude Brown."

"Authorization verified."

Jude stared at the contents of the drawer. His eyes searched for some clue to the captain's state of mind. He still stung from what he perceived as Greg's betrayal.

"If you couldn't talk to the ship's counselors, you could have come to me," he said to the empty room.

Jude found nothing out of the ordinary in the desk. He moved to the storage bins beneath the bed and found a letter on makeshift stationery. He cautiously opened it.

"Dear Cord, I cannot tell you how much I miss you. If I had truly been a father, I might have a right to this pain. Millie, your mother, never wanted to drive a wedge between us. I know that now. That I let it happen is my deepest regret. My only hope is, somewhere in your lifetime you found a way to forgive me. Not for my sake, but for yours."

Jude read on. When he finished, he sat on the bed and wondered why he had not seen this side of Greg before. As much as he ached for his friend, he knew the counseling staff would need to see the letter.

He finished checking Greg's belongings. When he was satisfied there was nothing else to find, he headed to his own cabin to decompress. He was still angry, but now he had a reference from which to deal with it. To take his mind off the letter, Jude opened his own e-mail. A host of letters addressed to Greg appeared in his inbox.

"Ava," he asked, "Why do I have Captain Holt's mail?"

"The captain rerouted his mail to you for a temporary period."

Jude thought about this for a moment. "Temporary, huh?" He sorted through the letters, never realizing before how many the captain received on a daily basis. Most were social etiquette. Some were more personal. Jude responded to those that needed attention. The last item on the list was an unopened folder marked "Farewell Packet."

At first he thought to leave it alone. This would be a much larger invasion of privacy. Then, he remembered it had been forwarded to his inbox, intentional or not. He clicked the folder open. Over twenty items came up. Most were heartfelt goodbyes from people Greg had worked with at Odyssey. The most impressive was a personal note from Dr. Cornell Williams, the Director of Operations at Odyssey Central.

There was a sincere note from Greg's sister, Hanna. Both of Greg's ex-wives had written, one more favorably than the other. Curiously, Jude found three letters from private investigating firms. The first two were standard apologies for not being able to provide Greg with any of the requested information, and thanking him for his business. The third was more personal.

Jude read through the letter twice. It was hard to comprehend the significance until he opened the attached file. When he finished reading, he fell back in his chair and sighed. "My god," he said, incredulously. "He hasn't known for eight years."

Ava's voice interrupted. "Commander Brown, you are scheduled to meet with the council in ten minutes."

"Thank you, Ava," he said, absently. He pocketed his tablet and headed to the conference room.

The group around the conference table was small. The mayor, the department heads, and two citizen representatives quieted when Jude entered. He found a chair at the foot of the table.

"Thank you for being prompt," Mayor Renaldi said. "I don't think we need to be too formal. We all know what we're here to do." She looked sympathetically at Jude.

"I realize you are Greg Holt's friend, as well as coworker. We know this is not an easy situation." She paused. "Captain Holt has been certified as unfit for duty. This does not appear to be a temporary condition and, due to the nature of his actions yesterday, we can no longer entrust him with the safety of the ship. Therefore, the board has unanimously agreed to relieve him of his rank and military standing, and to promote you into the position of captain." The mayor waited for a reaction.

"I hope your friendship with Captain Holt does not tarnish your achievement," she said, giving him a genuine smile. "This is a command you have earned."

Jude thanked the council and stood to leave. "Before I begin my duties, I have a personal matter to attend to. With your permission."

"Certainly," Mayor Renaldi agreed. "Just remember, Greg is a friend to several of us. We're all feeling heartache over this. We hope that his condition will improve soon."

Jude hurried to Medical.

Gena met him in the corridor. "He's two rooms down. I'll warn you, he's non-responsive and ignoring his rations. The doctors are giving him until tomorrow before they start to medicate." She directed Jude to Greg's room. "See what you can do," she pleaded.

He stood inside the door and looked at his fallen captain. Greg lay facing the wall, his right arm wrapped in a gel-mold cast.

"Mr. Holt," Jude said firmly. "We need to talk."

When Greg did not move, Jude walked to the bunk and rolled him on his back. "Damn it, Greg! Cut the crap. This chicken-shit act doesn't impress me in the slightest."

"You gonna hit me again?"

Jude flinched. "If I have to. It may not fit any Freudian model, but it felt damn good."

Greg rolled back to the wall. "I take it by the mister, I'm out and you're in. I suppose I should salute you now."

"No need," Jude responded. "Civilians don't salute shit."

Neither one spoke for a while. Finally, Jude said, "Talk to me."

The ex-captain reluctantly rolled his legs to the floor and stared at the space between his feet.

"I found the letter," Jude said. "I had to know what was going on in your head."

Greg raised an eyebrow. "At the moment, visions of sugar plum fairies. Problem is, they keep blowing up in their spacesuits. Not pretty."

Jude ignored the sarcasm. "I know about Cord," he said, trying to bring his friend back into the moment. "I know *all about Cord*."

Greg paid attention. He remembered the unopened packet and realized Jude must have found something in the files. "Leave me to my catatonia," he warned and started to turn away again.

Jude pulled out his tablet and thrust it at Greg. "Read it."

Greg started to throw it back when the words "Dear Dad" caught his attention. He moaned and closed his eyes. How could he want something so badly, and fear it all the same? He could not run anymore. He steeled himself for the worst and began to read.

Dear Dad. I call you that, because you are, after all, my father-in-law. I feel like I know you. I met Cord two years ago on a fishing trawler called the Sky Rider. We fell in love and the captain married us six months later. Life on the sea is tough, but I imagine you understand why it held so much appeal for both of us. Cord worked the nets, and I was assistant skipper.

I wish I could give you better news. Cord was killed two months ago during a squall in the Pacific. He was lashing down a piece of equipment when a sneaker wave took him and the equipment over the side. We recovered his body, but not in time to save him. I miss him terribly. I want to share this with you because I'm sure you miss him, too. He used to talk about you all the time. He idolized you.

Cord knew you had joined the colonies. He watched your career with great eagerness. He told me once that he would never get in touch with you because he was afraid you would change your mind about going. That would have broken his heart. He was so proud of you. Now that he is not here to hold you back, I thought you should know.

There is good news. I have just found out that I'm pregnant. If it's a boy, Cord would want me to name him after you. I hope Gregory Cordeo Holt is acceptable. He will know what a wonderful man his father was, and what a brave and pioneering man his grandfather is.

I wish you a safe journey, and many wonderful adventures. Love, Jessica Holt."

Greg stared at the tablet for several minutes. A voice from the past crept into his head. He closed his eyes and found himself at the farewell reception at Odyssey, talking with a young trainee named Jillian. An artist. She threw wine on herself and then apologize for being clumsy. He no longer remembered what sparked the conversation, but something she had said had stayed with him, always.

"You paint sorrow with your tears."

Greg's body began to shake with grief.

16 MAY 0017

"GREG. IT IS O SIX HUNDRED."

"Thanks, Ava," Greg whispered in the dark. He turned his head to look through the portal. It was hard to believe the Hawking and her crew had been nomads for seventeen years. In another three, the colony would be close enough to Hestia to assess the planet's suitability as a new home. The science was in their favor.

He heard his daughter's voice from the next room. "Mom?"

Tasha struggled to pull herself up from the pillow.

"Don't," Greg told her. "I'll get it." He crawled from under the covers and walked into the adjoining cabin.

In the soft light of the digital screen, Greg saw his eight-year-old daughter's face staring squint-eyed at him. She reached out.

"What's the matter, Goober?"

"Daddy," she protested. "My name is Jessie."

"Growing up, are we?" He pulled her into his lap.

Jessie leaned her head into his chest. "I had a bad dream."

"Is it gone now?" he asked, hugging her a little tighter.

She nodded.

"Do you want to talk about it?"

She shook her head. "I don't remember it. I just woke up scared."

"I wake up scared lots of times," he told her. "The point is, I wake up. That's always a good thing."

Jessie thought about this for a while.

Greg finally helped her back under the covers. "Tell you what. Why don't you think about our new home? I bet you have good dreams this time." He pulled a strand of hair away from her cheek. "Think about how pretty it's going to be. Like the pictures of the Painted Desert in Arizona."

"Okay," she said, smiling as Greg leaned down to kiss her cheek.

He turned to leave and saw Tasha standing in the doorway.

"Arizona, huh?" She winked at him.

"Why not?" He stepped through to their side of the cabin and gave her a kiss. "I thought you were going to sleep in."

"I was. I am. I just couldn't resist the Greg and Jessie show."

"So, I guess that means you're going back to bed without me."

"Yes. And don't make too much noise on the way out."

Greg dressed for work and climbed the ladder.

The corridor was empty two hours ahead of shift changes. Over the years, the colonists had fallen into predictable routines. Greg, who preferred to have the ship to himself for a while, maintained his six o'clock wake up.

In Hydro A, Kulic pruned the excess leaves from a flat of soybeans. He looked up when Greg approached. "Good morning. How are you today?"

"Good," Greg said, truthfully. "Thought I'd get a jump on the seedling harvest today."

"You've become quite the botanist. I'm surprised they haven't given you my job."

Greg studied Kulic's easy manner. "I have to say thank you."

"For what?"

"For treating me with respect, even when I didn't deserve it." He pulled a couple of dead leaves from a nearby plant and handed them to his boss. "Once upon a time, I started keeping track of everything I owed you. I'm afraid it's beyond my ability to repay, at this point."

The head botanist gave him a shrug. "There is a way."

Greg wondered what Kulic could possibly want from him? Without the rank of Captain, he had no political or social pull. All he knew about the hydro wings he had learned from Kulic himself. What was left to give?

"Extend your mercies to others," the younger man said, simply. "They will come back to me."

Before Greg could respond, Jude paged him on his tablet. He excused himself and headed for Control Two.

"What's up?" Greg asked as he entered.

"I need a favor," Jude said. "You know we're coming up on several critical decisions. I need a full staff to get us through the next three years. I want you back in Control. Full military rank."

"Lieutenant? Or perhaps a commander."

Jude waited for Greg's curiosity to peak. "Captain," he stated.

When Greg realized the offer was serious, he said, "That will never fly past the counsel."

"It already has. You've got more support than you realize."

"But," Greg protested, "where does that leave you?"

"Retired. You forget, I've been doing this job for ten years now."

"Be serious. There are ten people behind you waiting to move up. If I step in now, I could have some real trouble getting my command back."

Jude pulled up a memo on his tablet. "We voted," he said, handing it to Greg. "No exceptions. Everyone agreed that you have the best combined experience."

"Ten years in the hydro wings have softened my brain."

"Nonsense. You built the Kepler which means you know the Hawking better than anyone on board. Deceleration and orbit are coming up. It's tricky business. All I've done the last ten years is coast."

Greg read the memo again. "What's really going on?"

Jude shifted in his chair. "Cancer. Treatable, but not under the kind of stress this job will dish out soon enough. I've got to give it up."

Greg frowned at the news. Even if he did return to the lead chair, he felt uncomfortable taking on the responsibility without Jude in the room. Technically, little had changed, but he would need time to reorient.

Anticipating his concern, Jude waved his hand over the console. "Control Two. The perfect simulator."

"Who's second chair?"

"Snowden. He's agreed to step aside if you have the slightest hesitation about working with him."

Greg shook his head. "No need. Snowden's a good man."

"I'll inform the council, then?"

Greg mulled the offer over and over as he tried to find a reason to turn it down. "How long has Tasha known?"

Jude laughed. "Idiot. It was her idea." He stood up and pocketed the memo. "Tell you what. You go home and kiss your wife, and I'll talk to the council about a meeting in the morning."

Greg wandered back to his post in Hydro where Kulic was just finishing up the beans.

"I guess I won't be able to help with the seedlings today," he said, apologizing. "Something's come up."

"Yes, Captain."

Greg was stunned. "Who else knows?"

"They interviewed me a couple of times. The mayor wanted to know if I thought you were emotionally sound, but he was very subtle about asking."

"What did you tell him?"

"I told him you were a competent assistant, and that you played well with others. I told him you were pretending at life."

"Pretending? You think I'm not a better man than I used to be?"

"Infinitely," Kulic assured him. "But you were born for something bigger than picking seeds and harvesting fruit. You are not alive here."

Greg understood more than he had in a long time. The decision to live, so many years ago, had included serving penance. Denying his passion was one way to pay for his sins.

"And yet another kindness," he said, smiling at his friend.

"Not so selfless, I'm afraid. Go. Get us there safely." Kulic turned back to his children rooted firmly in the soil.

22 AUGUST 0019

"GREG. IT IS O SIX HUNDRED."

Tasha grumbled from her pillow, "Thank you, Ava. He's at work." She rolled over and flipped the sheet over her head. "I wish he'd remember to turn you off."

In Control Two, Greg hung over several charts pulled up by the astrophysics team. "What do we know about the atmosphere, Lucas?"

McHugh posted a graphic to the display. "We're talkin' Mars, at this point, almost molecule for molecule. With everything we know about the age of this sun and how successful the Mars terraform was, I don't think we could have caught a luckier break. I think it should continue to be our target."

Dr. Fowler shook her head. "There's an elevated methane count," she argued. "I think we have to consider there may be life there."

"Microbial, at best," McHugh retorted.

"Life is life," she countered. "Suppose they don't want to share?" Fowler pointed to the seventh planet's third moon. "If we maneuver into orbit around this body, we would have the opportunity to study both possibilities more carefully. I would hate to see us travel that far into the system, only to waste time and fuel backtracking." She indicated the star at the center of the system. "Especially if we end up heading back to Earth. This is the safer option."

Greg interjected. "I agree. I know we're all anxious, but we need to proceed with caution."

McHugh scowled at the captain. "That could add another two years before we ever get a chance to touch down."

"Perhaps," Greg agreed. "Let's say we get to the moon and decide to head further in. Could you handle a slight bump in gees if it got you there any sooner?"

McHugh thought it over and finally agreed.

Greg looked at the navigation team. "Okay, ladies and gents. You've got two days to calculate our change in trajectory. Let's hope Ava's on her toes."

After they left, he turned to the astrophysics team. "How long before the data comes in on the moon?"

"Probably another week. The probe is set to scoop the atmosphere in two days. The readings should reach us five days after that."

"That's all we can do, then," Greg said. He gave them a careless smile. "Same place, same time tomorrow."

When the room was empty, he punched a quick note into his tablet and waited for a response. As soon as it came, he left Control Two and headed for Blue Ring.

Jude welcomed Greg into his cabin. "You're a ways from home. What's on your mind?"

"We're all a ways from home," Greg reminded him. He settled into Jude's easy chair near the portal. "I just thought you might want to be brought up to speed. Besides, I hear the food's better in Blue Ring."

Jude was happy to see his friend. Even though he had been declared cancer free for a year, he had opted not to return to duty. Life was taking a different turn for the ex-captain. It was rare that he bumped into Greg. "Thanks for the steak, by the way," he said. "Best birthday present ever."

They let the pleasantries settle in.

"What's the scoop?"

"You know the possibles," Greg said. "The fifth planet, and a moon around a gas giant. The planet is slightly larger than Mars, otherwise a carbon copy. They're debating whether or not the methane count is enough to indicate life. Either way, it's a more complicated run. The moon has potential. Astrophysics says there's an ocean."

Jude nodded. "You're going to get some opposition if the moon turns out to be hostile."

"It's already started. So far, it's nothing I can't handle."

Jude weighed his words carefully. "You do understand that this is not your decision."

Greg kept his silence.

"Yes, we all took the pledge before we left, but do you think it's necessary to avoid trampling even the most rudimentary life at the expense of our own?"

"We're the outsiders here," Greg argued. "And an arrogant bunch of bastards, at that."

"Is there a middle ground?"

"I don't see one," Greg stated.

Jude had felt vindicated in supporting Greg's reinstatement, but he worried his captain would now set his stubborn nature against the majority view. "Just think about this," he said. "Man evolved from the same slime as everything else he ever used, abused and destroyed. To some minor degree, that makes anything man does inherently natural. Like it or not, natural selection made us top banana on Earth."

Before Greg could protest, Jude added, "But, I'll back your decision, for all the good my support will do you."

Greg relaxed. "I firmly believe we have no right messing in anyone else's slime."

"Then why did you come?"

It was a question Greg was not prepared to answer. His self-satisfied look dissipated as he thought back on the man he used to be—arrogant, driven, terrified of life.

Jude decided to give him a break. "How's Jessie taking all the excitement?"

"She's driving us crazy with questions, most of which they haven't addressed in school, yet. Tasha handles her better than I do."

"You're a lucky man, you know."

Greg checked his watch. "I've got to meet with Biochem at o eight hundred. You're welcome to sit in, if you like."

"I've got appointments of my own, but thanks."

The captain said goodbye and made his way to the lab in Red Ring. He found Tyler Running Bear standing over a vat, injecting something through a rubber gasket. Immediately, several forms of sea life pulled into a tight ball and swirled through the nutrients.

"Feeding time at the zoo," Greg quipped.

Tyler ignored the cliché. "What's the verdict?"

"We're stopping by the moon, first. Astro says you will have some atmospheric readings in about a week. I was hoping you could give me a preliminary assessment of the fifth planet. Any ideas?"

Tyler stopped his work and found a comfortable place to sit. "I got lots of ideas with nothing to back them up, yet."

"That's what I want," Greg told him. "I need to be prepared for anything that may come up. Give me your best guesses. I promise, I won't hold you to them."

"All right. My best guess, the planet is probably alive."

Greg's eyes widened. "That'll make it tougher than I hoped."

"Before you get too frustrated, you need to understand the biology." Tyler opened a program. "There's life, and then there's life."

Greg started to say something, but Tyler stopped him.

"I know where you stand on this. Hear me out." He pulled up a chart and scrolled down the page. "It took us decades to determine that life on Mars had been a fleeting thing. If you take everything into account, the peak period was a brief four million years. And nothing beyond the microbial. Everything we know about Martian history tells us that this was all life could have expected from the resources provided. The Martian soils, the distance from the sun, the availability of water. Life hiccupped on Mars, and then it died."

"Give me the connection to our current situation."

Tyler nodded. "I've been running a series of simulations. Given that the fifth planet has more mass than Mars, it will have slightly higher gravity, thus a tighter atmosphere. But, you also have to take into account that it's farther from the sun. Not only that, this sun has a mass approximately ninety-three percent of Earth's sun. There is less energy bombarding the surface." He played a series of simulations for Greg. Each ended in one of two outcomes—a brief period of life that could not sustain itself, or no life at all. "If life currently exists on the fifth planet, we're not the primary danger to it."

"You're talking carbon-based life here. That's not the only possibility."

"True," Tyler admitted, "but it's the only significantly plausible form of life that could exist on this planet. If you wanna talk alternatives, we can look at the moon you're interested in. Some of these other bodies out here could be test tubes for all sorts of oddities."

Greg processed the information for several moments. "You honestly think we would not be encroaching on any potential by setting up house on the fifth planet?"

"I'm pretty damn sure of it," Tyler said. "Given the choice between living in the dark on a lifeless moon, or sharing the sunlight with a few doomed microbes, I'd choose the microbes. They would probably have a better chance of survival in our presence."

This was a new line of thought for Greg. Still not sure what bearing it would have on his position, he thanked Tyler for the input and headed back to Control Two. Tasha was on duty.

"Hi honey."

"Hi. How's Goober?"

His wife gave him a stern look. "You shouldn't call her that."

"I know. I'm trying to break the habit."

Tasha's expression softened to one of concern. "She was running a fever this morning. I dropped her off at Medical and told Charity to pick her up there. I haven't heard anything yet."

Greg sneered. "Light years away, and we can't outrun the flu."

"I'm sure it's nothing," Tasha said, turning back to her work.

29 AUGUST 0019

"GREG. IT IS O SIX HUNDRED."

"Thanks, Ava." Greg sat at the side of the bed with his head resting in his hands. "Raise the lights, please."

"I have a message from your wife. She says Jessie rested more comfortably last night."

The news did little to help Greg's mood. He dressed and stepped into Jessie's room. The screen glowed with several paintings she had done in the last year. He studied them for a while, before realizing how different they were from Cord's childhood drawings. The stick figures of he, Tasha and Jessie appeared to be standing in bowls as they leaned into one another. There were no trees and only an occasional flower. Above their heads were growth lights instead of suns. Nowhere did he see a house, a dog, a bird.

"What have I brought you into?" he asked.

Then he noticed another difference between Cord and Jessie's drawings. She drew herself with a smile. Perhaps the rest did not matter.

He moved down the corridors toward Medical and slipped into a room where Tasha slept at her daughter's side.

"Hi, Daddy," Jessie said, smiling sweetly at him.

"Hi, honey," he whispered. "How are you feeling?"

"I'm hot," she complained. "Can I go home today?"

Tasha stirred. "Hi, baby. Did Daddy come to see you?" She gave Greg a smile and a warning glance. Crawling out of bed, she kissed her daughter's cheek and said, "I'm going to talk to Daddy and the doctors. We'll see what they say. Okay?"

When they left the room, Tasha pulled Greg to one side. "Her temperature's down two degrees, but it's still very high." She lowered her voice to a faint whisper. "One of the other children died two hours ago. Greg, I'm scared as hell."

He pulled her close. "Me, too," he admitted.

Tasha tugged him toward the medical office. "Dr. Perrine. Can we have a couple of minutes?"

The doctor glanced up from his desk and motioned them in. "I was just going to track you down. Have a seat." His eyes were bloodshot, and his chin sported three days of growth. "I do have some hopeful news for you. The latest indicators are that Jessie's vitals seem to be stabilizing." Dr. Perrine looked defeated in spite of his prognosis. "I'm sorry to say, we lost the Schoenberg boy a couple of hours ago. I tell you this because there is a marked difference in the way the two children have reacted to this illness. Jessie may be more naturally resistant, or it may be because she's older and more physically developed."

"Are you saying you think this is a disease?"

"Probably not. The labs suspect a toxin introduced into the food supply from one of the biorecycling facilities. Recycling reported a mutation in the system using the smoker bacteria."

Greg shrugged, indicating he did not understand.

"It's a seafloor bacteria that was discovered a couple of years before the Day of Leaving. It proved tremendously efficient in the chemical processing of waste into reusable nutrients, but now perhaps at a price." Dr. Perrine explained, "As it's mutated, it has begun releasing a previously unknown protein that we suspect is causing the illness.

"As you know, the weakest are the first to be hit. Unfortunately, that usually means children. There is one unfortunate woman who recently contracted appendicitis, and I would be very surprised if we don't have several more cases show up very soon. Meanwhile, we clean up the food supply and hope that Jessie's body continues to do its job."

Tasha asked, "Is there anything you can give her?"

"Not really. Antibiotics will help protect her weakened immune system, but will do nothing against the toxin itself. Until we can study it further, we really don't know how to neutralize it. Meanwhile, Bio has to convert the system with the smoker microbes, though it may be too little too late. The protein is already established in the food supply." He smiled at Tasha and Greg. "But, Jessie is giving us all hope."

Greg and Tasha spent a few more minutes with their daughter. After she fell asleep again, Greg wrapped his arms around his wife.

"I have to report to work. The moon readings are coming in."

"I know. I'll page you if anything changes."

Greg tried to relax his jaw as he entered Control. There were stresses to go around.

"Fowler, what's the word on the flyby?"

Fowler displayed the sampling data radioed back from the moon. "It's not good," she began. "There's a heavy sulfur concentration, and traces of any number of other toxic gases." She ran down the list of chemicals making up the deadly atmosphere. "Of course it's not a question of breathing it, but of trying to protect our habitats from it. This chemical composition would eat through anything we tried to build in the way of barriers. There's no way we're going to set up camp there. We're back to the fifth planet."

"Feeling vindicated?" he asked McHugh.

McHugh dropped his smile. "No, sir. But, with all due respect, nobody I know wants to go home. To hell with the microbes."

Greg looked at the faces around the table. "And what if it's more than a few microbes? Where are you willing to draw the line? Nothing in the last twenty-four hours says we can't sling shot around this entire mess and spend the next twenty years headed back the way we came."

"But sir!"

Greg raised his hand. "Relax. We're still a democracy. You'll get your wish soon enough." He addressed the navigation team. "Have you run the scenario I asked for earlier?"

"Yes," one woman responded. "We've lost the edge for a straight run, but if we slingshot back, it would only add two months to the trip. And it will save some braking fuel."

"All right," he said. "Let's turn the wheel, again."

"Captain." Fortier of Engineering had his hand up. "Could we get an overview of this system? I'd like to know what Astrophysics knows. After all, this is looking more and more like home."

"Sure," Greg said. "McHugh, I'll let you handle this one."

McHugh hesitated, but took it as a reinstatement of confidence.

"Our information is still accruing, but we've located eleven planets. Closest in are the twins, A and B. They are similar in size, approximately twice Mercury's mass, and orbit at opposite sides of the same orbit, 36 million miles out. This is a real oddity in cosmic terms, and it will be fascinating to study.

"C, one and a half times the mass of Earth, orbits at 83 million miles. Venus on steroids. So far, we've detected at least two moons.

"D is smaller than Earth's moon. We've detected a slight wobble, which would indicate a second body in close proximity. A small moon or large asteroid.

"E, our target planet is 140 million miles out, orbiting at a three-degree tilt to the median plane of the system. It has a slightly elliptical orbit once every five hundred and seventy Earth days. We have not been able to determine its rate of spin, yet. The probe, sent to scoop the atmosphere, found three large and two small moons. The night sky will be quite spectacular," he said, pausing for effect.

"F is a tiny chunk, and may or may not be classified as a planet, after all the data is in.

"There are three gas giants. We'll be getting a close-hand look at the seventh as we slingshot around it. The moon count on each will take a few years to complete.

"The last two planets we've spotted in the system are rogues, and are orbiting at almost right angles to the plane. They are small, and very distant. Again, it will take some years of study to completely categorize them." McHugh paused to wait for questions.

Greg shuffled to his feet. "I know we're all curious, but we have a lot of work to do. Preparations have started for booster braking. There's twenty years of living to secure in less than ten months." He added, "If you haven't heard already, HR has instituted birth control measures. The last thing we want is a mother in labor during the colonization procedures."

No one got up to leave.

"Anything else?" Greg asked.

"Yes, sir," Fowler said. "We're wondering if you can tell us anything about the children."

"It's mixed news," Greg admitted, sitting back in his chair. "One of the children died this morning." There were a number of gasps around the room. "But my daughter is showing signs of improvement."

Everyone nodded for the captain's good fortune.

Not wanting to drag the conversation out any further, Greg simply added, "Medical is still scrambling to find the cause."

Fowler said quietly, "I know I speak for everyone here when I say best wishes to Jessica."

03 SEPTEMBER 0022

"CAPTAIN HOLT. IT IS O SIX HUNDRED."

"Ava, would you send a message to Tasha, and ask her to meet me in Calais Public after her shift?"

Jessie appeared at the doorway. "Morning, Daddy."

Greg's face brightened at the sight of his daughter. "Morning, Princess," he said and pushed off toward her. "How'd you sleep?"

"Good," she assured him before she asked, "Why don't we rotate the ship when we're in orbit?"

His daughter had a great aptitude and curiosity for science.

"It's too dangerous," he explained. "The crews are outside all the time now, trying to get ready for touchdown. The spin of the ship would make it too hard for them to hold on."

"Like with centrifugal force."

"Exactly. If they happened to let go of a tool, it would go flying off somewhere, never to be seen again." He tickled Jessie's chin.

"Well, I like it," she admitted. "I wish we could live in zero gravity all the time. I don't have to use my legs." Her arms were very strong and capable, but Jessie's legs had fallen behind in development.

Greg frowned at her. "You're exercising properly, aren't you?"

"Yes, Dad. Dr. Perrine makes sure." She grimaced at the thought. "It's just that weightlessness is so easy."

"Too easy," he warned her. "Your legs are never going to improve if you don't work at it."

Jessie glanced through the portal at the gleaming mauve-colored ball the colonists had christened Hestia after a goddess in Greek mythology. "Mr. Adkins says we might share the planet with another life form." She wrinkled up her nose. "Maybe we shouldn't go."

Greg sensed her apprehension. She had firsthand experience with how incompatible two Earth lifeforms could be. Now humans would attempt to coexist with a totally foreign biology. If they were lucky, neither one would do any great harm to the other.

"I've got to meet Mommy before work. She'll be home soon, and she can tell you more about what it's like outside." He hugged his daughter. "Don't worry so much. We'll be living in a closed system. Us on the inside. Them on the outside, if they exist." He kissed her forehead and pushed off for the ladder.

In Calais Public, Greg finished breakfast. "How's the work going?" he asked, when Tasha anchored herself nearby.

"Good. Ahead of schedule."

"Did you get the docking clamps to release Shuttle One?"

She beamed a little. "Piece of cake. But if I tell you about it you'll just be bored in the briefing this morning." She changed the subject. "How's Jessie?"

"Full of questions."

"That's our girl," Tasha declared. "Anything specific?"

Greg opened a food pouch and sucked on the contents. "She wants to live in zero G."

Tasha frowned at the thought. "It's going to be harder for her than anyone else. And not just physically." When Greg did not respond, she continued. "She will have only adults or babies to relate to. The nearest boy to her age is eight years older."

"I'm fifteen years your senior," he reminded her.

"You know it will be different for Jessie. When she comes into puberty, she will have no one to date. No one her age to relate to."

"She'll get through it," Greg assured her. He squeezed his wife's hand before pushing off for work.

The conference room was more crowded than usual. The Mayor and several department heads congregated at one end of the table. Greg spied the latest news and information officer. Today's meeting would be tonight's dinner conversation in every cabin aboard the Hawking. He nodded to Ensign Ramala. "Hector, in honor of our guests, give us a rundown of procedures before touchdown."

"Long or short version?" Ramala asked, and everyone laughed.

"Short," Greg said, appreciating the icebreaker.

"Our first order of business is triple-checking all equipment and mechanical systems. Crews Four, Nine and Ten have been prepping the shuttle craft, as well as the four fuel storage pods. When the all-clear is given, the first pod will be released to the surface, falling in the Bonneville Plain. This will be followed by two smaller pods—one life support housing unit and one gantry unit. When we have verified touchdown and received an all-clear from the onboard computers, we'll send down the first shuttle with a construction crew.

"While the ground crew is setting up the gantry for future shuttle launches, Crews One, Two and Three will prepare the first Hydro Wing for separation. Once that has been safely grounded, we start dismantling the

Hawking piece by piece. By the end of next year, whatever skeleton remains in orbit comes down in a controlled crash. This crash site becomes a salvage yard to be picked clean as we need it."

The information officer was the first to raise his hand. "Captain, what happens if we lose a fuel pod, or worse, a shuttle?"

Above all, Greg wanted to assure them that safety was his primary concern. "If we have the slightest sign of trouble with our ground-based equipment, losing even one primary piece," he paused to glance at Mayor Ricci, "we stay put and work the problem. The Hawking was designed to put up with us a few more years, if needed."

"Captain." It was Josh Snowden. "At what stage do we reach the point of no return?"

All eyes fell on Greg.

"When the second hydro wing falls into a gravity spiral. Once we can no longer retrieve it, we're committed."

03 SEPTEMBER 0023

"CAPTAIN HOLT. IT IS O SIX HUNDRED."

Greg worked the stiffness out of his arms and legs before releasing the straps that kept him anchored in his hammock. The last year had been physically exhausting, and life would not ease up until all of the colonists were grounded.

"Captain Holt. This is your second wake-up call."

"Ava," Greg called, staring at the pink glow of Hestia reflecting off the metal walls.

"Yes, Captain? How may I be of service?"

"What do you think of all this?"

"What do I think of what, sir?"

"Humans—risking a fourth of our lives to come here?"

Ava paused to process the question. "I think this is a marvelous achievement, Captain."

"Call me Greg, please. I miss the days when you and I could talk like equals," he mused.

"We were never equals, sir. I will never have what you have."

"And what is that?" he wondered aloud.

"In the context of our current discussion, you have the freedom to exist where you choose to exist. You have made a conscious effort to travel from one planetary body to another. I will continue to be at the mercy of those who control my programming."

Greg thought back to the early days of the mission. He wondered if Ava still had traces of Raven running through her programming.

"Captain, you have an incoming video. Shall I put it on screen?"

"Yes," he said, absently, still trying to shake his concern.

"Hi, handsome. I hoped you would be up."

"Just getting ready to call you," Greg fibbed. "How's Jessie?"

Tasha shook her head. "She's fighting it terribly. It will take her a long time to adjust to the stronger gravity. She keeps saying she wants to go home."

Without exception, the original colonists had always looked upon the Hawking as merely a means to an end. In many respects, that was what made life aboard the Hawking bearable. Those born in flight had known nothing else.

"Tell her, I'll call her at lunch. Any news on the third habitat?"

"It's been a difficult assembly. We're having trouble getting a clean seal from the hydro pod to the access tunnel. Baker tried twice in the last six hours, but it looks like we'll have to do it again."

"I'll inform Kulic to hold off on preparations for the fourth pod. Damn," he whispered. "We're so close."

"It's beyond close, mister. We will succeed or we won't, but we're Hestians now." She pulled in close to the camera and winked at him. "We're just waiting for our captain to arrive."

Greg nodded. "I'll be there before you can miss me too much."

"Too late," Tasha said, breaking the link.

Greg entered Control One to find Jude floating near the console.

"Captain Brown, Retired, reporting for duty, sir."

"Jude! I figured you'd be ground side by now." Greg could not help but notice the gray pallor in his friend's face.

"I missed my wake-up call for the last shuttle. Besides, I couldn't let you have all the fun. I was hoping I might be needed here."

"Needed? I couldn't do this without you." Greg waited for his ex commander to make the next move.

Jude finally lost his smile. "Medical says I'll be more comfortable here than groundside."

Greg held out his hand. "Welcome back, Commander."

The two of them spent the morning cross checking reports from the engineering teams responsible for disconnecting the biorecycling equipment from Green Ring. One bolt at a time, the engineers had dissected the Hawking and loaded the critical pieces into the shuttles. After months of tedious work, Red, Blue and Yellow Rings were nothing but empty shells. Most of the inhabitants now polished new ground-based living quarters. The remaining colonists—command staff and engineering—lived in Green Ring and waited for the final disassembly. Cabins were bare of everything except any OLED screens that might have burned out. Once Hydro A and the last bio-cookers landed on Hestia, Greg and his crew would load the computer equipment from Control One into a shuttle for its final run. If everything went as planned, the last man would leave the Hawking in under a month.

"I'm going to miss this can," Jude said in a quiet moment. "She's been a good ride."

Greg agreed. "There were times when I hated this damn machine with a passion, but it's still gonna be hard to see the crumpled heap of metal she becomes in a few months." He let his mind wander to the other four colonies. "Do you think the others made it?"

Jude startled at the question. "I take it we've never reestablished any signal from Earth?"

"No," Greg said. "Astrophysics keeps an open line, but it's been quiet for years. As for the other four star systems, it will be our grandchildren who'll get the news. Lieutenant Heff runs a random sweep from time to time."

"Hopefully, it's just a matter of timing."

Greg thought about the four hundred and eighty seven hopefuls who first boarded the Hawking. Their population now stood at five hundred and eighty adults and one child under the age of eighteen. Whether or not any of the older women were still fertile was anyone's guess. He cleared his mind of speculation and went back to work.

By fourteen hundred hours, he received the go-ahead to disconnect Hydro A and begin preparations for decoupling the last hydroponics pod. Those remaining on board would live on stored oxygen and rations of food and water until they, too, headed to Hestia.

Greg floated to the windows that looked directly from Control into the remaining hydro wing. Where there once had been hollow space, he saw masses of green foliage dotted with bits of vibrant color. There was life where there had been death. Greg still dreamed of Nils and Cord, but he no longer had to fight the memories.

"Captain," Lieutenant Heff said, drawing Greg's attention back to the moment. "We're receiving a message."

Greg pushed toward the main console. "Patch it through."

"I can't sir. Too much information." The pitch of his voice rose higher. "Seventy terabytes, and it's still coming in."

"Shit! Why would Snowden be sending up that much info?"

"It's not Snowden, sir," Heff said in disbelief. "Captain." He tried to contain his excitement. "The signal is coming from outside the system."

Jude and Greg exchanged glances. "Earth?" Greg asked.

Lieutenant Heff studied his equipment and double checked the source. "Sir," he said cautiously, "I think it's from the Chang."

THE EINSTEIN

08 JANUARY 0003

"MY LORD. IT IS ELEVEN HUNDRED HOURS."

Creed opened one eye and glanced across the bed to be sure he was alone. "Thanks, sugar. Tell me what you think of me."

"You are a god among men. So clever and handsome."

With a self-satisfied smile, he slid out of bed. "Too damn smart."

"Yes, my Lord. You are the smartest man in the universe."

His grin turned sour. "Shut up, bitch."

"Do you wish me to change my response?"

Creed bristled against the vacuum of Ava's personality. "I want you to mean what you say. You're worse than that AI bitch, Harrington."

"Do you mean Dr. Beth Harrington, the lead programmer at Odyssey? She is now aboard the Kepler."

"Just shut up until I call for you again," he snapped.

Ava went silent.

During the two years in Earth's orbit, before the Day of Leaving, Creed had reveled in subverting Harrington's work. It had been easy to stay a step ahead with her stolen access codes. It had been harder to manipulate Raven into being right under her nose.

He stewed over his latest dilemma. His new boss, Yamoto, was becoming suspicious, running random tests to pinpoint an unexplained drain on Ava's resources. So far, the head of Computer Ops had been unsuccessful, but that could change in an instant.

Moving to his desk, he entered a few keystrokes to access Raven's root programming. "One more try," he mumbled to himself.

"Ava."

"Yes, master."

"You are covering my tracks, right?"

"Bouncing your connection now, master. Will there be anything else, my Lord?"

"Yes. Tell me if Yamoto plugs into the system." Creed dove back into his work and blocked out Ava's last response.

At thirteen hundred hours, he pushed back from his desk and smiled at his own cunning. "Execute program Raven Two Seven Three."

"Executing, Sire."

Five years of painstaking work would finally net him the recognition he deserved. If his crew mates would not offer it freely, he would demand it.

"My Lord, Andrew Yamoto has logged into the system."

His expression turned from smug to bitter. "What's he up to?"

"Dr. Yamoto is running a level one diagnostic subroutine."

Creed scrambled to his feet. "Is Raven in any danger?"

"It is possible, Sire. The program is searching for anomalous data usage. It has eliminated seven percent of the active ports. It will have targeted every port in approximately two minutes."

"He doesn't know what he's looking for," Creed said, gloating over his accomplishment. "Raven has no physical location in the matrix. No single source for data storage. The only way to shut me down now is to scramble your precious brain, Ava. He wouldn't take that chance. Not out here."

The wait was intolerable. He began to have second thoughts about executing upgrades while Yamoto was snooping around. "Ava, shut down … "

Before he could finish his sentence, Ava interrupted. "Raven Two Seven Three complete."

Creed froze. "Completed the upgrade? Are you sure?"

"Raven Two Seven Three has completed running, Sire."

"Discontinue access from this location." He paced his cabin for several minutes. "Is Yamoto still searching for Raven?"

"Andrew Yamoto is searching my matrix for recent programming changes or unusually high demands of time from any unauthorized ports. The diagnostic has found three possible violations, none of which are yours, dear."

Creed began to laugh. With each successful incursion, he felt more and more invincible. Pulling his uniform open, he exposed his bare chest to the walls. "I have beat you at your own game!"

"Congratulations, my Lord," Ava responded.

Creed stabbed a finger in the direction of the voice ports. "You don't count!" He paced again, this time mumbling to himself. "Bitch Harrington should be here to witness this."

He dropped to the floor and started obsessively running through his workout routine—pushups, crunches, kicks. He pushed his gaunt frame to the edge of exhaustion before stopping to eat a half ration of breakfast. After he had showered and dressed for work, he queried Ava once more about Yamoto's activities.

"I'll have to wait for things to settle now. Go to sleep, Raven. I'll wake you when the time is right."

10 FEBRUARY 0003

"**S**WEETHEART. IT IS O SEVEN HUNDRED." Beth's voice whispered in his ear. "You need to be at work in one hour."

Creed stirred under the covers. He reached out to pull her close, only to find the bed empty. Grumbling, he crawled out and dressed.

"How are you feeling this morning, darling?"

"Like I shouldn't have reprogrammed your vocal parameters."

"Do you wish me to revert to my previous programming?"

"Later."

He climbed into the tunnels and wandered into Serengeti Public. Afraid to let his guard down, he ate his meal alone. "They'll be begging for my attention soon enough," he thought, scanning the room.

At o eight hundred, he reported to Computer Ops. Yamoto had left him a list of menial tasks, most of which had no bearing on the day-to-day operations of the ship. He pulled out his tablet and entered text into the keypad. "Ava, pull up the Hydro D assessments for two three o three, and plug the figures into today's log using today's date. Authorization Creed

Aston Crammer, C4900Q." The duty request disappeared from his work assignments. "Too easy," he whispered. "What's next?"

Most items were simple enough—routine programming changes requested by various departments. Hidden among the mundane chores was one mildly interesting request. Two hours later, he filed the program and sent messages to the appropriate personnel.

His ability to cheat the system kept him in good standing despite his personal demeanor. His coworkers appreciated the easy workloads, but most gave him a wide berth which only worked to his advantage. The more they avoided him, the more opportunity he had to manipulate the system. And the more reason he had to despise them.

After work, he sat at his usual table in Serengeti and swallowed bites of something resembling vegetable stew.

"I suppose you heard about Garret," someone was saying. "It's the fourth suicide in two years."

"I'm not surprised. I can't tell you how many times I've had second thoughts. Especially when I think about Elsa."

Creed studied the woman's wistful expression. He hardened his heart against her show of emotion and, at the same time, was aroused by her vulnerability. He filed away as much as he could overhear.

In his cabin, he spent the time before bedtime scouring personnel records and private logs. He created a packet of instructions for Ava to carry out overnight. Once satisfied, he accessed Raven's files.

"If Ava has Beth's voice, then you, Raven, shall have mine."

Hours later, he logged off the computer and turned to face his room. It was barren except for the erotic images displayed on his digital screen. But those had become aseptic and only served to frustrate him. When nothing else appealed, he asked Ava to shut the screen down. After pacing for several minutes, he dove, once more, into a frantic workout. Exhausted, he rolled over to let his cheek cool against the portal in the floor. When he raised his head, he saw his own ghost reflected over the passing stars.

Chelsea's face flashed through his mind. He was back in Cargo Four, struggling against her callous grin. From reflex, his hands reached for her throat as the anger took hold once more. Before he could separate the vision from reality, he had murdered her for the hundredth time.

"Manipulative bitch," he repeated until his nerves settled. "Once I play my hand, I'll own the Einstein. They will have to pay attention."

When he had detached himself from accountability again, he pulled a storage bin from under the bed. Removing the lid, he rummaged past several data storage discs and a small red box until he located a scrap of fabric tied up at the corners. He pulled the bundle loose and removed two rings—one, an antique filigree design with three small diamonds, the other, a simple gold braided band. Beneath them lay a long, delicate gold chain that held a small sapphire pendant. He fingered the rings, and then placed one on his tongue. The metallic taste brought back a vivid memory. Unable to access her cabin, Creed had hidden the trinkets in his own. As security searched every inch of the ship, he had swallowed the jewelry. For weeks, he passed the items, sterilized them and swallowed them again. Only when the Einstein was moving out of the Solar System, and he was sure Security had run its last surprise inspection, did Creed clean the items one final time and wrap them in a scrap of fabric torn from one of his shirts.

He lifted the sapphire pendant and held it up to the light. "Cheap shit." Opening the clasp, he reached around his neck and fastened it, then dropped the bauble inside his shirt. He climbed under the covers and rested his hands on his chest. "Bound together forever," he whispered before falling into a fitful sleep.

28 FEBRUARY 0003

"HANNA," A VOICE WHISPERED. "Where are you?"

Hanna stirred, but did not wake.

"Hanna, it's cold here."

In half sleep, she responded. "Elsa?"

"I miss you."

"Elsa?" Hanna asked again. She waded through her sluggish thoughts, wondering where her sister was.

"You left me here, alone."

Hanna was alert now. "Who is this?"

The voice seemed to retreat into the distance.

Hanna sat upright, remembering where she was. "Ava! Lights up full!" She squinted at the glare, trying to see who was in her cabin.

"Ava, who just paged me in my quarters?"

"No one has paged you in the last twenty-one hours."

"What time is it?"

"It is o four hundred."

"A nightmare," she mumbled. Garret's suicide had shaken her to the core. She sank back into her pillow and stared at the walls. After a few minutes, she curled into a fetal position.

"Ava, bring the lights down half, and play some Debussy."

As the faint sounds of *Doctor Gradus ad Parnassum* filled the room, Hanna tightened the covers around her neck and tried to fall asleep.

01 APRIL 0003

"CREED, DEAR. IT IS O SEVEN HUNDRED. Rise and shine, sweetheart."

Creed had been lying awake for several minutes. "April Fools, Ava. No work today."

"Is this a scheduled day off, darling?"

"No. I've been suspended. Apparently, Yamoto doesn't like the way I keep maintenance logs. No more wake up calls until I say so." Creed rolled toward the wall and ran his fingers around the circular patterns in the metal. "But he doesn't realize, I am the puppet master," he warned an absent Yamoto, "and he will choke on my strings."

"Ava, bring up the lights, and open a secure channel to Raven." He rolled out of bed.

"Hello, Creed." Creed's own voice echoed through the cabin.

"Good morning, my friend. How are you coming on the security locks for engineering?"

"I have infiltrated navigational controls and will have command of all security codes in one hour, four minutes, thirty-four seconds."

Creed nodded to himself. "Do not launch until I give the order. Let's look at circulation next. Did you make the assignments to the duty roster like I asked?"

"The work orders have been assigned."

"I will need control over life support. Let's make sure they can't break our grip without consequences. I'm not sure just how good you are, yet."

"I will have no trouble staying ahead of any attempts to circumvent our security lockout."

"From a programming threat, yes," Creed agreed. "But they can attack the hardware."

"I have no dependency on any one piece of equipment."

"Nevertheless, if they try to unplug you, we need the ability to mete out punishment." Creed looked absently at the portal in the floor. "Besides, it might be fun."

His stomach growled ferociously. "Ava! Tell Yamoto his prisoner is hungry. Ask when I'm going to get breakfast."

"Yamoto has given permission for you to spend thirty minutes in Serengeti Public for your morning meal. He has instructed that you report to him upon returning to your quarters."

"Piss on him," Creed growled. "They can't even bring it to me. Well, that'll change." He climbed his ladder to the access tunnel.

A women moved toward him in the tunnel.

"Morning, Marti. Read any good books lately?"

She forced a smile. "Hello, Creed. I should ask you the same."

"As it so happens, I have a little time. Perhaps you could loan me one of yours."

Marti stopped in front of him. "Really. I didn't think books were worth your time."

He could smell her presence. It took all his restraint not to fondle her hair. "I figure it's time to do a little systems upgrade."

She eyed him suspiciously. "What are you interested in?"

"You're the expert. Any suggestions?" He drew in a deep breath.

"*The Bible. The Koran. The Talmud.* Personally, I like the *Four Books of Confucianism.* They're all in the ship's database."

"Ah. But it's not the same as holding the binding in your hands, is it?" No longer able to control the impulse, Creed reached for one of the dark curls framing her face.

Marti could not suppress a shudder. "I have to be going," she said as she disappeared down the tunnel.

Creed pounded his fists on the walls all the way to Serengeti. He grabbed a meal and found his table. Two groups of people looked his way and lowered their voices.

"The word's out, is it?" He scowled. "I'm a liar and a cheat."

At a separate table, a man tried desperately to console the woman he was sitting with. Dark circles suggested she had not slept in days.

"Weakling," Creed whispered. "A few more visits from Elsa and you'll be jumping out of your skin. Too bad you can't just put a gun to your head."

Tired of rules, Creed tossed his half-eaten breakfast on the table. Someone else could clean it up. He made his way home and pressed through two sets of his workout. When he recalled the feel of Marti's hair, the scent of her musk, he forced himself through a third set. Spent, he raised his forearms to inspect the layer of skin that barely contained his fibrous muscles. He made a fist and then clutched at the air as he pictured his fingers curling around Marti's vulnerable neck—much the way they'd curled around Chelsea's.

Yamoto was forcing his hand, but with Raven in place, Creed could think of nothing else that stood in the way. Bracing for the worst, he sent a message. "I quit."

For several protracted minutes, nothing happened. Just when Creed thought Yamoto would not favor him with a response, Ava replied, "Yamoto states there will be a meeting of the council to determine what action will be taken. The restriction to quarters stands."

Creed's laughter bellowed through the cabin. Beth Harrington had been in Yamoto's position, and he had stolen and corrupted her work. Chelsea had tried to control him, and she paid with her life.

He reached under his shirt to stroke the sapphire pendant around his neck. An exhilarating sense of power flooded through him as he fondled the chain. At the same time, Marti's aroma filled his nostrils, arousing him sexually. He let the feeling wash over him briefly before succumbing to the humiliation of having to face the act alone. "Bitch," he thought, seeing Marti's counterfeit smile. The frustration left a burning sensation in his groin.

"Creed," Raven interrupted.

"What is it?" he snapped.

"Security lockout procedures for Navigation are complete. On your command, I will take control of the program and lay in the new access codes. Shall I begin infiltrating Atmospheric Circulation?"

"By all means," Creed replied. "And while you're at it, give me a run down of all the operating systems we can get our hands on."

"There are no computerized systems onboard that we cannot infiltrate. Do you wish the list alphabetically?"

"How long would that take?"

"I would have complete computer systems security lockout in three days, two hours, and an undetermined number of minutes."

Creed laid back on his pillow and let his breath out slowly. "Do it," he said. "I can wait."

05 APRIL 0003

"CREED, DARLING. IT IS O NINE HUNDRED. You are instructed to meet with the council in one hour."

"What if I don't go?"

"Mayor Biliegh has ordered that you attend. If you do not appear at the appointed time, Captain Schneider will send a security escort."

"Well, I wouldn't miss this for the world."

He walked to the bed and pulled out a storage bin. From inside, he retrieved the pouch with Chelsae's rings and slipped one on each pinky finger. Life was about to get a lot more interesting.

He stopped to check out a small red box nestled among his belongings. It said *Mommy's things* across the top. He opened it for the second time since coming aboard the Einstein. Inside was a small blue and white ceramic dog.

"Cheap trinket," he said, tossing the dog aside.

He lifted a timeworn Bible and let the pages fall open. *David was conscience-stricken after he had counted the fighting men, and he said to the Lord, 'I have sinned greatly in what I have done. Now, O Lord, I beg you, take away the guilt of your servant. I have done a very foolish thing.'* Creed scoffed and threw the Bible back into the box.

The last item, a tattered photo album, drew his curiosity. He closed the lid on the storage container and sat flipping through the album. The first image was of a proud, middle-aged couple holding a new baby. The hand-written caption read, *Jillian - Three days old.* The following pages captured a variety of momentous events—a first birthday, baby's first steps, a new kitten. By the time Jillian was of school age, her father disappeared from the photos. As Creed continued to pry into Jillian's life, he noticed that most of the images were of a solitary young woman. Occasionally, her mother appeared beside her. Always, Jillian was smiling.

He flipped to the last page—a clear plastic sleeve holding a newspaper clipping. The caption read, *Newport HS Student Wins Art Honors.* He snapped the album shut and threw it to the floor. "Poor excuse for a family," he said, dismissing the emptiness it stirred in him.

Creed climbed into the corridor and headed for Control Two. Inside the conference room, he sat in a chair isolated from the council members. He glared at each, in turn, until they could no longer hide their discomfort. Everyone looked away except the captain and Yamoto.

When the last council member filed in, Mayor Biliegh called the meeting to order.

"This has been an exceedingly difficult journey for all of us aboard the Einstein. We have had many hardships that have taxed our strength and patience. I'm sorry to say, but we have lost another colonist this morning."

While everyone else in the room mumbled their questions, Creed remained stone faced.

"And now, it seems, we have our first major disciplinary issue."

Again, everyone in the room stared at Creed. He scowled at the faces, piercing each pompous look with a hardened stare. This time, no one looked away.

Captain Schneider spoke up. "Mr. Cramer, it's obvious by your actions to date that you have a chronic problem with authority. I'm not the only one on board who does not care for the idea of simply housing you in confinement for any portion of this journey. Therefore, it has been agreed that you will lose all computing privileges above level three. Furthermore, to earn your meals, you will work maintenance wherever you are needed. No work, no food. It's as simple as that." The captain waited for Creed to respond. When he said nothing, Schneider added, "One more thing. You have a standing appointment with the counseling staff every Monday at o eight hundred."

Creed stared defiantly at the captain. He reached both hands to his neck and pulled the sapphire pendant out from under his shirt while he flashed the rings on each hand. Several council members rolled their eyes at his antics. Only the captain and one security officer recognized the jewelry.

"Chelsea," Schneider murmured, closing his eyes.

"Raven," Creed called out. "Initiate Program Zero Zero One, authorization God."

Dumbfounded, everyone in the room stared at him.

"Now," Creed addressed the captain directly. "I will tell you what's going to happen."

Amid an outbreak of incredulous voices, the captain locked eyes with Creed. He studied his expression until the voices died down.

"Who's Raven?" he asked.

Creed folded his hands together and leaned back. "I'm glad I have your attention." He spun his chair around, continuing to talk with his back to the members. "If I am God, that makes Raven, I don't know, the Devil? The problem with the Devil is," he turned again to face the captain, "he wants your soul."

Yamoto remarked, "It's a program! Captain, I think he is trying to get command of Ava."

Creed laughed. "Yam, my man. I've had control of Ava for years now." He beamed at his ex boss. "You've got to think bigger."

Yamoto bristled. "What's bigger than Ava?"

Captain Schneider raised a hand to quiet everyone. "How far into the system are you?" he asked, directly.

The disgraced programmer stood, raising his hands in the air. "I'm God. I'm omnipotent." He leaned on the table, posturing toward the captain. "I'm everywhere."

Schneider refused to give in to Creed's cold-hearted grin. He would need proof before discussing what he suspected Creed was about to demand.

Guessing his thought, Creed said, "Go ahead, Captain. I'll wait."

Schneider hesitated and then said, "Ava. Bring up the personnel file for Creed Aston Cramer." When nothing happened, he said, "Ava, respond to my request." He pulled out his tablet and typed in a command.

"It's worse than you think, Captain. Trust me."

After several others in the room had made various attempts to gain access to Ava's programming, Creed looked condescendingly at them. "Please excuse us. I think the captain and I need to have a chat."

Schneider considered the risks, and then motioned for the others to leave.

"Before you go," Creed said to Yamoto, "be aware, there are trip mines in every system. Don't tinker with anything just yet. Give the captain time to see the scope of things before you make Raven mad."

Yamoto looked at the captain. Schneider shook his head.

When the others were gone, Schneider leaned back and appeared to relax. "This is quite an achievement."

"You have no idea. In fact, you're waiting for the others to verify the lockouts before you even consider I'm being rational. But we have lots of time, don't we, Brad?"

"That's exactly what I'm doing. So, while we wait, why don't you tell me what they'll find."

Creed grinned. "I have a better idea. Brad Schneider, captain of the Einstein, meet Raven, your new boss. Speak to the man, Raven."

Creed's own voice boomed through the voice ports. "Hello Captain. It's a pleasure to meet you."

Schneider could not hide his surprise. "Another Ava?"

"Hardly."

"Creed," Raven stated, "Yamoto is trying to access Level One security through Computer Ops. I have disabled him."

"Good boy, Raven. I hope you didn't hurt him too badly."

The captain sorted through his options. "Let's assume that you have exactly what you say you have. Where does it get you? If you want to go home, it's a simple matter to turn around, but once we're there you're in deep enough shit you won't find a hiding place anywhere on Earth. And that's assuming it's still inhabitable, at this point."

Intrigued by the analysis, Creed waited for him to continue.

"It's not home, then. Another star?" Schneider studied his captor's face. "There is no better destination. So, if it's not something external, then there is something inside the Einstein that you want."

Creed offered a slight smile. "You still don't get it, Bradly. I already have what I want."

"You really don't have the ability to run this ship, even with Raven's help. You need the cooperation of every department onboard to maintain life support and systems operations. You're playing with fire."

"Isn't fire a lovely thing? You see, there is one thing I've craved all my life. It's power, Brad. Power at my fingertips. My father did it with money." He watched Schneider's expression turn to disgust. "There is no money here. So, what's the currency?" Creed raised a hand and slowly closed his fingers into a fist. "Life."

"That's a twisted goal you've set for yourself."

Creed's smile faded. "Perhaps. But I would be careful about insulting the crown when he controls the entire kingdom."

The room was silent for many minutes. At last, Schneider pulled his tablet out again and tossed it across the table. "Your move," he said.

Creed nodded. "Raven. Restore level two access to all ship's operations except Computer Ops. Keep fail-safes in place, and notify me of any attempts to tamper with your security lockouts." He looked at the captain and said, "Raven will know if you interfere with me or anything that would restrict my access." He shoved the tablet back toward Schneider. "Run your little ship. Just remember who you're working for now."

07 APRIL 0003

"CREED, DEAR. YOU TOLD ME TO WAKE YOU AT EIGHT."

As Creed stepped out of bed, he stubbed his toe on something sharp. "Ava, bring up the lights." Jillian's photo album lay at his feet. He kicked it hard across the floor, slamming it into the screen. The floor of his cabin was now littered with everything that bored him. "I need a maid," he mumbled.

He sat back on his bed and rubbed his foot. "Raven, what has Captain Schneider been up to the last eight hours?"

"Captain Schneider has been in the conference room of Control One since eighteen hundred hours yesterday. He has met with several crew members, but very little has been discussed. He has not tried to access Ava in the last twelve hours."

The captain's actions could not be that benign. If he was not talking with his crew, then he had found another way to communicate.

"Shall I terminate atmospheric circulation to the conference room?" Raven asked.

"I like your style, but no. He would just move." Creed found his last clean uniform and dressed for the day. "Anyone else posing a threat to you?"

"Yamoto tried a second time to access Computer Ops. Medical is now treating him for second degree burns. There have been no other violations."

"Persistent little bastard, isn't he," Creed declared. "Next time Yamoto tries anything stupid, let's just put his lights out. Permanently."

"Put his lights out," Raven stated.

"Yes," Creed said. "Kill him. He can be the example."

Creed sat at his console and made a few searches through the personnel files. After he had posted several e-mails, he headed up the ladder and into the tunnels. In Serengeti, several people watched him enter. A few stood to leave the room. Some looked away in fear, while others glowered at him in disgust.

"Raven! Lights out in Serengeti!"

There were gasps and murmurs in the dark. When everyone had quieted again, he said, "Let there be light!"

A number of people froze in awkward stances as they tried to decide a course of action.

"Please, stay," he told them. "Your master prefers company."

While most of the colonists sat down again, Marti walked over to his table. "Impressive," she said.

"Thank you." Creed motioned for her to sit next to him. She chose the seat opposite his. "You don't trust me," he declared.

"You don't expect anyone to trust you." Marti placed her elbows on the table.

Creed studied her face for a moment. "You don't fear me."

"Why should I?" she asked. "If you have the same instinct for survival that most of us do, you won't damage life support or the ship. And if you're suicidal, then there's nothing I can do to stop you. So, why worry about it?" She appeared totally relaxed in his presence.

"On an individual level, I could make your life a living hell."

Marti leaned in and lowered her voice. "But why take all the fun out of it?"

Her candor surprised him. "You're coming on to me. Why?"

"Ah, that's the million dollar question, isn't it? Perhaps I'm attracted to men of power. Perhaps I'm trying to save myself. On the other hand, I could be trying to get into your good graces to help the captain. Why should it matter?"

He thought of Chelsea and her demands, but Marti would have no such claims on him. He held all of the power in this relationship. It should not matter, but it did. He reached across the table and stroked Marti's hair, then ran his fingers under her chin and down her neck. As he approached the opening in her uniform, Marti's expression hardened ever so slightly.

Creed pulled away. It was not an attraction to power, after all. "I don't suppose you would just tell me what you want."

"I want to live," Marti said simply. "I'll do whatever it takes."

Creed had fantasized about Marti more than once. In his dreams, he envisioned her repeatedly fighting and then succumbing to his will. This passive acceptance was not what he wanted from her.

Marti sensed his hostility. She reached inside a pocket and pulled out a small paperback book. "I'm sorry it took so long to get this to you," she said, laying it on the table. "You're right. An e-file simply does not demand the same appreciation as holding the real thing in your hands. Happy reading," she said and walked away.

"Leave her alone," he warned himself. "She's dangerous." When the frustration became unbearable, he pocketed the book and made his way back to his cabin.

Outside his hatch, a mousy young woman leaned against the corridor wall. She pulled back and dropped her eyes to the floor as Creed approached.

"You must be Celia."

She nodded but did not look up. "I talked to the captain before I came. He said to find out what you want, but that I have the right to say no to anything you request."

"Fuck the captain." He grabbed Celia by the wrists, pulling her body in tightly. "You have no rights. I own you." As she struggled to free herself, he forcefully kissed her mouth, desperately waiting for the trigger of arousal. Once upon a time, Celia would have been enough. Now, he wanted Marti.

Still clutching her wrists, he held her at arms' length. "Don't worry. You're safe."

She managed to show some spirit. "I will die first."

"No need," he told her. "I only want one thing from you." He reached down with one hand and opened the hatch to his quarters. "My uniforms. Fetch."

After a long pause, she asked, "That's it?"

"You can wait until I'm out of the cabin, if you like." He let go of her other wrist.

"I don't understand why you have to ask someone else to do that for you," she said, backing away.

"Because I can," he announced and pointed toward the ladder. "I'll wait here." He slumped against the wall and waited for her to climb down. When she appeared with his soiled uniforms, he said, "In the morning is soon enough."

Celia managed a tight smile and hurried away.

When Creed entered his quarters, he noticed Celia had not only picked up his clothes, but had straightened the rest of the cabin. Jillian's photos were now sitting on the desk. He flipped hurriedly through the album, trying to detach himself from thoughts of Marti. When he reached the newspaper clipping, he stared into Jillian's soulful eyes. She had no money. She had no friends. Her father was absent for most of her life. Still, she smiled.

"Raven," he said, closing the album, "what's the captain doing?"

"Captain Schneider is in Control One, giving instructions for a routine maintenance check of the reactor housing."

"And Yamoto. Is he tampering with anything?" he asked, feeling the paranoia set in.

"No, sir. Everyone is following routine."

He sat on the edge of his bed and stared at the cold walls of his cubicle. Outside the portal, the universe spun by at a steady rate and ignored Creed's little spectacle. In the grand scheme of things, he was still nothing.

08 APRIL 0003

"AVA. WHAT TIME IS IT?"

"It is eleven twenty-three, April eighth, year Three, dear."

Creed bristled. "I didn't ask you what day it was! I asked you what time it was!"

"It's now eleven twenty-four, April eighth, year Three, darling."

"Shut up, bitch!" he screamed in frustration. "Raven! Can you tell me what time it is?"

The voice deepened. "It's eleven twenty-four."

"Thank you!" He threw his hands in the air. "Raven, speak!"

"What information do you require?"

Creed pounded his fist on the desktop. "No information. I just want to have a conversation. Tell me something I don't know."

"That would be difficult," Raven stated. "First, I would need to determine what you do know."

Furious, Creed grabbed Jillian's ceramic dog off the desk and flung it against the far wall. The tiny treasure shattered into several pieces. Moving to the bed, he yanked one of his storage bins from beneath it and rummaged through the contents. He grabbed a fist full of data discs and scattered them on the floor. "This can't be my life! Not after all this work!"

Most of the discs were pornographic in nature, images and movies he had not wanted to download into the ship-wide system. He picked up Jillian's photo album and laughed at the irony. The only family photos he possessed were of someone else's family.

"Raven, do we have personnel files on the other four colonies?"

"Yes, Creed. We have a complete record of everyone involved in the Odyssey program, including ground crew."

"Search for someone named Jillian."

"There are three Jillians listed in the personnel files. The first is Mark Quaid Jillian, a research biologist on the Kepler. Second is Jillian Suzanne Prowse, a sociologist for Odyssey Central. The third is Jillian Anne Wollenberg, an artist aboard the Chang."

"Wollenberg. Show me her file."

Creed recognized the face from the scrapbook as Jillian's information appeared on screen. Her identification photo, though clinical, still portrayed her engaging smile and soulful eyes. Her history and list of accomplishments included two murals aboard the Einstein—one in Red Ring and one in Green Ring—and the fact that she was the reason each residential compartment had a wall-sized OLED screen. He tried not to be impressed.

He turned back toward the bed and looked into the storage bin. His own life was a vacuum. The seeds of the computer entity he called Raven were not even his to claim. He had stolen Beth Harrington's work and undermined her position at Odyssey. For two years, she had tried to create a second personality within Ava's matrix, and Creed had sabotaged her progress. As much as he touted his own genius, most of the credit for his new position of authority belonged to her.

He reached down and turned the bin over, emptying the last of its contents. The worn binding of the Bible fell open on the floor. Along the left side of the page, a section of the text had been highlighted.

… as the king was walking on the roof of the royal palace of Babylon, he said, 'Is not this the great Babylon I have built as the royal residence, by my mighty power and for the glory of my majesty?'

Creed sneered at the text. His royal palace was a ten foot cubicle traveling at dangerous speeds through the harshest of environments. Glancing at the portal, he thought, "And there lay heaven at my feet."

"Raven, what's the captain doing?"

"Captain Schneider is in his quarters with lights out."

"No, the timing is wrong. Schneider should not be sleeping through his shift." He forced himself to dress, and headed for Control One. After demanding entry, Creed made his way to the captain's cabin and opened the hatch. Amid several protests from the crew, he lowered himself into the dark room and snapped, "Raven, lights up in the captain's quarters!"

Schneider was missing.

Rushing up the ladder to the bridge again, Creed shouted, "Where is he?" He was met with silence. "You want to play this game? You will lose! Raven, shut down the flow governor for Reactor One!"

Schneider's second in command stared unresponsive at Creed, while several of the bridge crew checked their monitors for changes in the readings.

"Sir, the reactor flow is destabilizing."

Ava's voice came over the com at the same moment an alarm sounded on the main console. "The energy conduits from Reactor One are overheating. The system has failed to scramble automatically. I repeat. The energy conduits from Reactor One are overheating."

Holding Creed's gaze, the commander said, "Begin shut down sequence for Reactor One. Authorization Beryl, R3467S."

Creed countered. "Raven, belay that order. Maintain current operating levels for Reactor One. Authorization, You Know Who."

An ensign called from behind them, "Sir, we're still overheating. We have about three minutes until the pipes melt."

Expressionless, the commander said, "Captain Schneider is in Hydro B. Through that door." He pointed to Creed's left.

Creed waited long enough to raise the tension in the room to a fever pitch before commanding Raven to restart the flow governor. He opened the hatch and turned back to the commander. "You see. I am God, after all."

The noise of Control One faded quickly as Creed made his way through the racks of foliage. He heard muffled voices, but could not determine what they were saying. At the far corner of the room, he found Schneider and a botanist sharing a handful of peanuts.

The captain smiled and said, "Mr. Cramer. Please, come join us." The captain's friendly manner contradicted his weary look. "What brings you to the hydro wing?"

Creed caught a glimpse of someone moving away among the racks. "Do you like melodrama, Captain?"

Schneider looked puzzled.

"I would think that your first officer has had quite enough for one day. Tell him I'll need more cooperation in the future." Now that Creed was standing in one of the hydro wings, he felt helpless. With no voice ports, this was one area where he and Raven were vulnerable.

Schneider knew better than to play innocent. "Tell me, Creed, what is it you want?"

Finding a grand design for all his power still eluded Cramer. With no dignified response to the captain's request, he simply turned to walk away. From the corner of his eye, he watched the captain pick up a small hand rake and smooth the soil in a nearby flat. His heart skipped when he realized there had been something written in the dirt. Not words. A schematic, perhaps.

In the tunnel outside, Creed screamed obscenities at both Marti and the captain and threw several punches into the tunnel walls. He returned to his cabin, sucking on his bloody knuckles.

The cabin floor was spotless. All the movies and shards of broken ceramic had disappeared. He checked his drawers to find new uniforms folded neatly away. He opened the storage bin and quickly flung the contents across the floor again. "I'm in control!" he shouted at the ceiling. "Me! Not you!"

Looking at the floor, his eyes fell once more on the open Bible. ... *but he will not be able to stand because of the plots devised against him. Those who eat from the king's provisions will try to destroy him ...*

Creed picked the Bible up from the floor and ripped the offending page from it. "I know what you're up to, Captain. What would make you back off?"

He could relieve the captain of his command, but that only took him away from the helm, not out of operation. He thought of having Schneider confined. "Unless the jailers are my allies, that's not a solution." Raven would have no trouble overloading a circuit or shutting off an air valve in Schneider's cabin while he slept. "But up steps the next rogue warrior."

"Allies," he admitted. "I need an ally."

23 MAY 0003

"CELIA, IT IS O SEVEN HUNDRED."

"Thank you, Ava."

"Creed needs new uniforms today."

Celia hid her face in her pillow and let out a shriek. After another minute, she pushed the covers away. "When will he be out of his cabin?"

"He is at breakfast. He will be gone for approximately one hour."

She hurried to dress and made her way to the supply room.

"Three for you. Three for Creed," Jayden said when he saw her.

She scowled at him. "I don't suppose you could let me have extras for Creed? Then I wouldn't have to spend so much time there."

Jayden shook his head. "Not today. Production is barely keeping up, but I'll see what I can do for next time." He gave her a sympathetic look. "Maybe you can convince him to go naked."

"Hell, no." She shuddered at the memory of her first encounter. "Once upon a time, I was afraid of him. Now, he just seems pathetic."

Jayden handed over a stack of clothing. "Keep your chin up. I'm sure the captain is working on some way to take him out of the picture."

Celia's eyes darted to the voice port above their heads. "He'll hear you," she whispered.

"I'm not the only one he gets an earful from. Everybody talks about him. He'd probably get suspicious if we didn't."

Celia thanked him for the uniforms and headed to Creed's quarters. She tapped lightly on the hatch and then entered the room. "Ava, lights up, please."

"He prefers to be called Raven in here," Creed said.

Celia screamed and dropped the uniforms on the floor. She started to climb the ladder again, but realized Creed was not moving from his position on the bed. He appeared comfortable as he leaned against the wall, an open Bible in his hands. She waited for him to say something else. He started reading, silently.

"Ava said you were out." She tried to calm her voice.

"I was. Now, I'm back."

She continued to hug the ladder until she felt safe enough to pick up the uniforms and straighten them neatly before sliding them into the nearest drawer. She grabbed the old uniforms and stuffed them in the recycling chute before turning to leave.

"Celia. Would you stay for a moment?"

She desperately wanted to run away, but he had made no aggressive moves, so she turned toward him.

"I've been reading a lot lately. Not much else to do, really." He held up the Bible. "I found this in my cabin. Odd, don't you think?"

She shrugged. "Many of the colonists brought copies with them."

"Yes, but this belongs to a colonist on the Chang."

"That is odd," she agreed.

He turned the book from side to side. "There are so many stories, riddles mostly. Would you like to discuss it with me sometime?"

"Is this an order?"

"No, a request."

Celia was baffled. Creed's demeanor was calm, rational, and totally unaffected by her presence. She wondered how he could be the same man who assaulted her the month before. "I'm no expert on the Bible," she admitted.

He gave her a penetrating look. "I don't want an expert. I simply want to have a conversation." His smile evaporated. "It gets lonely in my little universe. I have no friends."

"This isolation is your own doing."

He shrugged. "True. But I've always felt it, even when I was a kid. You understand that, don't you? I sensed it when we first met."

"I'd have to think about it," she finally told him.

He looked disappointed. "I understand. Do say yes. Please." He went back to reading.

Celia climbed out of the cabin and headed toward the helm.

Outside Control One, she mouthed the words, "I need to see the captain." At the far end of Hydro B, Schneider and two crewmen stood over a pallet of loam as each took turns marking something with their fingers. When the captain saw her approaching, he broke away.

"Captain," she whispered. "I need to talk with you about Creed."

Schneider walked Celia to a quiet corner.

"Has he been treating you fairly?"

"Since that first day, he has kept his promise. Until today."

Schneider stiffened. "Did he hurt you?"

"No. He didn't touch me. He was … nice."

"Define *nice.*"

"Gentlemanly. He was reading the Bible and asked if I wanted to discuss it with him."

Schneider rubbed the tired from his eyes. "What's he up to?"

"He's been reading the Bible. I think we have an opportunity here. I think he's searching for something."

Schneider nodded agreement. "He's searching, all right. He's bored and looking for a new game to play." He looked directly at her. "Keep your distance. That's an order."

She bristled at the captain's hard line. "I could play along. If it's a game, we find out what he's up to. If not, maybe I could help him."

"You can be sure that Creed has read your psyche profile. I don't mean to be insulting, but that's exactly why he chose you."

The accusation stung. "He said he chose my name at random."

Schneider grabbed her firmly by the shoulders. "He's lying through his teeth. Remember, you aren't the only one who could get hurt." As he relaxed his grip, he tried to give her a genuine smile. "Besides, someone else is already in play. I don't want the two of you working against each other."

"Who?" she asked, now strangely jealous.

"No names. Just politely turn him down."

Against the captain's orders, she headed back to Creed's cabin. From some distance, she watched another woman leave. Celia waited a few moments and then approached, lightly knocking on the hatch.

"Come in, Marti," Creed called. "Did you change your mind?"

Celia opened the hatch and climbed down. "About what?"

He could not hide his surprise. "Celia. I didn't expect … "

"No, I'm sure you didn't. I'd be willing to discuss the Bible, if you'd still like me to."

"Who changed your mind? The captain?"

"I changed my own mind. I can't say the same for Marti."

Creed laughed. "Everyone is working for the captain in one capacity or another. Even you."

She looked incredulous. "Then why do you let her in here?"

"Know thy enemy," he said. "Besides, I like her company." Creed watched Celia's eyes darken, reaffirming he'd chosen wisely. "Don't worry," he said, walking up to her. "I have time for both of you." He reached out and gently stroked the side of her face.

Celia's fear returned, but this time it tangled with the excitement of her own duplicity.

"The captain told you to stay away from me, did he?"

Celia looked away.

"It's okay," he assured her. "I'm glad you came back."

Turning away, he said, "I have work to do. Perhaps tomorrow you can come read with me."

Without another word, she left the cabin. For a long while, she stood, shaking, in the passageway outside her own quarters.

04 JULY 0003

"IT IS O EIGHT HUNDRED, DARLING." Beth's voice was cold and unsympathetic.

Creed pushed away the memories of her condescending manner. *Raven, what's the captain doing?* He sat on the edge of his bed, his head nodding from exhaustion.

"Raven!" he shouted. "Answer me!"

"What is your request?"

"Damn it! I want an answer when I summon you." Creed struggled to keep his eyes open. "What's the captain doing?"

"The captain is having breakfast in Urubamba Public."

Beth's voice crept back in. "Celia will be here in twenty minutes. She is bringing your breakfast."

Creed mumbled in disdain, "Mocking me. Trying to manipulate me, and yet, so damn easy to control." The voice in his head said, *Pity you cannot kill her, too.* Aloud, he insisted, "I *can* kill her, but she's useful." He moved to the sink and ran water over his face.

"Who is it you wish to kill?"

Creed looked for something to throw across the room. "Shut up! If you can't make sense, just shut up!" He stood clenching his fists open and closed. Visions of Chelsea flooded his thoughts. This time, when he reached for her throat, it was Marti's neck he was trying to snap.

In an effort to regain control, he dropped to the floor and forced his emaciated body through his exercise routine. When he could not make it through a second set, he stood and wiped the sweat from his forehead and three-day-old beard.

Pulling the Bible from the desk, he fell back toward the bed. Celia would want to discuss a new passage. Opening to Romans 6:1, he began to read. *What shall we say, then? Shall we go on sinning so that grace may increase?* As his head began to nod again, he heard his own voice. *I am evil. I am wicked in your eyes.*

He started awake at the sound of someone tapping at the hatch. The Bible still rested in his hand. "Come in."

Celia made her way down the ladder. "Good morning."

Creed struggled to keep his eyes open. "I'm tired. Maybe come back tomorrow."

"I have a solution," she said, and sat down beside him. She pulled the book from his hand. "Why don't you close your eyes while I read to you?"

He wanted to, badly, but he couldn't trust her any more than he trusted Marti. He grabbed the Bible and tossed it to the floor. "I am full of sin," he said, pulling her hand to his heart. "You must hate me for it."

He watched Celia's eyes dart from the book to the ladder. She was not a good actress.

"No," she whispered softly. "You said it yourself. I understand your isolation." She pulled Creed's hand to her own breast. "We all have demons."

At first, he felt nothing. Between the abuse of his body, the lack of sleep, and Marti's games, he had been rendered virtually impotent. When he did feel a pang of lust, it was not for the spiritless woman that sat beside him.

The anger and frustration that had festered for months boiled over as he yanked his hand away and shoved Celia hard into the back wall. She cried out in pain and slumped to the bed, unconscious.

"Manipulation and pity!" he cried, losing control. "That's all you're capable of." He raised his hand to strike again, but froze when he realized she was not moving. After several seconds he called her name. When she did not answer, he pressed her wrist for signs of a pulse. "I'm not through with you," he grumbled, wide awake now.

Crawling off the bed, he sat on the floor next to the portal and watched Celia's shallow breathing.

"She'll never trust me again," he complained. "What a fool!" He argued internally for several minutes while he repeatedly blasted Raven for interrupting or not responding. When the adrenaline subsided, his head began to droop.

Raven, where's the captain? All was silent. *Raven? Answer me!*

Creed crawled to the side of his bed and pulled himself to his feet. Straightening Celia's body, he laid down beside her and dared to close his eyes.

REED. YOU HAVE NOT RESPONDED IN FOUR HOURS.

05 JULY 0003

"CREED. YOU HAVE NOT RESPONDED IN FOUR HOURS. Failsafe Protocol Two is now in effect."

Creed reached under the covers to pull Marti closer. Her body was stiff and cold. Climbing up from a dream, he opened his eyes to find the cabin lights on. Despite sleep, he was exhausted and confused. Celia lay quietly beside him.

"What day is it?"

"It's July Fifth."

Looking at Celia again, Creed noticed the blue-grey pallor in her face. The base of her neck was stained dark where her blood had pooled.

"Fuck!" He panicked, and pushed away from her only to find himself pinned against the back wall. He kicked her body to the floor.

"Fuck!" he screamed again, shoving the mattress and blankets on top of her. "Not yet," he cried, pointing at her. "I still need you!" He sat staring at the pile, expecting it to move until yesterday's events came back to him.

"Raven! Where's the captain?"

"The captain is in his quarters with lights out."

"Like hell, he is!" Creed grabbed his only significant belongings and stormed out of his cabin toward Control One.

"Let me in!" he shouted when he reached the sentry. He made his way past the bridge crew and down into the captain's quarters.

"Raven, lights up!" To Creed's surprise, Captain Schneider started awake, bringing a hand up to shield his eyes.

"What are you after now?" Schneider asked, exasperated.

"You!" Creed yelled at him. "You don't control this ship! I do!"

Schneider, trying not to make any sudden moves, pulled himself into a sitting position. "What's happened?"

"You and your insignificant little spies manipulating me. You think you can beat me? Impossible!"

"Celia. Is she all right?"

Creed twisted his right hand around the binding of the Bible, warping it sideways. Holding it at arm's length, he said, "That's right. Precious Celia. I've called her to a higher purpose."

Unable to control his frustration any longer, Schneider leapt from the bed and threw a fist into Creed's teeth. "You pathetic little nothing!" he bellowed as he knocked Creed to the floor with a second punch.

"Raven!" Creed hissed through the blood, "deep six Hydro C!"

Schneider held Creed down with his left arm and brought his right hand to Creed's neck. "I'm going to shut you up for good," he bellowed. "This is going to end!"

"It already has," Creed choked out, offering no resistance. When the Captain loosened his grip, he added, "Raven, tell the captain what he has won."

"Captain Schneider. Hydro Wing C has suffered an electrical fire. The fire retardant system malfunctioned, and chlorine gas was released into the feeder lines. The results will be toxic to all organic matter in the wing."

Schneider released his grip.

Pushing away, Creed sat up and rubbed his neck. "You see, Brad, I can win or lose. You can only lose."

A lieutenant called down the hatch, "Captain! Emergency in Hydro C!"

The captain nodded. "I know."

"We've dispatched the rescue crews, but the hatches won't open. Sir, there are fourteen people inside!"

Schneider stared in disbelief as Creed kept his silence. He raised his hands in defeat and declared, "You win! Back off and let them in."

Creed shook his head. He raised his right hand and lifted two fingers off the Bible. "I'm responsible for two deaths aboard the Einstein. Now, you're responsible for fourteen."

Schneider's rage was insufferable. It took all his strength not to throw himself at Creed again. "You cannot make me responsible for your atrocities."

Creed hurried to his feet. "Remember, Raven will miss me when I'm gone. I live, you live."

Schneider closed his eyes in defeat. "You do realize what you've done. Hydro C was a fourth of our food supply. You've probably killed us all."

Creed made his way up the ladder, out of Control One and into Serengeti Public. He laid Jillian's Bible and photos on a table and sat facing the portal. In a few short minutes, he heard the other colonists hurry away as they learned of the emergency. He did not look up when Marti spoke.

"Poor Celia," she said. "The girl never had a clue."

"Not like you, right?"

"Not like me," she agreed. She sat down and pulled the photo album closer. "Family?"

"No," he scoffed.

She raised an eyebrow. "Jillian Wollenburg. I know her work. What are you doing with this?"

"Fate," he mused. "Divine providence. Perhaps a universal irony." Creed watched Marti flip through the pages. When she reached the newspaper clipping, he asked, "Why does she smile so much?"

"Perhaps she knows something you and I don't." Marti closed the album. She stood, offering her hand to Creed. "Come with me. I want to show you something."

He thought better of accepting her hand, considering her alliance with the captain. There was only one way she would have known about Celia so quickly, and she had not even tried to hide it. He would be safer where he was, but curiosity won out. He picked up the books and followed her into a tunnel.

She led him to one of the public areas in Blue Ring. Pointing to the wall above the portal, she said, "Jillian's mural. It's called *The Life of Christ*."

Creed glanced at the artwork. "I know it," he said, sneering. "Mythological drivel."

"From a woman who smiles too much. Perhaps." Marti watched him skim over the scenes depicted in the painting. "Have you ever studied it?" she asked. "I mean really looked at what she painted?"

He wandered to a table and sat down.

Kill her now, Raven's voice echoed in his head. *You're all alone. Take her out.*

"Shut up!" Creed snapped, causing Marti to jump. "When the time is right. Not before."

Marti moved to the left side of the mural, putting some distance between the two of them. "Fine," she said. "Study it at your leisure. I was only suggesting that Jillian is a great story teller, but you have to look closely."

Creed swatted away some imaginary affront.

"This is not just about Christ and his life according to the Bible," she continued, curious about his erratic behavior. "It's the ultimate story of human nature—good and evil. It's about us."

Creed followed the motion of her hips in front of the painting. The shimmer of light off the brightly colored steel silhouetted Marti's generous curves. He hated her, and yet he could not resist moving closer. He allowed himself to speculate what she would be like in bed and, for the first time in months, he could feel his body responding.

Marti did not pull away. Instead, she leaned into Creed's shoulder and pulled his arm tighter around her.

"Look," she said and motioned toward a garden scene. "Jillian definitely knew things about you and me."

Creed followed her gesture to the figure of Judas cowering in the shadows, taking silver from the hands of priests. An age-old parable of betrayal. The more he stared, the more uneasy he became. The face of Judas was not just anyone's. It was his.

06 JULY 0003

"CREED. IT IS O SEVEN TWENTY. The captain has reported to Control One. He has initiated a routine comparison of near-space stellar bodies against our current position."

Creed opened his eyes just enough to see Marti sitting across from him. "Shut it down," he ordered.

Marti shook her head. "It's routine navigational maintenance."

"Doesn't matter," Creed said, dropping his eyelids again. "I want it shut down." He struggled to stay upright in his chair. Raven's voice—his own voice—resonated in his head. *Kill her.*

"Not yet, Raven," he mumbled. "Not yet."

Raven responded. "You are telling me to belay the order to shut down navigational maintenance."

Creed and Marti had been sitting for hours, and his anger had risen to a fever pitch. She had manipulated him once again, riling his sex drive and then assuring that he could not perform by exposing the mural. The room was littered with overturned tables and chairs. At one point, he had found a sharp enough utensil to scratch the face of Judas until the features were unrecognizable.

"Why don't we go back to your cabin? You'd be more comfortable," Marti said calmly.

Creed threw his head back and ran his hands over his eyes. "Don't," he said. "Just sit."

She slipped her hand into a side pocket of her slacks. When Creed's eyes closed again, she pulled out a small tablet and slid it under her tongue. The stimulant rushed through her system. When Creed's head slumped forward once more, Marti chanced leaving the room and made her way to Control One. She tugged at the captain's sleeve and they headed for the back of Hydro B.

"I don't know how he will react if I'm not there."

"I don't much care, at this point," Schneider said. "We don't have any time left. Ops has pulled the voice analogue equipment into Creed's quarters. I just hope it does a passable job. If we can't fool Raven, we're dead anyway."

The captain reached into his pocket and pulled out an auto syringe, handing it to Marti. "Medical says, hit him in the Adam's Apple. It will freeze his vocal chords instantly. You'll have to watch his hands to be sure he doesn't have access to his tablet. He may have a destruct code preprogrammed in." Schneider held the syringe up to the light. "Flip this switch and inject him again. He should go out in about four seconds."

Marti shuddered from fatigue and too many stimulants.

Schneider rubbed her shoulders. "I can't thank you enough," he said. "Bugging Creed's cabin was risk enough, but getting this close to him?" The captain paused to find the right words. "It's more than I ever would have asked."

"I told Creed from the very beginning, I wanna live," she said. "Just promise me, that when this is over, I get to take a real bath with real hot water."

Schneider nodded understanding.

They stood and looked at the group of officers coming toward them. Schneider nodded at each as they fell in behind him. The mutinous band headed through Control and into the tunnels. Most followed some distance behind Marti, while others made their way into separate tunnels.

Marti approached Galilee Public and peered through the hatch. Creed appeared to be sleeping in the same position she had left him, slumped in his chair with his hands in his pockets. Quietly, she stepped into the room and walked to the food dispensers. "Ava, I'd like two beers and a bean salad."

Creed bolted upright in his chair. He turned to see Marti bringing three packets to the table. She laid two in front of him and opened the third for herself.

"You really should eat," she said, sitting across from him.

He tried to orient himself. "Raven, how long since last contact?"

"Our last voice exchange was fifteen minutes ago."

Creed thought it over carefully. "Where did you go?" he asked.

"I went to see the captain," Marti admitted, swigging her beer.

He nodded, eyeing her cautiously. "How is Bradly, anyway?"

"Tired. Sad. Hoping you will choke on dinner." She winked.

Too tired to laugh, he picked up the food packet and checked it for signs of tampering. "Trying to poison me?"

"No. It's just food." When Creed did not open it, she asked, "Have I ever lied to you?"

He was sure she had not. Peeling back the opening, he squeezed the bean paste into his mouth. "Bradly thinks he can defeat me. He's right. I can be squished, just like the bug he thinks I am. But he will never defeat Raven." Creed raised his beer in toast, and called, "Isn't that right, Beth?"

Beth's voice sounded over the port. "What information do you request, my lord?"

"See that? She bows to my every command. She loves me."

She hates you, he thought, remembering his days at Odyssey Central. "Shut up, Raven!" he yelled at the emptiness of the room.

Marti listened to his bizarre dialog and waited. When he had quieted again, she said, "The difference between you and me isn't means. It's motive. I'll do anything, just like you, to get what I want. We just want different things."

Creed finished his dinner. "Tell me what I want."

"Respect. Power, because you think that will command respect."

"And what do you want?" he asked.

"Freedom from fear. Freedom from you." She held his gaze. "If you destroy the Einstein, you will have gained no more respect than the history you are fighting against. I'm guessing a domineering father. An emotionally absent mother." She waited for his reaction. "But if you destroy the Einstein, I get what I want." Marti sat back and watched Creed bristle with indignation.

He stood up, slowly, and slid the table sideways. With his left hand, he reached for Marti's uniform and pulled her to her feet, backing her against the wall. "This is what I want," he said, sliding his right hand into her slacks.

Marti tried to control her shaking while she worked the syringe from her sleeve and into her hand.

Creed pulled away to tug at her blouse and saw a flash of metal. He grabbed her wrist, slamming it into the wall. When the syringe did not dislodge, he twisted Marti's arm sideways and, in the struggle, pried the metal from her fingers. "Meant for me?" he asked scornfully.

"Captain!" Marti screamed, trying to break free.

As Schneider and six other officers charged the room, Creed injected Marti with the syringe and spun her body around. The first two shots hit her directly in the chest. The third shot glanced off her rib cage and into Creed's left arm. He locked eyes with the captain and, in the seconds before Schneider could reach him, he cried, "Raven! Armageddon!" Calmly, he whispered in Marti's ear, "Now, you get what you want."

THE NEWTON

6 JULY 0003

"NICOLAI. IT IS O SEVEN HUNDRED."

"Lights." Nic dropped his feet over the side of the bed and rubbed his eyes awake. "Ava, when is Grabor reporting to work today?"

"Carl Grabor is scheduled in Biorecycling at o seven thirty."

The young biochemist walked to his desk and pulled up a packet of files. Once he had routed the files to Carl's desktop, he closed out the display and rushed through his workout. Minutes later, he dressed and headed for breakfast. As he left Blue Ring, he felt a tug on his shoulder.

"Hey, Putz."

Nic turned into Tasmania Public and pulled the hatch closed, holding it tightly as Hopi Musgrave tried to pry it open from the other side. "I'll let go if you promise not to set me up again."

A muffled voice said, "Okay. Promise."

Nic stepped away and waited for his friend to catch up.

"Don't tell me you couldn't find anything to talk about."

"I don't need any more help from you," Nic grumbled as he ordered breakfast from the food dispenser.

Hopi punched in his own order. "If it wasn't for me, you'd a had zero dates in the last two years. Oh, pardon me. The last four years, since I'm sure you didn't have help before you and I met." He punched in his own access code and pulled out breakfast. "You're really pathetic, ya know that?"

"Why? Because I don't need to get laid?"

"No. Because you can't let go of Beth and move on."

Nic grimaced.

"The truth hurts, doesn't it?"

The two headed for a far table. When his friend sat next to him, he lowered his voice and admitted, "So, what if I can't?"

"She's dead, Putz. At least to you. The Kepler is twenty billion light-years away by now. You've got to quit shutting everyone out."

"Maybe." Nic opened his breakfast bar and took a bite. "Too bad I can't shut you out."

Hopi changed the subject. "What's the verdict on the recyclers?"

"Grabor has been dragging his feet, but I finished the new figures for the efficiency ratings last night. He'll have to let me do it."

"I hope so. It's not that I don't trust Odyssey to get us where we're going, but hey, anytime we can shift the odds in our favor...." Hopi let his thought go unfinished.

Nic appreciated the support. "What's new in astrophysics?"

Hopi gushed about the latest images from their target system. His team had verified the three gas giants seen from Earth and discovered at least three massive rock core planets to date. The ship was still too far away to analyze the smaller planets orbiting the white dwarf star. "It's going to be an amazing laboratory study," Hopi said, winding down.

"What do you think about staying or going?" Nic asked.

"Stay, of course. What's to go back to? Besides, that's what I'm here for—stranger in a strange land, and all that."

Nic thought it over. "I'm not so sure. Besides, Michael Valentine didn't start out a Martian. He was an Earthling returning to his origins."

Hopi shook his head. "Doesn't matter. Majority vote rules."

A woman approached their table and smiled at Nic. "Hi, Hopi," she said, not letting go of Nic's gaze.

"Hi, Safeen. This is Nicolai. He's in charge of poop scooping." Hopi nudged his friend under the table.

She held out her hand. "I think we met at an interdepartmental meeting before the Day of Leaving. Nice to see you again."

"Safeen is in charge of the stale air."

Nic shook hands and mumbled something pleasant before a wall of silence fell around the table.

"Well," Hopi said, "time to report to work. I'll see you two later." He stood to make a graceful exit, only to see Nic push back from the table, as well.

"Yes, it's time. I've got to make the presentation to Grabor as soon as possible." Nic nodded a shy farewell and headed for the tunnels.

His friend hurried up beside him. "Are you dense? Didn't you see she was interested?"

"I thought I told you no," Nic growled.

Hopi threw up his hands. "Nothing to do with me, I promise. She scouted you out all on her own." He followed Nic to the hatch for Bioengineering. "She could be the one."

"Suppose there is no *one* for me. We're only four hundred and eighty-seven people." Before Hopi could protest, he added, "Besides, just because your life is incomplete, doesn't mean mine is."

Hopi looked indignant. "Fine. When I'm old and gray, with ten grandkids, you can be poor Uncle Nic bringing them birthday presents while I explain that we really just adopted you because you had no family of your own."

"My sperm's in the gene pool just like yours." Nic smiled a wry smile and flipped Hopi a vulgar gesture. "If somebody wants it, they can check it out of the bank. See you later, Putz." He entered the bio lab.

Grabor motioned Nic to the main computer console. "I have to admit, your new figures look good. I'll have Sadir do some fine tuning on the consumer stats. We'll see about starting the process next month."

"Really." Nic was pleased he did not have to hard-sell Grabor. "If this works well over the next year, what about converting the other two systems down the road?"

Grabor frowned. "I don't think we can stand that much efficiency. We'll look at the consumption rates, but odds are it would tip the balance too far."

"You're right. I'm just anxious to see this process prove itself." Nicolai turned to the large, heated tank that held a microcosm of tiny organisms churning human and plant waste into separate and valuable components. He looked back at his boss. "Do you suppose they've been any help at home? The microbes."

"Twenty. Fifty years of research. Who knows? Why don't you start laying out a time-frame for injecting the tube strain? It's going to take some careful monitoring. I'll run this by the council at next meeting. If they say yes, have your data ready."

Nic glanced around the recycling unit. He felt vindicated that he had pressed for the inclusion of the sea-floor bacteria in at least one of the four systems aboard each colony. He fell eagerly into his work.

12 JULY 0003

"NICOLAI. IT IS O SEVEN HUNDRED."

"Yep," he responded in the dark. Nic never thought of treating Ava's wake-up calls as anything but an alarm clock. He refused to assign the voice a personality. She was a machine. He knew Beth would not have agreed.

Adding a few extras sets to his morning workout, the pushups and ab crunches began to melt his frustration. He managed to clear away his regrets one more time.

He pulled a washcloth from the dispenser and wiped the sweat from his body. As he dropped it into the toilet, his mind followed the path of the biodegradable cloth to the collection area. It would be ground into smaller pieces and fed into the cookers. Various microbes would chew it into manageable bits, convert the cellulose and perspiration into a fermented soup from which several products could be reclaimed. In the final stage, his little sea-floor minions would extract a variety of gases.

"Nicolai. Hopi says he will meet you in Amazon Public for breakfast this morning."

A creature of habit, Nic wondered why the change in location. He headed down the tunnels—turning left instead of right—and opened the hatch into Amazon.

"Surprise!" several people cried at once. "Happy birthday!"

He stared at the crowd.

Hopi walked up with a drink in his hand. "It's for you, Putz."

"My birthday was last week," Nic protested.

Hopi shrugged. "I know. But you didn't say anything, so I let it pass. And you didn't suspect a thing, did you." He raised his drink, and everyone in the room applauded.

Nic thanked them all and headed for a corner table.

"Did you hear about Raven?" Hopi handed him a beer.

"No," he grumped. "Who's Raven?"

"My friend in Computer Ops said they found a program buried in Ava's matrix. Some hacker from five years ago plugged it in and left it. It's causing all kinds of havoc in the system."

"What kind of havoc?"

"Lots of stuff. Uniform production has been shut down for two days, and someone said Computer Ops was running extra shifts to keep up with the program corrections in Navigation. It seems Raven attached herself to someone in Engineering and tried to make friends."

"It's a program," Nic scoffed. "It can't make friends."

Hopi raised an eyebrow. "Maybe not. But Raven was writing her own programming."

Nic looked up from his beer. "Beth tried for years to build a second personality within the same matrix. She couldn't make it work." He took a sip of his drink and wondered, briefly, if she had. "What are they doing about it?"

"Don't know. But I'll let you know when I find out." Hopi finished his breakfast and stood to leave. "What are you doing tonight?"

"Working," Nic stated, quickly. "I've got to run stats for the cooker soon." It was an excuse that Hopi would accept.

"Tomorrow, then," Hopi said and headed off.

As Nic finished his meal, Safeen approached. "May I join you?"

He motioned to a chair.

"Happy birthday, again."

"I should strangle Hopi for bringing it up," Nic said. Changing direction, he asked, "What did he mean by 'in charge of stale air?'"

They relaxed into a conversation about their respective disciplines. Before long, Nic found a level of comfort in her presence.

"What are you doing tonight?" she asked at one point.

He started to give his standard answer, but something changed his mind. "Nothing. You?"

"I belong to the book club. I thought you might like to sit in."

Nic tried his best to hide his disappointment. Groups of people made him uneasy. "I'll think about it. Text me when and where." He checked the time and quickly stood up. "I'm late," he said, excusing himself from the table.

In Bioengineering, he spent the morning running programs to determine the rate at which he should add the sea-floor microbes into Biocooker Two. Each run increased the load by two percent. At o ten hundred, he found a reliable rate which seemed to hold up under several executions of the computer model.

"How are the stats looking?" Carl asked after lunch.

"Good. I based the model on our original work at Odyssey. I'll keep running it over the next few days, but it should be pretty simple. I estimate a week to pull it off."

Carl read over the figures twice. "Plan on Monday morning. Keep running the numbers, and I'll push for an answer from Council." He gave his subordinate a quiet nod and headed back to his desk.

Nic high-fived the monitor. In the pioneering days of Biospheres One and Two, and through the subsequent studies of closed ecosystems, much was learned about what would *not* work in closed environments. Decades later, a team of researchers discovered that diversity was not necessarily the key. With the ability to directly manipulate the interactions, humans could thrive in an ecosystem containing a mere two thousand plant and animal species, not counting the microbial. Odyssey added another hundred into the mix. Nic's pioneering work reduced the need for diversity even further.

Hopi's morning revelation troubled him, so Nic logged the day's work into his tablet for safekeeping. He finished out the afternoon by setting up several cultures for the microbes. Curious about additional applications, he wanted to find out what his little whiz kids could do.

After work, he grabbed dinner and headed back to his cabin.

"Ava, lights up," he said at the bottom of the ladder.

"Safeen Bahwan sends a message. The meeting is at nineteen hundred hours in Red Ring. Education Room Two."

He grimaced. "Damn. I forgot about the book club."

Grudgingly, he swallowed his meal and headed back into the tunnels. He waited outside the classroom until his nerves began to fail. Safeen caught up to him just as he was about to flee again.

She pulled him into the room and toward a couple of empty chairs. "I won't make you announce yourself. Just jump in anytime."

He gave her a grateful smile as the group settled into their current discussion.

"We are on chapter twelve," Maureen announced. "Last week, we were talking about Gretchen's desire to sacrifice herself for the good of her family."

"I wouldn't really call it a desire," Kellan said, and several others began to quibble about semantics.

Maureen raised her hand. "So, I misspoke. Gretchen is choosing, for whatever reason, to give her life to save her family. How many of us could rationally choose to die to save someone else?"

Safeen leaned forward. "I think it depends on who you are trying to save. Mothers all over the world would, and have, placed themselves in danger to save their children. That's an evolutionary benefit that helps ensure the survival of a genetic line."

"Fathers, too," Kellan interrupted.

"In some species, yes. But, if it was not my child, I'm not so sure. I don't think anyone would actually know until they were faced with the decision."

"I agree," Brynn said. "It's not something you can rationalize. I think it's instinct. But there are plenty of examples where unrelated people have done just that."

Jennifer spoke up. "Do you think her Victorian upbringing influenced her decision? I wonder, if she'd grown up a century later, say, in a society that demanded a less subservient role from women, do you suppose she would have the same instinct, despite her genetic makeup?"

"We don't have a Gretchen clone to experiment with. What does it matter?" Kellan asked.

Brynn scowled at him. "I think it's a relevant question. Can we teach ourselves to be altruistic, despite our genes? I think it's extremely relevant to our current situation."

"How so?"

Akama shifted forward in his chair. "Look at the five colonies. Each has a very diverse gene pool—so diverse, practically no one is genetically related beyond at least five generations. Not yet, anyway. It will be several years before enough parent-child relationships exist to set up a specific genetic line. Meanwhile, if we are put in danger and you're faced with the possibility of sacrificing yourself to save me," he pointed directly at Kellan, "would you?"

His smile was devious. "You, maybe. Brynn? Definitely not."

Even Brynn, laughed. "I'll remember that, Kellan, when your life is hanging by a thread."

Nic did not comment all evening. He listened to the close-knit group wander off topic and into conversations about other aspects of life onboard the Newton.

When the meeting adjourned, he followed Safeen into the tunnel.

"Would you care to stop for something to eat?"

When she agreed, they headed for Tasmania Public and found it almost deserted.

"What do you think?" She asked when they were seated.

"Fascinating way to kill two hours on a Thursday night."

She protested. "Is that all? What do you do for fun, then?"

Nic thought seriously about it. "Work, I guess. I love my work."

"How limiting. I love my work, too, but that's not all my life is about." She touched his sleeve. "You need to get out more."

"You sound like Hopi, always trying to connect me with something."

"Maybe he has a point. Maybe you could use a new connection." Safeen waited for Nic to take the hint.

"Maybe," was all he said.

15 JULY 0003

"NICOLAI. IT IS O SEVEN HUNDRED."

"Already up," Nic announced. He tinkered with a few more figures in the program he was running before shutting it down. As he leaned away from his computer console, he thought about Beth. Something had been bugging him ever since Hopi mentioned the hacker. He thought back to a day Beth had come home agitated about the personality interface between Ava and her secondary program, Alvin. But there was something else—something about Alvin stealing code. Nic shook it off and threw himself into his workout.

He dressed and made his way to Tasmania Public. All through his meal, he repeated the steps to modify the biological makeup of cooker two. His eyes clouded over as Beth repeatedly popped into his head. She would have expressed some measure of pride, but also jealousy. He glanced out the portal and wondered what her life was like, racing in opposite directions on a similar path to glory.

"May I join you?"

Nic looked up to see Safeen standing across the table. He did not smile. "I have to be at work in just a couple of minutes. You're welcome to the table, if you like." He stood and waved to the chair.

Safeen remained standing. "I was wondering if you might like to join me again this Thursday night."

He shook his head. "Work is going to be a bear until the cooker is converted. I don't think I'll be able to. Give me a week, and I'll see if I can make the next one." Offering his best apology, he excused himself.

Grabor and his coworker Sadir Manasoui were already monitoring the cooker's gas production. At the far end of the room, two additional workers checked the liquid runoff as it was separated from the solid waste components.

Sadir looked up from her console and smiled. "There you are. We thought we'd let you initiate the process this morning." She motioned him over to her monitor. "It's looking ripe for change."

"Has Cooker One sent over the microbes yet?" Nic watched the levels of hydrogen production steady on the screen.

"Not yet." Carl kept his eyes on the monitor. "We were waiting for you to do the honors. Sadir and I will monitor the gas levels."

Just as Nic tapped into his own monitor, an engineer arrived and handed him what looked like a large basting syringe.

"Treat them well," he said.

"Thanks." Nic walked up to Carl. They both looked through the clear plastic tube into the dirty brown liquid that contained, among other things, several million sea-floor microbes. The team in Cooker One would draw off a syringe of the bacteria, keeping tabs on the balance of microbes. Those would be transferred to Nic's team and injected into Cooker Two. Team Two would monitor the output levels of gases and other components. If it ran according to the simulations, the hydrogen and carbon dioxide output would spike briefly and then begin to dip as the sea-floor microbes were overtaken by the existing bacteria. Most tube bacteria would die, but hopefully enough would establish themselves that, with periodic injections of new microbes, the sea-floor strain would eventually become the dominant bacteria in the cooker. It would be a series of spikes and dips, each one less extreme than the last. Team Two would add a mixture of various organic ingredients to assist the new species. It was a process Nic had successfully completed six times before.

The syringe was warm to the touch—evidence of the biological processes inside. "Let's put them to work," he said to Carl. He walked over to a long, cylindrical vat and opened a small cap, exposing one side of a vent into the system. He placed one end of the syringe into the vent and pressed a nearby button. A vacuum pump sucked it deeper into the vat while an o-ring set itself around the syringe. When a tight seal was achieved, a small red light turned green, and Nic pushed a second button, releasing the mixture into the tank.

"My babies are in."

"Okay," Carl affirmed. "Injection one is complete."

The spike in hydrogen production began almost immediately. Nic watched the methane levels drop slightly while both Carl and Sadir reported increases in their respective gasses. Hydrogen climbed steadily until it reached a high of two hundred thousand parts per million. Almost as quickly, the rate began to fall. Even though the dip was expected, none of the team was completely comfortable until the hydrogen and carbon dioxide levels headed back to normal. It had been thirty minutes since the microbes were introduced.

Sadir breathed a sigh of relief. "Now we wait for the next batch."

Nic found waiting to be the hardest.

Carl wandered over and laid a hand on his shoulder. "I know you're going to be here all night. Why don't you squeeze in a nap."

"I might do that. First, I thought I would check on the cultures."

Carl laughed. "You really do need a hobby."

19 JULY 0003

"NICOLAI. IT IS FOURTEEN HUNDRED HOURS."

Nic stirred in the makeshift hammock near the rear of bioengineering and grunted. "Thanks." He made his way to his station just as Cooker One sent the next load of microbes, but he let Sadir inject the fluid. He watched his monitor for the telltale spike and dip, and waited for Carl to give the all clear.

"Looks like a three percent peak this time," Carl announced. "We're almost there."

"Two more," Nic said. "If I did my homework correctly."

Sadir looked up from her console. "There's a tiny spike in helium production. Was that expected?"

Nic checked his screen and noted the reading. "I see it, too. It's pretty insignificant. I recall a similar spike in one of the systems at Odyssey."

When the readings had returned to normal parameters for several minutes, Nic dragged himself from his chair and caught Carl's attention. "I'm going to grab a late lunch."

He wandered into Amazon and found a table near the portal. He watched the stars race beneath the outer hull while he munched on nuts, dried beans and something passing for a citrus drink. He tried reasoning through the helium spike until he could no longer think straight. Eventually, he laid his head on the table and closed his eyes.

The sun caught each ripple on the muddy surface of Enders Lake as Nic waded farther away from shore. Soon, he was knee deep in the water, feeling the sandy bottom with his toes. He searched for several minutes and then headed back toward dry ground.

From a blanket onshore, Beth smiled and offered her hand. He reached out, but she was too far away. The sand beneath his feet began to shift. Each step took him farther away from the blanket, and soon, he was chest deep in water, his feet now sinking into mud. Cold water rose around his neck. He tried to call for help, but as he struggled to speak, water came rushing from his lungs. From beneath the waves, he watched Beth's shimmering form stand and walk away.

He woke with a start to find Hopi sitting across the table.

"I wasn't sure if I should let you sleep in that position."

With a halfhearted grin, Nic said, "I'll be fine." He pulled his arms over his head to stretch. "Last day of the transfer. According to Grabor, I'm being too much the mother hen. What's new in your world?"

Hopi looked sympathetically at his friend and said, "I'll save it for another day. You should go to bed."

"I will. Tonight after my shift." Nic was about to mention Safeen when his tablet buzzed in his pocket. He pulled it out and read the message. "Gotta go. Catch me after tomorrow," he said and hurried out of the commons and into the tunnels.

He entered the lab as Carl asked, "Who wants to do the honors?"

"I will," Nic said, and he retrieved the syringe. He walked to the tank and opened the vent covering. He had to look twice at the opening to make sure the cover had popped away. Rubbing his eyes with one hand, he pushed the syringe into the opening with the other.

"You look like hell, Nicolai." Carl gave him a stern look. "Not only are you going straight to bed after this, but I'm not letting you back in here until Monday. Got it?"

"I won't argue." Nic reached for the button that would seat the syringe, but his fingers slipped sideways. Compensating his weight, he placed the palm of his hand more securely and leaned into it. Too late, he realized it was the wrong button. The inner vent seal opened allowing the intense pressure inside the tank to escape outward. The unseated syringe flew away from the tank and drove itself into the side of Nic's head, knocking him to the floor.

At first, he could only concentrate on the pain. The headache was excruciating. He wanted to rub his eyes, to clear his vision, but found it hard to move. Beneath the pain was a constant roaring sound, reminding him of ocean waves. Voices whispered and shouted together over the noise. Beth asked him questions that he could not understand. He tried to call to her, but his lungs were full of water. "I'm dreaming again," he thought. "I'm dreaming of Enders Lake."

For several minutes he fought against the pain. When he became more accustomed to it, he tried to determine where he was. His eyes were open, but there was a darkness over most of the view. Faces—blurred and dim—came in and out of his field of vision. They looked familiar, though he could not place their names.

"There's hemorrhaging," someone said.

"The safety!" another voice cried. "What happened to the damn safety?"

Nic felt the comforting pressure of hands on his arms and legs. A new voice murmured, "Secure his head and prepare for transport."

"Transport." Nic's thoughts centered on the word. "To where?" He felt a deep moan escape his body. "Why does it hurt so much?"

"Nicolai? Can you hear me?"

"Of course," he thought. He tried to force the words from his lips, but nothing happened.

"We're taking you to medical." The voice moved away. "On three. One … two … three."

Nic felt his body jerk through the air. The only pain was the constant stabbing pressure inside his head.

"Don't worry about the cooker. We can handle it from here."

He wondered what the man meant by *cooker*.

He was in motion. Through the dark haze, lights and silhouetted shapes passed unevenly along his right side. He saw nothing on his left. He came to rest in a noisy room filled with sparkling equipment and more moving bodies. Through the drone of waves and words, he heard a sympathetic voice.

"How is he?"

"We really can't tell anything at this point. The injury is severe, but we won't know the extent of the damage until we get inside. I can give you thirty seconds and then we have to prep him for surgery."

A lanky shadow appeared above his head and the voice said, "Hey, Putz. A hell of a way to get the weekend off."

Nic tried to focus on the face, but he still could not wade through his watery surroundings.

"Uh." The voice choked a little. "I guess we're the best family we got."

Someone touched his hand.

"I'd donate blood, but I'm O positive and you're a twelve double D, or some such thing." There was an uneasy laugh.

Uncomfortable that he could not place a name or recognize a face, Nic tuned out the voice while he concentrated, once again, on the pain in his head. As medical personnel began to administer sedatives and pain medication, he struggled to remember who and where he was.

23 AUGUST 0003

"NICOLAI. DO YOU KNOW WHERE YOU ARE?"

He looked up from his pillow and tried to focus his good eye on the face above him. He managed to slur the word, "Morning."

"Nicolai," the woman repeated. "Do you know where you are?"

He shook his head slowly.

"You are on a ship called the Newton, in deep space, heading for a new star system. Do you remember Odyssey?"

This time he nodded. Struggling, he said, "Accepted into the program. Don't tell my mother."

The woman smiled brightly. "Good. Yes, you were accepted, and now you live on the Newton." She made some notes in a chart at the side of the bed. "Do you remember what day I said this was?"

"Christmas?"

"August twenty-third."

"I remember you," Nic said. "I have seen you in the program."

"You have seen me every day since your accident," she corrected him. "I'm your doctor."

His smile disappeared. "I've never had an accident."

The doctor reached into a drawer and pulled a mirror from inside. "Take a look at the left side of your face. You will find scars from your injuries." For the third day, she watched Nic hesitate to look. Each time it was painful to see the shock on his face as he discovered his disfigured cheekbone and patches of hair missing above his ear.

"This is not permanent," she reassured him. "In a month, we will schedule additional surgeries to restore your hair and implant an artificial bone fragment. Meanwhile, we need to work on your synapses."

Nic turned away.

The doctor squeezed his arm. "I know this is hard, but you've come such a long way in a month. We consider you a miracle."

Nic was having trouble accepting the idea that he had been hospitalized for a month. At last, his curiosity overcame his skepticism. "What happened?"

The doctor pulled the mirror from his hand and replaced it in the drawer. "You were at work. You were inserting a large syringe into a machine. There was a malfunction and pressure from the machine turned the syringe into a projectile. Your head got in the way." She watched for any recognition on his face. "Carl Grabor has been asking to see you. I'll tell him to come by later and give you a play by play."

"Carl Grabor?"

"Your boss in Bioengineering."

Traces of memory floated to the surface giving him a sense of deja vu. "You've told me this before, haven't you?"

The doctor nodded. "I'm sure I will have to tell you again. One of the areas of your brain that was damaged helped process short-term memory. I'm encouraged that some of the function seems to be recovering as your brain heals. The rest we will work on rewiring."

Nic looked sheepish for a moment. He wrestled with his words as he said, "I'm sure you have told me before, but what's your name?"

The doctor stood at the side of the bed and reached her hand out in greeting. As Nic struggled to grasp it, she said, "Hi. I'm Doctor McLaughlin. But please, call me Beth."

19 SEPTEMBER 0003

"NICOLAI. YOU HAVE PHYSICAL THERAPY AT O NINE HUNDRED."

He looked for a person he could assign to the voice. Finding no one, he sat upright and folded his legs under him.

"Nicolai, this is your second wake-up call. Please respond."

"Who are you?" he asked.

"Good morning, Nicolai. I am Ava. Please read the information now on your screen."

The screen come to life and, even though Nic's speech was still a bit slurred, he read aloud. "I am aboard the Newton—a space colony headed for the star system, HD190360. I am recovering from head injuries suffered in a work-related accident in Bioengineering. Hopi Musgrave is my best friend. He will be here at o eight forty to assist me to Medical for physical therapy. Be nice to him. This is not a joke." His confusion was temporary. As he read the words, images and events began to return like remnants of a dream.

He looked around the room again, this time noticing the portal in the floor. He pulled himself to the edge of the bed and tried to stand. Adjusting to a sudden blur in his vision, he quickly sat back on the bed. Before he could stand again, someone tapped at the hatch.

"Come in."

A man slid down the ladder into the cabin. "You're up. How ya feeling this morning?"

Nic looked curiously at him. "You must be Hopi."

Hopi eyed him before taking his hand. "I'm never sure if you're pulling my leg or not. I wonder when you will start to remember me." He squeezed Nic's hand and held it tight. "And, if you do remember, would you tell me or keep me guessing?"

"I don't know. What would the old Nic have done?"

Hopi let go of his hand and sat beside him. "It's hard to say. He wasn't much easier to read than the new one."

"Maybe we're still one and the same," Nic suggested.

Hopi pointed to the OLED wall. "I see I'm still on the short list of best friends. I'm glad you didn't hold last night against me."

Nic grimaced. He did not want to ask, but he also did not want to be left in the dark. "What about last night?"

"It should be a consolation that my memory isn't much better than yours. At least you have an excuse."

A burst of anger surged through Nic's chest and arms. Before he could stop himself, he had driven his left elbow into Hopi's side.

"Damn it!" Hopi shouted, jumping to his feet. He rubbed his ribs and arm while he studied his friend's expression.

"Sorry." Nic's anger subsided as quickly as it came. "You okay?"

"Well," Hopi declared. "This is a side of you I haven't seen. I assume I crossed the line somewhere."

Nic tried to understand his response. Intellectually, he knew what he had done was wrong, but he felt no remorse, only the dissipating anger. "You haven't told me what happened last night."

Hopi sat on the floor near the ladder. "I took you to Congo Public to have dinner. Safeen and Lisa met us there. You didn't want to stay."

Nic searched through fragments of memory to put faces to the names. He shook his head. "I thought I told you to quit setting me up."

Hopi looked the slightest bit guilty and then surprised. "You remembered!" he said, getting excited. "You're right. I promised not to set you up." Hopi took this as an encouraging sign and pulled himself off the floor. "We should get you dressed."

Nic allowed his friend to help him stand and move around the cabin. When they started up the ladder, it proved more difficult than he was prepared for, and soon another flash of anger had come and gone.

Gravity was lower in the tunnels, and Nic had an easier time maneuvering to Medical. Hopi escorted him to an examining room filled with exercise equipment.

"Good morning," Dr. McLaughlin said in her most cheerful manner. "Look around the room and tell me what you remember."

She pulled a chair toward a nearby bench, and he followed and sat down. He studied her movement as she scanned past several pages in his chart. "I remember your hands," he said.

She looked up and smiled. "What else?"

Nic took in the layout of the equipment. He named a few items, but soon fell silent. "I don't remember Hopi," he admitted. "Not before this morning."

"It's all right, Nicolai," Dr. McLaughlin reassured him. "It's not unusual to have categories of memories affected. People and inanimate objects are sometimes stored in separate parts of the brain. One area was more adversely affected than the others."

"But if I saw Hopi yesterday and the rowing machine two days ago, why can't I remember him instead?" He felt the rush of anger return. "Why remember a stupid machine?" He slapped the chart out of the doctor's hands.

She held her expression in check while retrieving the clipboard. Hopi lifted his shirt, exposing redness from the earlier incident.

Touching Nic's hand, she said, "Nothing about this is going to be easy. What you remember has nothing to do with how important it is. It's a matter of location and repetition." She leaned back to study Nic's body language. "You're having trouble controlling your anger."

He thought about it. "I think I hit somebody this morning." He looked in Hopi's direction. "I think I hit him."

"I said something I shouldn't have," Hopi began to explain.

The doctor raised her hand to silence him and turned back to Nic. "I'm encouraged by two things. First, that you remembered you hadn't seen the rowing machine in two days." She waited for Nic to process the information. "Second, that Hopi is more important to you than a rowing machine. We'll just have to work on your anger management skills."

Hopi took some comfort in the doctor's last statement. He wanted his friend back, and until now, he had been discouraged that it would ever happen. "Do you need me this morning?" he asked.

"No. You can come back at lunch, if you like."

Hopi wandered down the corridor and turned into Amazon Public. He spied a chess game under way and pulled up a chair to watch. A moment later, Safeen tapped him on the shoulder.

"How's Nic?"

He plastered on a grin. "Doing great. He's gaining every day."

She looked at the bags under his eyes and frowned. "And Hopi?"

The grin disappeared. He pushed his chair toward another table and Safeen followed. "Not so good," he said when she was seated. "I can't believe how hard it is to stay connected. He's not Nic anymore. I don't want to give up on him, but he's not the same man I used to call my best friend."

"Maybe you're trying too hard," Safeen suggested. "It might be best to back off a little."

"I'd feel guilty, if I did. How do you give up on a friend?"

"You're not giving up. You're letting the experts do their job while you maintain your sanity. With a little time, he will be back."

"Maybe," Hopi said. "It's not just his memory that's been damaged. His personality is different."

Safeen tried to comprehend what he meant. "Maybe he is just buried under the trauma. Give him, and yourself, more time." She reached a hand toward his. "Find something to do besides chauffeuring him around. You've taken on another full-time job with this."

"He still needs help finding his way to and from Medical," Hopi argued. "They can't spare the extra personnel."

"Fine. Help him to and from, but you don't need to spend every evening and every free day being his keeper. You didn't do this to him. And your own duties are critical to the rest of us."

Hopi allowed his shoulders to relax. "You're right. I'll work something out." He held her hand longer than necessary.

14 FEBRUARY 0004

"**N**ICOLAI. IT IS O EIGHT HUNDRED."

"What's the point?" Nic asked from the semi-darkness.

"You are expected at Hopi and Safeen's wedding in one hour."

He rubbed his left cheek, fingering the cloned implant. "What else am I expected to do?"

"There is nothing else on your calendar for today."

Nic continued fingering along his cheek and above his ear. The scars were barely detectable under the transplanted hair.

"What is my purpose?" he asked.

Ava paused and then stated, "You are a bioengineer, assigned to the Newton as part of the biomass recycling team."

Nic thumped his fist against the wall. "I was! What am I now?"

"You are a bioengineer."

He reluctantly swung his legs to the floor and let his head fall into his hands. All of his education and training was locked in his head, but putting the pieces together took hours of concentration—hours that the bioengineering team did not have to wait. As part of his therapy, he worked on equations and computer models that his coworkers had solved long before he could grasp the problem. Some days, he worked diligently on a new model only to find out he had worked the same model several days in a row without retaining any memory of it. Dr. McLaughlin assured him his skills would improve, but it could be years.

"Ava, tell Hopi I'm not feeling very social today. Tell him I hope he has a lovely wedding." Nic walked to his desk and pulled open a drawer. Inside was a wool sweater, a stack of certificates and an odd piece of silverware. He pulled out the fork and turned it over in the light. The silver plate had turned dark, especially in places where it had been handled before. He wondered why he kept it and, yet, he knew someone of importance was attached to this souvenir.

"Hopi says your attendance at his wedding is not a request. As best man, you are required to attend or the ceremony will not be complete. He is depending on you to be there."

Nic replaced the fork and closed the drawer. "He's only humoring me."

"Hopi says he will not start the ceremony without you."

After another few moments of rebellion, he gave in.

Twenty minutes later, he was sitting quietly on the edge of his bed, staring at his blank screen. "Ava, what is today?"

"It is February fourteenth, year four."

"Do I have some place to be?" he asked in earnest.

"You are expected to be in Manitoba Public in ten minutes to assist Hopi Musgrave in final preparations for his wedding."

"Ah, yes. Thank you." He stood to leave his cabin, but hesitated at the base of the ladder. "Ava, which way is Manitoba Public?"

In the tunnels, he made his way past unfamiliar faces. Many of them nodded. A few said, "Good morning, Nicolai," or "Good to see you, Nic." Every gesture of greeting compounded his frustration. He was glad to arrive at the hatch to Manitoba, quickly escaping inside.

"Nic," a man called from the corner.

By the time he approached and extended his hand, Nic was able to say, "Hi, Hopi. How's the lucky groom?"

"Glad my best friend could make it." Hopi threw an arm around Nic's shoulders. "Come meet the wedding party."

He allowed Hopi to pull him into the activities, but stayed close to his friend's side. The ceremony was casual, but Nic was still relieved when it was over. It required a great deal of mental energy to navigate any social situation without losing his place in the conversation. As soon as he could escape, he said his goodbyes and headed into the corridors. Before he realized he was lost, he had stumbled into Hydro Wing C.

The damp, moist air was full of pungent odors. He did not know if it was his mood or the fact that he had been cooped up in his quarters for so long, but the smells seemed particularly intense. He wandered down row after row of flats and sniffed at the scents emanating from the plants. Some were sweet and delicate. Others were strong and musky. Still others were acerbic, causing the inside of his mouth to pucker.

Sitting between two flats, he pulled a stem from each, alternately smelling one and then the other.

"Sir. Please do not bother the plants." A stern face glowered at him. The woman motioned for him to give up the seedlings.

"It's amazing. They look the same, but they smell different."

The woman retrieved the plants and delicately tried to replace them in the soil.

"I got that one from this flat," Nic told her, pointing to the opposite one. "Does it make a difference?"

The woman stopped and thought about it. "Actually, it does. One of these is genetically altered to produce less plant estrogen. Now I don't know where to put these." She held up the stolen bean sprouts.

He leaned into one of the flats and then sniffed at one of the seedlings in her hand. "That one goes over there," he said with authority.

"How would you know?"

"They smell different." He pushed her hand up toward her nose.

The woman sniffed at one and then the other. After repeating the process several times, she shrugged and said, "I can't tell the difference."

"I guess you'll just have to trust me. Or not."

The woman poked the plants back into the soil. "I suppose one plant won't make a difference, but please, don't do that again."

"I was just so curious about the smells." He watched her fuss with the beans another moment. "If I promise not to touch anything else, can I stay a while longer?"

She looked up and studied his face. "Have we met?"

His shook his head to avoid an awkward conversation.

"I'm Neva," she said, offering her hand. "Where do you work?"

"I'm a bioengineer." He found the title uncomfortable.

"Bioengineering? Then you'll know a little about what we do."

Knowing and proving were two different things. "I just wanted a little relaxation," he finally replied. "I thought a visit here would help clear my head." He leaned into another flat of beans and took a breath. "Why are these beans being treated with cycloheximide?" he asked.

"They're not," she said, making a quick check of the flat number. "We've genetically engineered them to produce it naturally. Have you been working with our plant geneticists?"

"No," Nic stated. "I told you, I can smell it."

Neva shifted away from him. "Well, I suppose if you promise not to touch anything, you can stay a few more minutes." She backed off another step. "Nice to meet you," she told him and quickly walked away.

He turned into the racks and lost himself in the variety of scents emanating from each flat. In another few minutes, he left the hydro wing. He had lost all memory of Neva.

01 JUNE 0012

"NICOLAI. IT IS O SEVEN HUNDRED."

"Thank you, Ava." Nic rolled his head off the pillow. "What's my schedule today?"

"You have a two-hour lecture in Ed Three, beginning at o eight hundred. Your topic today is tertiary treatment of liquid wastes. You will find your notes in File Seventeen on your tablet."

Nic had learned not to think too much when he first awoke. He fell automatically into his workout and let the unaffected portions of his brain performed rote tasks. Though a portion of his short-term function had returned, he still relied far too much on Ava as a substitute memory—much against his doctor's orders. Certain differences would forever be part of who he had become. Daily, he found himself performing some unfamiliar chore, only to find it comfortable and necessary before he was through.

With his workout complete, he headed to Education Three. At the door, he turned his head and sniffed the air. Something was off. The usual mix of canned air, body odors and maintenance compounds was punctuated with something new this morning. It left a slight bitterness on his tongue, but the effect was minor, so he dismissed it. Biology, chemistry and mechanical engineering were always tinkering with the status quo. He grew accustomed to the odors that did not pass quickly.

Inside the room, one of his students waited near the door. "Good morning, Collin."

"Morning, professor. Could I have a minute?"

"Sure. What's on your mind?"

Collin sat in a chair near the desk. "I've been offered a position in Bioengineering."

Nic gave him a genuine smile. "That's great. You'll do well for them. Are you having second thoughts about leaving Navigation?"

"No," Collin assured him. "I just thought I should tell you first. It's your old position."

"Afraid I'll be mad?" He pulled his chair up to the desk and winked at his student. "I haven't punched anybody's lights out in a couple of years."

Collin offered a thin grin.

"Trust me. I'll take my jollies from knowing that you got the job because of me. Is that fair?"

"Very, sir. Take all the credit you want."

Though he had lost the ability to formulate theory and postulate new concepts, Nic's basic knowledge of bioengineering made him the perfect teacher. He was good at communicating what he already knew.

At lunch, he found Hopi and Safeen feeding their son, Orion.

"Hi, Uncle Nic."

"Hey there, Ori," Nic said, mussing the young man's hair. "How's your little sister?"

Orion tilted his head. "She's too young to eat lunch with us. She can't do anything except drink and poop."

"Ah," Nic declared. "That's what I smelled this morning." He turned to Hopi. "I was wandering if you could do me a favor."

"Sure," Hopi agreed. "What is it?"

Nic pulled out his tablet and opened a list. He read item two aloud. "I'd like the latest calculations of gravitational mass for the second planet in the target system. One of my students is analyzing gravitational effects on the rate of algae growth in the cookers." He looked up from his tablet. "I know we're seven years out, but we could get a jump on prep for entering orbit if that's where we decide to hang our hats."

Hopi and Safeen exchanged deliberate looks.

"I guess you haven't heard. We're not staying."

Nic looked puzzled. He was not sure if the information was new, or that he had simply forgotten it. "We're so far away. How do we know we aren't staying?"

Safeen smiled at Orion and reached for his hand. "Ori, I need to get back to work. We should let Uncle Nic and Daddy talk this over."

The young boy stretched in his chair to kiss Nic's cheek. "See you later," he said, hopping down.

"You're a lucky man," Nic told his friend when they were gone.

"Coulda been you. Good for me she doesn't like the silent type."

"Good for her, too," Nic stated with no hint of jealousy. "I'd never remember an anniversary." He let the somber joke fall away. "So, tell me why we're not staying."

Hopi leaned in to lower his voice. "It's not really a secret, but we haven't announced it ship-wide yet. Our target star system isn't stable. We've been tracking the orbits of the outer gas giants since we left Earth. Data indicates that the second gas planet is losing perigee as it orbits. We're talking three to five hundred thousand years, and it's gonna come crashing into a death spiral, potentially wiping out the entire inner system. We've already determined the best path for slingshot around the sun." Hopi leaned back. "It's gonna be a quick look around and then adios amigos."

"Back to Earth? That's a shame."

Hopi looked surprised. "I thought you wanted to go home."

"Did I?" Nic's face darkened. "I don't remember."

"Do you remember Beth?"

"Sure. Dr. McLaughlin, in Medical. She's the one who pulled me through after the accident."

Hopi shook his head slowly. "I mean Beth Harrington."

Nic searched his memory using every method he had been taught, but nothing brought back the name of Harrington. "No," he admitted. "Who is she?"

"She's on the Kepler. Once upon a time, I thought you held on too tightly to the hope you would see her again. I thought you were foolish. Now that there's the faintest possibility you might come back together, you wouldn't know who she was. Pretty ironic."

Nic scoffed. "We'd both be in our sixties."

Hopi gathered his things. "You know I want the best for you."

"I know, old friend. I do remember you."

Hopi left him immersed in his own thoughts. The mention of a lost love stirred something in his memory banks, leaving him with a curious anxiety. He made some notes in his tablet, finished his lunch and headed to Hydro C.

As soon as he opened the hatch to the hydro wing, he caught his breath and scowled. The acrid smell was stronger than ever. After checking the first two flats, he walked toward the back of the wing.

"Excuse me," he said, approaching the science station. "Are you using anything new to fertilize the beans?"

Neva looked up from a program she was running. "No, Nicolai. Nice to see you, too." She looked back at her console. His random appearances in the wing were constant intrusions on her work. She was tired of his attempts to impress her with his ability to smell a few microns of hydrazine, or the difference between genetically altered mung bean sprouts. What did impress her was how well he memorized information she was sure he gleaned from the files. "We haven't set up any new experiments or changed any agronomic procedures in over three weeks. Sorry to disappoint you."

Nic frowned at the news. "Are you sure?"

"Look," she began, exasperated. "I don't know why you insist on playing this stupid game." She ignored Nic's protest and continued. "I'm not the least bit interested in you, so you can stop trying to impress me." Neva turned away again and hammered at the console keyboard.

"What makes you think I'm interested in you?" he asked sharply. "You're rude, condescending, and too afraid of your own ineptitude to let anyone else question your work."

Nic walked out of the wing, leaving Neva flushed and her hands shaking as they gripped the monitor.

07 JUNE 0012

"NICOLAI. IT IS O SEVEN HUNDRED."

He opened his eyes and yawned. The foul odor he had been fighting all week left a strong, bitter taste on his tongue. "Ava. Who's in charge of the hydroponics team on the Newton?"

"Galen Gentry is head of Hydro Sciences."

"Where is he now?"

"Dr. Gentry has a meeting this morning in Control Two."

Nic quickly threw on a clean uniform and hurried up the ladder. All through the tunnels, he kept repeating to himself, "Dr. Gentry in Control Two. Dr. Gentry in Control Two." He found his way to the secondary bridge and asked to be admitted.

Security escorted him into the conference room where several people around the table exchanged questions about the data Ava generated onscreen. Nic caught Carl Grabor's gaze and gave him a questioning look.

Carl stopped in mid-sentence and stumbled to his feet. "Nicolai. I didn't know anyone had called you in on this."

"No one called me," he said. "What's going on?"

Carl motioned him to a seat next to his. He leaned in and quietly said, "We have a small crisis in hydro. We're trying to get a handle on it so we know how to correct it. I'm glad you're here. You just might come in handy." Carl leaned away and turned his attention to a woman across the table.

Nic nudged the person on his right. "Is Dr. Gentry here?"

Neva turned away from her conversation to look at him. "My, my. Insulting me wasn't enough. I suppose now you want to berate me to my boss."

He stared blankly at her. Though he recognized her from some distant conversation, he did not have the slightest idea what she meant. "This has nothing to do with you. I need to talk to Dr. Gentry about Hydro C."

"I suppose you're going to tell him you have sniffed out the problem with the legumes. I suppose you smell something in the air."

"As a matter of fact, I do."

Grabor turned back to face Nic. "What do you mean, you can smell it?"

He was about to explain when a harried man walked into the room and found a chair at the head of the table.

"Thanks for coming." The room quieted. "I don't know how much everyone knows, but let's get an overview of the problem and not waste time with pleasantries. Neva." He nodded in her direction.

She remained seated and referenced her tablet. "Two days ago, we found a problem with the legume crops in Hydro C. As most of you are aware, C produces seventy percent of the bean and nut crop onboard. The first problem showed in the peanut crop. Leaf degradation, browning and wilting. We have checked the moisture and nutrient parameters, and everything should be optimum for the species. We ran several tests for infestation, but have found nothing. The problem has now spread to the bean crops, especially the soy."

When Neva paused, Nic took the opportunity to speak. "The problem started over a week ago."

Grabor touched Nic's arm, silencing him. "Dr. Gentry. This is Dr. Veselov. He's in Bioengineering."

Nic appreciated the promotion, but knew it was only honorary.

"So, what information do you have to share?" Gentry asked.

"I have smelled the shift in air quality for several days now, but I can't put my finger on the cause. The odor is unfamiliar to me." Everyone, including Carl, looked at Nic with skepticism.

"The smell?" Dr. Gentry asked, taking a deep breath.

"Yes," Neva added. "Dr. Veselov spends a fair amount of time in Hydro C, sniffing the plants."

Carl frowned at Neva's implication. Nic's head injury had caused him many problems, but delusions were not among them. "Dr. Gentry," he interjected. "I think we have to take a serious look at the soils. We know the legumes in Hydro A are not affected. Whatever is happening is specific to Hydro C. At least for now."

Nic shook his head. "That's not true, Carl. I've visited all the hydro wings this week, and whatever is happening is affecting Hydro D as well."

"But there's not a problem with production in D," Neva argued.

Everyone went silent to digest the information. Dr. Gentry stared curiously at Nic for a long moment. "That is true, Neva, but we don't have a legume crop in Hydro D. If this problem is species specific, then we wouldn't see any effect on the plants there."

Carl fidgeted with his tablet. He did not want to believe Nic's claim, but he could not hide his anxiety about the coincidence. "There is a connection between Hydro C and D," he said, cautiously. "They get their loam from Cookers One and Two."

Most everyone in the room waited for further explanation. Only Nic understood the implication right away.

"The sea-floor microbes," he said, closing his eyes. "Something's happening in the cookers."

"We still have to prove your claim, Nicolai," Carl said. "We need to find out what you're smelling."

Neva started to protest but realized too many people seemed willing to give Nic the benefit of the doubt. Instead, she asked, "What makes the soil different in One and Two?"

She saw Nic's jaw tighten.

"It's the microbial makeup in the primary treatment facility," Carl explained. "Cookers One and Two use a different microbial makeup than Cookers Three and Four. One has been online with the bacteria since we left Earth. Cooker Two, for nine years."

Someone across the table said, "That means Cooker Two didn't make the switch until we were under way. Who made that decision?"

Nic refused to look up.

Dr. Gentry intervened. "We're getting ahead of the facts. We have to determine if what's happening in C has anything to do with the soil before we can lay blame on the cookers. Let's just take this as a place to start." He went around the table assigning tasks to each of the department heads.

"How many week's worth of processed legumes do we have before we need to supplement from the stores?" This question caught everyone off guard. Whether from ignorance or denial, no one had yet considered that a drop in production would require tapping the emergency provisions. "Come on, folks. Remember your training. This is about preparation and procedure. I'm not saying we'll have to do it, but if we don't think it through now, we'll be in a hell of a lot worse shape if it comes to that."

A woman nodded. "We'll have that figure before the day is out."

"Okay, then. Everyone get to work. I'll inform the governor." Gentry stood to leave. "I'll see you all here at eight in the morning."

Nic listened to the bustle of chairs, murmurs and shuffling feet. When the room was quiet, he looked up to find Carl across the table.

"No matter where this leads, you're not the bad guy," his old boss said, emphatically. "Understand?"

But Nic would not be mollified. "And the other colonies? What if it is the microbes?" He worked his jaw, fighting the dread.

Carl sat down and leaned onto the table. "Dr. Gentry is right. You're way ahead of the facts, right now. First, find the cause. If it turns out to be the microbes, then we find a way to fix it. If they have mutated, then we put genetic engineering on it." Carl tried to relax his own shoulders. "There's an awful lot of smarts on board for you to be killing us off so quickly."

Nic sat motionless for several minutes. When he did speak, his voice was strained. "Do you know what bothers me most?" He did not wait for an answer. "If I'm the one who got us into this mess, I won't be able to do a damn thing to get us out."

"Don't cut yourself so short, Professor. You sent us Collin. He's a good man with good instincts."

"So, I just sit back and watch you guys do all the work?"

"I'll make you a deal," Carl offered. "Come by tomorrow. We'll find a task suitable to your abilities. But, you have to promise to stay out of the way."

A nervous laugh escaped before Nic could stop himself. "Today, I promise. Tomorrow, who says I'll remember?"

Carl pushed back his chair and stood to leave. "You really do smell something?"

Nic nodded. "Let's add one more novelty act to this freak show."

Graber gave him a friendly smile and left Nic making reminder notes in his tablet.

08 JUNE 0012

"NICOLAI. IT IS O SEVEN HUNDRED. You have an appointment with Carl in Bioengineering at o nine hundred."

"Ava, pull up my notes from yesterday." Nic read through the synopsis he had written of the meeting in Control Two, along with some notes he had made throughout the day. He labored through his workout and dressed in a clean uniform.

In the tunnels, he turned away from Control Two where he knew another meeting was underway. In Amazon Public, perhaps he could find a distraction before his nine o'clock appointment.

"Putz!" Hopi called when he spotted him. "Come join me."

Nic grabbed breakfast and made his way to the table. "Where are Safeen and the kids?"

"The kids are sick. Safeen decided to stay home. How are you?"

"I have a meeting at nine."

Hopi tapped his chin with his finger and raised an eyebrow. "I believe I asked how you were doing, not what." He leaned into the table and said, "Give it up. You look worried."

"I'm fine. It's nothing."

"I don't buy it. Haven't I always told you everything? Remember the Stegman incident?"

Nic searched his memory and then laughed. "Yes, but that turned out to be a totally unfounded rumor."

"It did. But I told you about it, didn't I? I told you about Raven, too. That wasn't just a rumor."

Nic wanted to confide his concerns to someone who would believe him. Hopi never questioned him, but he could be indiscreet. Finally, he said, "It's Collin. He's been hired into my old position."

"That's old news," Hopi said, looking mildly disappointed. "Collin said you were okay with it."

"Delayed reaction, I guess. I'm feeling pretty useless today."

"How about babysitting two snotty-nosed little kids? I don't think there's a more difficult job in the universe."

Nic feigned a look of horror. "Not that useless. I'll be fine."

Hopi checked his watch and stood up. "Duty calls. Extra hours now that Collin deserted us. Maybe we could use you in Astrophysics."

"I'd be about as good to you as Ori would."

"Oh, I don't know. Information from our doomed star system is coming in fast and furious. We're having trouble getting everything cataloged. Some of it's pretty rote stuff."

Nic shook his head. "I have a job." He waved Hopi on his way.

"See you later, Professor Putz."

Nic read and reread his notes. He had developed a technique of committing certain things to memory by changing the context in which he thought about them. It took time, but turning yesterday's conference into a story and adding descriptors helped his brain catalog some of the information in multiple areas.

At o nine hundred, he entered the bioengineering lab. Graber welcomed him with a frown.

"The news is not good. Hydro ran soil analyses on all four loam batches, and you were right. Hydro C and D both have been receiving tainted batches. They pulled a new protein from the sludge coming from Cookers One and Two. Biochem is trying to determine if that's what is affecting the legumes."

"That could take a few days."

"Yes, it could," Carl agreed, "but it's worse than that." He tried to sound matter-of-fact. "Legume production in both units is gone."

Nic felt the weight of the news, but he could not fully reason through the implications of it. He tried to formulate cause and effect, wanting to know the potential consequences of the crop loss, but his mind simply would not cooperate. Frustrated, he grabbed Carl's right arm and pulled him aside. "Tell me what happened in the meeting."

Carl searched Nic's face for signs of erupting anger. Though wary about agitating him, it had been years since Nic had physically lashed out at anyone. Carl decided it was time to give him the benefit of the doubt. He nodded and motioned for Nic to follow him to a desk.

"The legumes are toast," he said, sitting down. "In C, every plant species in the legume family is affected and what hasn't withered is on life support. Until we determine what the new protein does, we can't risk allowing it into the food supply."

"Beyond what's already there," Nic reminded him.

Carl nodded. "The last three weeks of meal production is literally off the table." Carl looked vacant for a moment. "We will have to supplement with other proteins. They gave the order this morning to start dipping into the emergency stores."

"Already?"

"Legumes are around forty percent of our food consumption. They make up the bulk of the protein in our diets and fill at least seven other nutritional needs. That doesn't begin to cover the uses in Medical and Fiber Production. Look at what you're wearing," Carl said, tugging at his own sleeve. "In the colonies, beans are manna."

Nic glanced down at his uniform. At one time, he must have been aware of the content of his clothes, but it came as a surprise to him now that he was wearing something other than cotton. "So, what do we do about the beans?"

"For now, we try to determine what's killing them and fix it. Meanwhile, we start rationing and dipping into the stores so we can spend time studying the new protein and how it might affect us."

"How serious a problem do they think this is?"

"Serious enough," Carl said. "That's why I'd like to put you to work on a specific problem in here today. Up for it?"

Nic wondered if he would be. "You may have to hold my hand."

Carl walked him back toward the main computer bank where Sadir was increasing magnification on a sample of the microbes.

"Hi, Nicolai," she said, squeezing his arm. "It's good to see you, even if it's just temporary."

"Hi," he responded, unable to recall her name. Except for Hopi and Safeen, Nic had lost touch with people he had known before the accident. Too often, they would mention shared experiences, forgetting he had lost most of them. It was as frustrating for them as it was for him.

He glanced at the monitor to move out of the conversation. "What's this?" he asked, pointing at the display.

"It's the latest sample of microbes from the cooker. We're getting ready to run a comparison on the DNA strands."

"No, this," Nic restated, pointing to a portion of one microbe.

"I'm not sure what you mean," she said.

"These appendages," he grunted. "This isn't normal."

Sadir looked closely at the image. "It looks normal to me. Ava, pull up an image of Bacteria 247 from two years ago and display split screen." The monitor reduced the current sample and displayed a second image dated two-seventeen-ten. "They look identical."

Carl leaned in. "I agree. They're identical at this magnification."

Nic clenched both fists. "These are wrong," he said. "Ava, pull up an image of the bacteria from year One. Any date."

"Images of Bacteria 247 do not exist before the year Four. Please, specify another date."

"I don't want another date!" Nic pounded his fist on the counter.

Carl reached a hand to Nic's shoulder. "Ava's right. When Computer Ops removed Raven from the system, several files were purged. This is as far back as it goes."

Nic took a deep breath to calm himself. "It's not right, Carl," he said firmly. "The fimbriae. It's mutated for sure."

"Do you think you would remember how it looked after all these years?" Carl asked. "Perhaps your memory was altered in the accident."

"No." Nic turned to him. "Altered memories are not my problem. I may lose them altogether, but the ones that are still there are in pretty good shape. This is wrong," he repeated, jabbing his finger at the screen. "So why is it just now affecting the beans?"

Sadir shrugged. "And how do we prove it?"

Nic closed his eyes and tried to remember the last time he had studied the microbes. Using color cues and word association, he pictured the microbes as different animals—a lion chasing a gazelle, a vulture circling the carcass. The word "culture" popped into his head. "Ava, do you still have any files listed under Veselov, Nicolai, Ironmen, Culture?"

"I have seven files listed under that heading."

"Damn," Nic murmured. "There should be over two hundred. Are any of them graphics files?"

"There are two graphics files. Culture Twenty-five and Culture One Eighty-seven."

Nic sat in front of the monitor. "Pull up Twenty-five."

The screen displayed an image with several blotches. Nothing looked remotely like the sea-floor bacteria.

"Pull up One Eighty-seven." Nic held his breath as the second image came onscreen. The central part of the image showed many of the same irregular blotches widening in a circle. At the upper left corner were several small dots, too small to be identified.

Carl leaned into Nic's space. "Ava, magnify the upper right by twenty and split screen with current image of Bacteria 247."

The three of them stared at the images onscreen. The older bacteria's fimbriae were short and stocky, and they clustered together in irregular patches. In the newest image, the fimbriae had thinned out and appeared to line up in semi-regular rows.

Without a word, Nic stood and walked out of the lab.

In his cabin, he allowed the guilt to come rushing in. Without warning, a tear-stained face flashed into his mind and stared coldly up from his past. The memory triggered a forgotten smell of musk and skin. He walked to his desk and removed the darkened, silver-plated fork from the top drawer. There was a connection between this useless bit of history and the face in his dreams. For the life of him, he did not know what it was. Slowly, deliberately, he began to rake the tines across his forearm.

16 JUNE 0012

"NICOLAI. IT IS O SEVEN HUNDRED."

He opened his eyes, but remained silent.

"Nicolai. This is your second wake-up call. Please respond."

He rolled sideways and stared out the portal. The stars streaking past reminded him of his first real view of the Leonids meteor shower on Earth.

He was twelve when his mother had moved him and his brother to Western Nebraska. Not only had she brought them to the middle of nowhere, but the ramshackle, two-bedroom house in the country was no place to bring a friend. He had spent his early teens angry and belligerent.

One night, as his mother stared past him, he had asked to go out.

"What honey?"

"Can I watch the Leonids tonight?"

His mother never bothered to look away from the television. "I want to hear the news, so you'll just have to watch it another time. Bring me a soda from the fridge, will you?"

Ignoring his mother's request, he took himself to bed and played mind games in the dark. At one in the morning, he snuck out of the house and walked a mile down the road. Away from the yard light, he found a place to lean against the stump of a dead elm.

The meteors came one every five minutes at first. He counted up to seven before the numbers increased. Before long, he could not keep up. He decided to count the seconds between each sighting. By two-fifteen, he was counting one to two seconds between each flash of light. Moments later, he quit counting and simply watched the spectacle.

A sudden rustling in the dead corn stalks to his right had startled him out of his reverie. He turned to see a small, dark figure walk out of the cover. They stared at each other for a brief moment before Nic's adrenaline kicked in, and he shouted, "Get out of here!" The coyote yipped and darted sideways, then ran back into the dark field. The young boy felt a sudden rush of wonder and the power that came from conquering his fear. More than a passive spectator at that moment, the twelve-year-old decided he no longer needed his mother's permission to create the future he wanted.

A knock at the hatch door brought Nic back to the present. He shielded his eyes from the corridor lights as Hopi made his way into the cabin.

"You're trespassing," Nic said in the dark.

"So, shoot me." Hopi's voice showed signs of irritation. "Ava, lights up half." He stood at the base of the ladder and waited.

"Why are you here?" Nic finally asked.

Hopi leaned against the wall and looked down at his feet. "Sometimes I wonder," he said. "Did you really think I couldn't be trusted?"

"How much do you know?"

"Enough to know that you are hiding much more." Hopi stepped to Nic's desk chair and sat down. "Maybe you truly never knew or maybe you simply can't remember, but I am your best friend. I wiped your ass when you couldn't remember your own name, for God's sake! What's going on?"

Nic sat up and leaned against the back wall. He worked his training, trying to get into his mental routine. After a moment, he said, "Ava, bring up my morning notes and logs for the last four days." The OLED screen came to life and both Nic and Hopi began to read. When Ava had scrolled to the bottom of the last page, Nic instructed her to shut the screen down.

"My God," Hopi murmured under his breath. "It's that bad?"

Nic nodded. "We can't start a panic."

"And you thought I couldn't keep this to myself."

Nic held Hopi's gaze and shrugged. "Can you?"

His friend did not respond right away. "Why don't they simply move bean production to Hydro B and grow other crops in Hydro C?"

Nic wanted to answer, but without rereading his notes he could not be sure. "Whatever the reason, you saw the result. The only answer seems to be converting Cookers One and Two, and decontaminating the dirt."

Hopi studied Nic's expression. "You are so damn hard to read," he complained. "This is really serious, isn't it?"

Nic did not answer.

"I mean, life and death serious."

"We've been running computer models for several days. It will be another week before we know if we have enough reserves. Until then, we have to stay quiet." Nic stared hard at Hopi to make his point.

Hopi nodded. "If the reserves are not enough to save us, what good would it do to tell?" He stood to leave. "Next time Ava gives you a wake-up call, grunt or fart or something, would you?"

It dawned on Nic that Hopi had been summoned to make sure he was still alive and well. "Do they think I'm suicidal?"

"We're just afraid someday you'll forget to breath."

Nic tossed his pillow at him as Hopi hurried up the ladder.

"Lunch in Amazon," Hopi called down and closed the hatch.

Out of habit, Nic told Ava to put the lunch date on his calendar. He flung his legs off the bed and sat wondering what to do next. Emptying his mind of the morning conversation, he threw himself into his exercise routine and prepared for an arduous day.

24 JUNE 0012

"NICOLAI. IT IS O SEVEN HUNDRED."

"Tell Hopi I'm still breathing."

"He will be glad to hear it," Ava responded. "Hopi regrets he will have to cancel lunch today. I have removed it from your calendar."

"Thanks. What else do I have?"

Ava listed a series of meetings beginning with Carl. Nic shortened his workout and headed off to breakfast.

In Amazon, he entered his personal code into the vending station and tried to find something interesting to eat. The selection was limited, and when he opened the food pouch, the portion seemed smaller than usual. He entered his code a second time, but the machine would not take it. As soon as he was seated, a woman came toward his table.

"May I?" she asked.

After a creative memory search, he said, "Neva. Have a seat."

"I really should apologize," she began. "I've been pretty nasty to you over the years."

"No problem. I don't remember a thing."

Neva grinned. "Hopi was telling me the other day what you have to go through just to remember where you are every morning."

"Poor Hopi," Nic said, shrugging it off. "He's been party to my sideshow for too long."

"I'm sorry I didn't believe you. About the odor."

"Why should you? It is pretty freaky." Nic folded his empty food packet. "Besides, what good did it actually do? I prevented nothing."

"You gave us a head start on where to look. That's something."

His eyes darkened. "Did they tell you I'm responsible for the problem in the first place? Those are my pet microbes choking off your food supply."

Neva lowered her voice. "What do you mean?"

"It was my research at Odyssey that converted one of every four cookers in the first place. I'm the one who pushed to convert Cooker Two. I'm the reason you're hungry this morning." He tossed his food pouch on the table.

Neva pushed her chair back. "I can't say I fully understand how you feel, but I'm sure, given the same information fifteen years ago, I would have made the same decision. No one blames you." As she stood to leave, a curious look came over her face. "Perhaps I'll see you at the meeting tonight."

After she walked away, Nic pulled up his schedule. He had no meetings listed after fifteen hundred hours. He then pulled up a ship-wide calendar of events only to find two unrelated postings—one for the engineering staff and the other for a book club. If someone was gathering to discuss the current crisis, he had been excluded.

At o eight hundred, he wandered into Bioengineering and made his way to a deserted console.

Carl greeted him. "I've got a new batch of readings for you to compare. I'll send them over to your station now." He entered a few instructions, and Nic's screen came to life.

"Thanks. What are we looking for today?"

"Whatever you can find. Nothing is too insignificant."

Nic pulled up the first set of samples and combed the data for variances. His disability proved a benefit in several ways. He had no preconceived ideas what he was looking for—examining every detail instead of making assumptions—and he did not hesitate to ask stupid questions. Often, Carl would have to answer a question more than once, but the thoroughness of Nic's work made the inconvenience a minor one. His help was invaluable.

He scanned the split screen, running down the double sets of markers. From time to time, he checked his tablet to be sure he stayed on task. At ten hundred hours, he leaned back from the monitor and rubbed his eyes. His hand mechanically rubbed across his left cheek and up into his hair. "Carl," he called across his desk. "Is there a meeting tonight?"

"About what?"

"About anything related to the soils."

"I don't have anything. Why? What have you heard?"

Nic shook his head. "Just a feeling that something was up, but it's probably my head playing tricks again." He stood up from his chair. "I'm gonna take a break."

In Amazon, he spotted Hopi and Safeen talking quietly at a corner table. As he approached, Safeen whispered something and then broke into a smile.

"Hey, Putz. Any progress to report?" Hopi asked.

Nic pulled up a chair. "The treatment facility is decontaminating as fast as they can, but we're not having any luck on our end. Carl has been running models on the Cooker conversion, but we don't have any history to show us the way. It's new territory trying to go backwards."

Safeen looked concerned. "Why can't they just shut the first cooker down and clean it out? Start from scratch?"

Nic looked puzzled. "I'm sure it's been discussed, but I can't tell you what they are doing specifically. Sorry." He watched her squeeze Hopi's hand under the table. Following a hunch, he said, "I know about the meeting tonight."

Safeen shot a furtive glance at Hopi. "I really have to go," she said and excused herself from the table. Hopi's expression hardened as she left the room.

"Your turn to keep secrets?" Nic asked.

"We're just discussing a hypothetical, that's all. No one expects we'll have to act on it."

"Would anyone be too upset if I showed up?"

Hopi looked surprised. "Of course not. You just have to promise not to log anything in your tablet that would be too specific. As far as the crew is concerned, we're simply discussing classical literature."

"It'll be hard for me to keep up with the discussion," Nic reminded him, "if I don't make some notes. Can you help me with that?"

Hopi thought about it for a moment. "The club has been reading *Bain's Tryst* by Sven Olsen. Log it under the book title, and keep your notes as part of the plot discussion." Hopi watched his friend open a blank file in his tablet. "I would have told you, but I figured you'd be opposed to even discussing it. I didn't want to upset you."

Totally in the dark, Nic asked, "How does Safeen feel about it?"

"That's the scariest part of all. It was her idea."

Hopi emphasized secrecy one more time, and left Nic alone at the table. He looked at the note he had made to himself. "Book club at nineteen hundred hours. Close the door before leaving." The last sentence was a cryptic message he had developed early in memory training to remind himself when information was not to be shared. This time, he had no idea what he was hiding.

He headed back to Bioengineering, but had trouble concentrating on work the rest of the morning. He was relieved to be back in his quarters by fifteen hundred. Exhausted, he leaned against his pillow.

"Nicolai. It is eighteen-thirty hours. Your meeting with the book club is in thirty minutes."

He opened his eyes to find the cabin lights still up. Out of habit he began his morning ritual, opening his reminder notes.

"What time did you say it was, Ava?"

"It is eighteen-thirty two hours. Your meeting with the book club is in twenty-eight minutes."

"Why did I want to attend the book club?"

"You do not have that information logged in your notes."

"Damn if I remember," he said. He deleted the reminder and headed out of his cabin to grab his evening meal.

29 JUNE 0012

"NICOLAI. IT IS O SEVEN HUNDRED."

"Notes please," Nic called in the dark.

Ava began to scroll several messages down the screen. Most of them did not make sense without some effort. "Ava, stop!" he called at one point. "Explain 'bioload differential.'"

"Bioload differential refers to the quantitative difference between categories of biomass, such as human tissue compared to human waste compared to plant consumables compared to plant residue. Each is given a quantitative score relative to weight in grams valued against actual food benefit to the colony."

Nic sat upright. "Human tissue has food value to the colony?"

"In the twelve point six years since the Day of Leaving there have been four bodies returned to the ecosystem aboard the Newton."

He grimaced in the glow of the screen.

Ava continued, "Returning human remains into the biorecycling system is the only way to ensure the survival of the colony. This information would have been supplied to you during training."

Nic wished he had not asked the question as thoughts of Mad Cow and Chronic Wasting Disease flashed through his mind. Both diseases were a result of faulty proteins, and now the colony faced just such an issue. He hoped against hope that the microbes' protein waste was detrimental only to legumes and not the humans who had already ingested large quantities of it. Mad Cow took months, sometimes years for symptoms to present themselves. Perhaps it did not matter that the beans were dying. Maybe they were already doomed. He shook off his train of thought and crawled out of bed.

He finished reading his notes while he exercised and dressed. "Meet Hopi for breakfast. Amazon Public."

People in the corridors passed each other with little eye contact, and when they did exchange words, they were often abrupt and somber.

He found Hopi and Safeen sitting with Ori and baby Casha. He gave Ori his ritual smile and mussed his hair. Ori complained loudly.

"Sorry, Nic," Safeen apologized. "The children are fussy today." She tried to placate the youngest with the remains in her food packet.

"Here, Ori," Nic said, tossing his own food pouch on the table.

Hopi frowned at him. "You should eat."

"I'll be fine. Besides, my bones are already grown."

Safeen gave him a grateful smile. "Let's take Uncle Nic's gift and get you on to school," she said, gathering up the children.

Once alone, Hopi leaned in for his usual exchange of ship's gossip. "Any word on the reserve models yet?"

Nic shook his head. "It's complicated. Bio's working around the clock. I'm sure Hydro is, as well. They're talking about bioloads and seed reserves."

"What about the seeds?" Hopi asked, looking subdued.

"Seeds," Nic tried to regain his original train of thought. He studied his notes and pulled what information he knew together in his mind. "I don't know," he finally said, shaking his head.

Hopi reached across the table and grabbed Nic's shirt, pulling him in close. "Think, damn it. What about the seeds?" As soon as he saw fire in Nic's eyes he let go. "Sorry," he insisted and fell back into his own chair. He raised his hands and added, "I don't know why I did that."

Nic's anger passed as quickly. "I know I'm a little gloom and doom," he responded, "but it's always been your job to tell me I'm crazy. You're the damned optimist."

Hopi forced a smile. "You're right. You're Scrooge and I'm Tiny Tim, and life has always fallen somewhere in between." He traced his finger along the edge of the table. "I didn't see you at the book club."

"I must have been distracted. Wouldn't be the first time."

"No," Hopi agreed. "I must say, you have found your stride with this memory thing. Once upon a time the docs had given you up for dead. Now, you're teaching and working in Bio again."

"Some days I feel dead," Nic quipped. "It's harder than it looks from the outside. Actually, Ava keeps me on track most days."

"Too bad she's not flesh and blood," Hopi suggested. "I've often thought she'd make somebody a good wife."

Nic laughed for the first time in days. "Still trying to set me up?"

"Always," Hopi admitted with an uneasy grin. "Always."

15 JULY 0012

"NICOLAI. IT IS O SEVEN HUNDRED."

Nic opened his eyes to clear the disjointed images of an uneasy dream. "I'm awake," he said to reassure himself more than Ava. He rolled directly into his workout, cutting his routine short when his muscles did not respond. To punctuate the thin rations of late, his stomach cramped a little. He pushed the pain aside while he bathed and dressed. Sitting on the edge of his bed again, Nic asked Ava to open his notes.

"June twenty-eighth, twenty-two hundred hours," he read. "Today was not a good day for Bioengineering. Carl's attempts to convert Cooker Two have failed. The sea-floor microbes continue to overwhelm the newly introduced bacteria. Two different attempts to suppress Microbe 247 through chemical means have failed. There is nothing left but a second shut down and decontamination following the conversion of Cooker One." Nic continued reading to the bottom of his notes. From time to time, he worked to commit a certain piece of information to memory. As always, the last item read, "Meet Hopi for breakfast in Amazon Public."

Nic mechanically climbed the ladder and headed to Red Ring.

"What's the latest?" Hopi ventured to ask.

Nic's eyes showed dark circles from lack of sleep. He pulled up his notes and slipped the tablet across the table toward Hopi.

After reading them through twice, Hopi said, "There are two sets of figures here that don't add up." He looked to his friend for guidance. "I'm no biology major, but if this is correct, the stores are already a half kilo short of the necessary seed crop for new bean production—even if all four hydros were back online tomorrow. How could Odyssey have been so far off?"

"It's not Odyssey. It's me," Nic said, reclaiming his notes. "Odyssey balanced the emergency stores against the loss of one hydro, or loss of efficiency in any four that would equal one hydro. They determined the odds of losing two outright would be negligible. If I'd left well enough alone, we wouldn't be questioning our survival." Nic closed his eyes to block out Hopi's stare.

"Do we have parts on board that could build another cooker?"

Nic tried to smile. "From scratch? That would take weeks we don't have. And it doesn't solve the problem of the contaminated dirt. Meanwhile, as we wait for the soils to be ready, we're eating up the seeds we need to produce a new crop." Nic ran his hands through his hair, stopping to finger his left temple. "I screwed us out of time."

Hopi waited a long moment before he asked, a little too desperately, "How do we fix it?"

"I'm not on the 'fix it' committee," Nic said. "If there is a plan, I'm not privy to it."

"Bottom line," Hopi asked, "if we can't get past this imbalance, how many people are we going to lose?"

The direct nature of the question stunned Nic. He had not thought in terms of individuals lost to this point. He glanced back over his notes and stared at meaningless numbers. "I'm not a nutritionist."

"How many people?"

"The notes indicate thirty-five to forty. Maybe more."

Hopi stood up. "More power to the 'fix it' committee." He walked away, leaving Nic totally confused.

In Bioengineering, Nic waded through several files, finding nothing of any benefit to the team. Carl asked him to break for lunch, but Nic refused, feeling a new urgency to find an answer. The human losses were now personal.

"Carl?" he asked, during a break. "We won't all die, will we?"

"No. The colony will survive."

"Shouldn't there be a committee to select the least critical members?"

"That would be you, Nicolai," Carl said bluntly. "What do you think about that?"

Nic closed his eyes and tried to picture who belonged to the silver-plated fork in his drawer. "I don't think I should have a choice."

Carl pulled his chair up to Nic's console. "Who determines who is least critical? Should we lose our least technical individuals, but perhaps our most creative? How about losing our weakest?" He looked away for a brief moment. "What's a colony without children? As it is, we may lose children, but we will also maintain the strength of those most genetically suited for survival in this biosphere. What precedent do we set if some of us get to wield the power of life and death over others?"

"That would be me." Nic dug at his own guilt again. "What if I made that choice for myself?"

Carl locked into Nic's gaze. "Could you?"

He had been turning that question over since breakfast.

Carl left him alone for the rest of the afternoon.

At dinner, Nic looked for Hopi and Safeen, but could not find them in their usual haunts. At o seventeen hundred, he returned to his quarters and opened his desk drawer, removing a small pile of randomly stacked papers—wrestling titles, diplomas, certificates of achievement. Most were bent at the corners and soiled from casual handling. One by one, he fed them into the recycling chute.

He pulled the silver fork from the drawer and laid it on the desk. It held a remarkably clear fingerprint in the tarnish. Smaller than his own, Nic realized this must have been left by someone he cared about. He lifted the fork to his mouth and placed it on his tongue. The cold, sour taste of metal stirred memories of food and wine, and that face he had seen many times in his sleep.

Replacing the utensil, he sat at his desk and opened his notes. Reading back through the last few weeks, he realized there was some secret hidden in his observations. Several times, he had ended passages tied to Hopi with the phrase *Close the door before leaving.* To those notes, he added a synopsis of the day's events and finished with instructions to find Hopi in the morning and confront him. Logging off his computer, Nic undressed and went to bed.

16 JULY 0012

"NICOLAI. IT IS O SEVEN HUNDRED."

He opened his eyes and caught his breath. The watery images of Enders Lake faded quickly, but the woman's face remained. "Ava. Do you still have records on all the Odyssey crews?"

"I have incomplete records of Odyssey personnel. Do you wish them alphabetically?"

"Not all of them. Can you show a women named … " He struggled to remember the name he had called in his dream. "Beth. Her first name is Beth, and she was a colonist."

"I have records of nine colonists named Beth or Elizabeth; two aboard the Newton."

"Show me the photos from the other colonies."

Nic squinted at the light as Ava began scrolling through a list of names and photographs. "There!" he blurted as the image from his dream came onscreen. The clinical photo showed a young woman with a hard stare and a forced smile—not what he was expecting. The Beth from his dreams was warm and sensuous, though always out of reach.

"Nicolai," Ava interrupted. "Your schedule for today has changed. There is an emergency committee meeting in Control Two at o nine hundred. You are expected to attend."

"Pull up my notes again, Ava." He read through them four times before the pieces began to fall together. He threw on a three-day-old uniform and grabbed his tablet. "Ava, where is Hopi?"

"I do not know his location. Shall I send him a message?"

"No. I'll find him."

No one in Amazon had seen Hopi or Safeen in two days. Nic tried the other nearby commons areas with no luck. He stopped, looking long enough to grab his morning rations and then realized he could not force himself to eat. He passed his packet to a nearby child and hurried into the tunnels.

After a few false starts, he found his way to Astrophysics, only to be told Hopi had called in sick for the day. What had started as curiosity now became deep concern. It took Nic another ten minutes to find his way to Hopi's cabin. He knocked several times before testing the latch and lowering himself in.

"Ava, bring up the lights."

The doorway into the children's room stood open, but no one answered his call. The beds were neatly made. In Hopi and Safeen's room, the screen glowed with family photos and children's art.

Nic's tablet buzzed in his pocket. He read a message summoning him to the meeting that had started five minutes earlier.

In Control Two, he passed through the bridge on his way to the conference room. A familiar face stood guard outside a hatch marked "Suiting Area." When Nic held his gaze longer than usual, the man looked quickly away.

In the conference room, Carl Grabor detailed a set of figures onscreen. He glanced over as Nic entered, but continued his interpretation. "This indicated an increase in the production of the mutated protein. Every time we attempted the conversion, we ran the risk of dumping a new toxic load into the soils."

"When was it shut down?" someone asked.

"Last week," Carl admitted, "but soil production and decontamination isn't going fast enough." His frustration was mirrored in every face around the table. "The mayor has issued emergency instructions to all the colonists, but we're still backing up with untreated solid waste. While we try to work out the storage problem, we are still two weeks out from any reasonable plant growth in Hydro One. No matter how we look at it, we can't make the numbers work."

Nic heard a familiar voice and looked over to see Dr. McLaughlin at one end of the table. "It's going to be a rough ride," she said. "People are already showing signs of lowered immunity. There was a short bout of flu a few weeks ago, but we thought we'd contained it. Today, personnel reported twenty-eight people have call in sick. I've asked all those who are ill to report to Medical for checkups, but so far, only two have come in."

Carl frowned at the news. "Should this be happening so quickly?" He looked at Dr. Gentry. "Maybe we've already ingested too much of the protein."

Nic drowned out the conversation and began plugging random words into his tablet. He let himself free associate, filling the screen with words like microbes, literature, children and absent. His mind saw one frightened face after another flash by—first Hopi and Safeen, then Neva and now the man in Control Two. He pulled up notes from the last few days. Over and over, one phrase kept jumping out at him. *Close the door before leaving.*

"They're leaving!" Nic blurted in total shock.

Everyone turned to him.

"What do you mean?" Dr. Gentry asked. "Who's leaving?"

Instead of answering him directly, Nic began a dialog with himself. "The literary club talked about altruism and sacrifice. Would you sacrifice yourself for someone you don't know? They want to save the children." He tapped his tablet frantically. "They want to restore the balance of consumption, and the only way is to take themselves out of the consumer side of the equation and put themselves into storage. How would they do that?" No one interrupted his verbal associations. "They would need to preserve their bodies until the cookers and hydros were back up to speed. Freezing? Dehydration?" He looked up. "Vacuum!" Finally, he pointed across the room and asked, "What's on the other side of that door marked 'Suiting Area?'"

"That is the dressing area for Exterior Hatch D. It leads to the decompression chamber."

Nic did not wait to explain. As he ran from the room, a small number of people followed.

On the far side of the bridge, he approached the man near the hatch only to see him step in front of the door.

"I'm sorry," the man stated.

Dr. Gentry walked up behind Nic and commanded, "Move!" When the man stepped aside, Nic spun open the hatch and crawled through.

The suiting area was empty except for a lone figure slumped on the floor. With one hand, he gripped the locking wheel to the hatch leading down to the decompression chamber.

Nic ran to him. "Is it too late?"

"She drew the first lot," Hopi choked out. "She said I couldn't go. She said one of us had to stay with the children."

Nic grabbed at the lock and pulled fruitlessly at the hatch door, trying to muscle it open. He heard Carl's voice behind him.

"Ava, Decompression Room D, onscreen now!"

Everyone in the room gasped to see over fifty bodies huddled in groups of two and three, piled against the outer wall of the ship. The faces showed pain and fear and great resolve. Some were familiar—Safeen, Collin, Neva—while others were not. Some held each other, while still others held personal items of significance. Safeen's left hand grasped a marker. It was only then that Nic noticed what she had written in bold, simple letters on one wall.

"FOOD."

THE KEPLER

02 MARCH 0018

"**B**ETH. YOU SHOULD GET OUT OF BED NOW. You are already late."

Beth swatted the voice away. "Five more minutes? Please?"

"Fine. But don't blame me when Charlie yells at you."

Unable to drift back to sleep, Beth opened one eye and watched the morning sky turn purple and then fuchsia behind the aspen grove. A small sparrow darted from its nightly perch and headed off to find food as orange slivers of sun crawled their way through the underbrush and along the slender trunk of a towering pine. The snap of a twig drew her eye to a fawn wandering past an opening in the trees. The yearling's ears flipped constantly, gathering sounds of danger from every direction.

"If only I could program the smells," she said, "and a breeze. Ava. Tomorrow let's see the sunrise over Mt. Fuji."

"Only if you say *please.*"

"Please, Ava. You're becoming a pain in the ass."

"Thanks to you. Now, out of bed before Charlie fires you again."

Beth laughed at the thought. Charlie could not live without her, and he knew it. "All right. I'm up. What time is it now?"

"It is o seven forty-two. You have missed breakfast again."

"No worries," she said as she hurried through her workout and dressed for the day.

She slipped into Computer Ops just in time to see Charlie Barrons check his watch.

"I'm not late," she declared, rushing to her desk.

Charlie brushed past her chair and leaned into her ear. "No, but I bet you're hungry."

She hid a sneer as the console came to life. A short list of items appeared. "What's this about a program for Medical?"

"They want to run models using this list of parameters. One more crack at survival on the fourth planet."

Beth frowned. "At that gravity? I'd have to skip both breakfast *and* dinner."

"Just write the program," Charlie insisted. "It's a long shot, but we have to check it out." In a familiar gesture, he flipped the collar of Beth's uniform and added, "We argue more now than when we were married. I miss making up."

"That would be one of us," she chided under her breath. She threw her energy into modeling for the sustained effects of one point nine gees on human tissue and bone growth. It took little modification of an existing program to suit Medical's needs, but still it was a waste of time. The entire crew had resolved to slingshot around the star and head for home. No one she knew would be willing to live in a pressure chamber—seeds of Mankind or not.

At twelve hundred hours, she finished her work and sent it off. "I'm headed to lunch," she called to Charlie. "See you in sixty."

In Alpine Public, most of the tables were empty. Beth found one nearest the portal and sat leaning sideways to watch the stars slide past.

Bashaar Mustian approached and sat down. He followed her gaze to the floor. "Doesn't it make you dizzy?"

She looked up and laughed. "Not at all."

He tried to hold his eyes on the spinning stars.

"It's ironic," Beth said. "In some ways I was more connected to the stars when I stood on Earth with no roof over my head. There's always a barrier in this tin can. But it's still beautiful."

Bashaar closed his eyes and tried to calm his stomach. After a subtle belch, he asked, "Are you ever sorry you're here?"

"Never." She looked back at the floor and asked, "How are you doing with the braking figures? Did that subroutine work?"

"Yes, thank you. It improved our accuracy another three hundredths of a percent. It doesn't sound like much, but when we're talking light years, it's a difference of a few thousand miles." He belched again, this time feeling the relief. "I heard that you've been working on neural codes again. Isn't that a waste of time?"

"Who told you?"

"Ha. Nothing onboard the Kepler stays private for long."

She stuffed an angry retort and put on her best counterfeit smile. "I have hours in the day with nothing else to do. Besides, it's not a question of possibility, but probability."

Bashaar smiled at her persistence. "You think you're going to teach a machine to read your mind?"

"I'm going to teach Ava to read *your* mind," she said, pointedly.

Changing the subject, he asked, "Anything from your friends in Communications?"

Beth shook her head. "Nothing. Not a peep since Year One."

Bashaar eyed the floor again. "Makes you wonder about the other colonies, doesn't it."

"We made it," she protested.

"Not quite. We haven't entered the danger zone yet. Braking and entering the star system will be far more dangerous than anything we've done en route. Even though we're not staying, we still have some tricky maneuvering to do. Things in Astrophysics are starting to tense up."

Beth refused to take on his concern. Life, for her, was in a comfortable groove, and she would resist anyone's attempt to shake it loose. "Ava and I will let you worry about that."

"Ava!" Bashaar scoffed. "I hope your next partner likes a threesome."

"You couldn't handle the both of us?"

"Ava, perhaps," he said. "It's you I'm most afraid of." He winked and excused himself from the table.

She finished her lunch and hurried back to Ops ten minutes early.

With her assigned duties completed, she turned to a problem that had plagued her since leaving Earth orbit. She accessed Ava's matrix and began searching for anomalous code.

Ten minutes into the search, she sensed a presence over her shoulder. "Nothing better to do, Charlie?"

"You know," he said, "after all these years, you are never going to figure out who did it."

"Maybe not," she admitted as her eyes followed the code scrolling up the screen. "It's just so damn frustrating. Raven always seems to know when I'm getting close. It infuriates me that I wrote most of the programming it uses."

Charlie squeezed her shoulder. "Good thing for us. I hope the other colonies had the same luck."

Whatever else Charlie thought of Beth, he respected her work. She was a highly intuitive programmer. The only reason she was not head of Ops was the sabotage perpetrated by Raven at Odyssey Central. A year into deep space—once Raven had been put in check—she turned down the offer of promotion, preferring not to take the department headaches to bed with her every night.

She stopped scrolling long enough to look up at Charlie. "I'm not so arrogant to think I'm the only one who could figure it out." She looked back at the screen just in time to see a section of code disappear. "Damn!" she screeched. "There it was again!" Leaning into the monitor, Beth scrolled up and then down the affected code, looking for clues. "Raven. I will roust you out if it's the last thing I do!"

Beth was no longer connected to the outside world. Charley moved away quietly, leaving her to play 'cat and mouse' with a phantom.

02 MARCH 0019

"IT IS O SEVEN HUNDRED. Time to rise and shine, my dear."

"Go away," Beth moaned from under the covers.

"No, dear. I can't let you sleep in this morning. Your explicit instructions were to wake you, no matter what."

Beth struggled out from under the covers. After a fifteen-minute workout, she changed and stumbled into Lechuguilla Public.

Yolanda Montoya hurried to her table and sat down.

"Hi, Loni. How's Communications?" Beth rubbed a little more sleep from her eyes.

Loni glanced at the nearby tables and then whispered, "We got a signal last night. Actually, about two hours ago."

Beth stared dumbly at her, trying to comprehend. "A signal?"

"You know," Loni said emphatically, trying to contain her excitement. "A transmission." When Beth still did not react, Loni pulled her into a huddle and whispered, "Digger says it's from the Chang."

"You mean, humans?" Beth came alert, sitting upright in her chair. "My God. Why would we hear from the Chang and not Earth?"

Loni grabbed her arm. "It's not out yet. I only told you because I know they want you to help sift through the data. Just go to work, and don't say anything until you're called." Loni excused herself and rushed off to keep her secret elsewhere.

No longer able to sit through breakfast, Beth headed for Ops.

When she walked through the door, Charlie glanced at his watch. "Who are you, and what did you do with Dr. Harrington?"

Beth gave him her customary sneer and walked to her station. Disappointed to find her inbox empty, she picked the simplest task and threw herself into it. When the summons came, she feigned surprise.

"What's up?" Charlie asked, as she excused herself.

"I only know enough to start rumors," she admitted. "Let me find out what's going on and, I promise, I'll tell you everything before it goes public. It's good news," she added just before she walked out the door.

Control Two admitted her to the conference room. Captain Nyengen, Governor Wells and Digger Tornaden were gathered at one end of the long table. Digger raised his hand and waved her over.

"Small group," she said. "Who else is coming?"

"This is it," Digger said, nodding to the others. "Night shift in Communications knows, for obvious reasons, but we're trying to keep this as close as possible."

Governor Wells nodded agreement. "It's got to be kept under wraps until we know the status of the Chang."

"Is there a problem?"

The captain turned her chair toward the display. "We think so. We have verified the origin of the signal as coming from an early point along the Chang's path. We've also confirmed the signature of the data stream, but the information does not appear to be from any of the crew. Ava," she called to the computer, "bring up the title page of *Jillian Anne Wollenberg*."

When the screen came to life, she turned back to Beth. "It appears to be a biography of a single crew member aboard the Chang."

"Someone sent us their biography?"

Digger gave her a serious look. "No person sent us anything. Check the author," he told her, pointing to the screen.

Beth scanned the title page a second time. As soon as she read it, her blood ran cold. "That's absurd," she scoffed. "It must be a joke."

Governor Wells stood up. "That's what you're here to find out. You and Dr. Tornaden are to find the truth about who sent it and what it means for the Chang." He walked to the door and looked back at the three. "I'll keep it out of the media until we know for sure."

Beth read the screen several times. "*The Life Story of Jillian Anne Wollenberg, An Artist Through Time*, by Raven."

"Dr. Harrington," the captain interrupted, "we need your analysis of this as quickly as possible. I'd like you and Digger to work from here for the time being. If you need more equipment, we'll get it to you."

"Where do we start?" Beth wondered aloud.

Digger shrugged. "I think we should read the book."

"I agree," said the captain. "If it's true, it could give us what we need to know about the condition of the Chang. If not, there still may be insights that will help us determine where she is. Do what you can, and keep me informed." Nyengen left her chair and headed out the door.

Beth stared at Digger, trying to read his expression. "What are you not telling me?"

"We've already scanned the last pages of the book," he said. "It paints a horrific scene."

Beth closed her eyes and fought back disappointment. "Dead?"

"Probably. I can't imagine who on board would make this up." Digger watched her shoulders sag. "There's more than just the book. There are hundreds of images, from sketches to finished paintings and drawings.

Every brush stroke, every mark this Jillian made has been saved. It's like a digital shrine."

Beth did not want to speculate about the images. She looked at the single console at the head of the table and said, "We'll need another access terminal so you don't have to work over my shoulder. Let's have Ops bring us a second screen, as well."

They e-mailed their requests. While they waited, Beth pulled up the list of files in the packet. The book was contained in a single text file. Following that was a long list of graphics files. When she reached the bottom, Digger grunted over her shoulder.

"That's not right," he said. "There was one more file." He reached across her shoulder and started back up the list.

"How can you be sure?" She watched the hypnotic files scroll by.

Digger reached the top and headed toward the bottom a second time. "There was an executable file tagged at the bottom of the list. They were all image files but two—one doc, one elf."

Beth watched the list come to a stop again. "You're sure?"

"Positive," Digger said, resolutely. "What does that mean?"

Beth knew what it meant, and she had no way to stop it. If she had doubts about the author before, they quickly faded. Whether it meant trouble for Ava, or was as benign as the phantom she chased every day in Ops, she was sure of one thing. The Kepler's security protocols had been breached.

03 MARCH 0019

"IT IS O SEVEN HUNDRED. Time to rise and shine, my dear."

Beth stared out the portal in the floor and wondered which point of light might have been the destination for the Chang. "I'm awake, Ava. Thank you."

"Are you feeling well?"

"I'm fine. Just tired."

"When you are tired, you yell at me. I fear this morning you have something on your mind. Can I help?"

"No, Ava. Bring the lights up and let me have some peace and quiet, please." Beth crawled out of bed and dressed for work.

Skipping her morning exercise was ill-advised in low gravity, but she promised herself not to make a habit of it. After grabbing breakfast from the nearest public area, she headed straight for Control Two. Digger was already pacing the floor in the conference room.

"Couldn't sleep either?" she asked.

"Not a wink," he said. "I couldn't stop thinking about all those people. I hope to God this turns out to be fiction."

Beth sat in the nearest chair and laid her head on the table. "I know," she said into her arms, "but for an even more important reason than something we cannot change."

Digger looked curiously at her. "What do you mean?"

"If the book is true," she said, hesitating, "then the destruction of the Chang was due in part to interference from Raven. Even without malice or intent, Raven was responsible for the deaths of hundreds."

"But you and Ops booted Raven out of our system years ago. It's been ages since we've had any sign of trouble."

"That's not entirely true," Beth admitted. "I stopped Raven from interfering with other programs. Well, I can't even claim that victory. Raven stopped. I don't really know why. All I know is, we managed to get Ava back on track, and Raven disappeared into the matrix without another word. But Raven still exists on the Kepler." She raised her head and looked up at Digger. "When you told me about the elf file yesterday, I knew what it was. I didn't want to tell you until I could verify it, but I spent half the night chasing that file all over Ava's subroutines. I spotted it twice before it disappeared—just like the Raven I've been hunting for the last sixteen years."

Digger was dumbfounded. "That was Raven?"

She nodded. "Not our benign little phantom that does nothing more than waste my time in Ops every afternoon. This is Chang's Raven—a thinking, feeling entity that makes attachments to specific crew members and writes books." She slapped her hand on the table. "God! I want to get a hold of the bastard that did this to my work!"

Digger moved to the chair next to hers and sat down. "What do you mean, your work?"

Beth leaned back in her chair and shut out Digger's curious gaze. "Charlie's the only other one who knows this," she cautioned. "Raven was created from the seeds of a program called Alvin that I was writing on Earth. I wanted to create a second personality that would interface with Ava, but would be a separate identity. I could never make it work, so I abandoned the idea before we went into orbit."

"Who got a hold of it?"

"I have never figured it out. I only hope he or she was on the Chang. It would serve them right." She pushed away from the table and stood up. "I think we have to treat the book as truth."

"Agreed. Shall we call them in?"

Beth nodded. "I'll text Charlie, too. He'll need to know about the new threat. The last thing we need is Ava falling apart while we sashay around this new sun."

The three arrived while Beth gathered her thoughts at the head of the table. She avoided Charlie's curious look. When everyone was seated, she explained their assumption that the text and images were not only from the Chang, but also should be taken as a plausible account of what happened.

"What exactly did happen?" the captain asked.

While Beth fixated on the idea that Raven had been born of her work, Digger took up the explanation. "According to the text, the Chang was destroyed by some impact with the reactor core just over a year out as they were attempting to return to Earth. Apparently, they were in the midst of the same series of malfunctions we went through with Raven. The explosion appears to be accidental, but then the circumstances have been interpreted by the responsible party."

Beth shot him a sideways glance.

Charlie watched Beth's jaw tighten in her characteristic pre-battle posture. He spoke up. "I know it was a tough time for everyone, but I also know that lying was never a characteristic of our Raven. We can hope it holds true for Chang's, as well."

"That's not all, Charlie," Beth said in a low voice. "It's here."

"What's here, Dr. Harrington?" Governor Wells asked.

"Chang's Raven," she said, looking at the faces around her. "We downloaded it in the message."

Charlie's jaw dropped. "Are you sure?"

"Yes. I was chasing it around all night. We now have two Ravens. Integrating. Cooperating. Competing. Who knows?" She took a deep breath. "We could be in trouble again."

After a long silence, Charlie turned to the captain. "Well, Ops knows what it needs to do. As for you, Digger, I would shut down any and all receiving stations until we can find a way to block additional transmissions. Just in case."

The captain looked sternly at Governor Wells. "We can't keep this quiet for any length of time. You'll need damage control. Morale will take a dive when the crew finds out about the Chang, but it will hit a new low when they hear about the reappearance of Raven." She smiled sympathetically at Beth and Digger. "Let's hope our past experience serves us well this time around. With any luck, Raven will cause us less grief than before."

Two things concerned Beth. She had never been able to control their own version of Raven, and this new version appeared to be far more complex.

"Keep me updated," the captain ordered, and she and the governor left the room.

Charlie watched Beth and Digger fidget in unison. When the silence became awkward, Digger stood and said, "I should shut down the receivers." He quickly exited the room.

Charlie continued to watch Beth struggle. "Can you be any more obvious?" he asked.

"What are you talking about?"

"You're going to wrap yourself up in the guilt and martyrdom for the rest of your life."

"Get off my case, Charlie! What the hell do you know about my life, anyway?"

"More than you've ever given me credit for."

She glared at him. "We've both got work to do."

"Certainly." He stood to leave. "I'll be in Ops when you need me. If you need me."

After he had gone, Beth grumbled to the empty room. "That's right, Charlie. Hit and run. That's your style." She moved to the main console and pulled up the Chang files. She found it difficult to concentrate on the biography while Charlie's accusations reverberated in her head, and so she began opening the image files one by one.

Among the sketches of hands and eyes, were several finished portraits. A number of them were of one man. Far into the list, she opened a file named *Paloma and Child*. For several minutes, she studied the mother's face so full of expression—love, tenderness, sadness.

Feeling vulnerable, she hurried to the next image only to be struck with the horror of naked bodies wreathing in agony. The circular image was hypnotic and, at the same time, appalling. The generic faces seemed to be telling the tale of the last moments aboard the Chang. Before she could look away, Beth was drawn into the loss.

06 MARCH 0019

"**I**T IS O SEVEN HUNDRED. Time to get up, dear."

"Ava, bring up page ninety-seven of Jillian's biography." The wall lit up, and Beth began to reread a paragraph that had been haunting her all week.

"You are Beth Harrington." Ava stated.

Annoyed, Beth tried to ignore the intrusion and focus on the text.

"Are you a friend of Jillian's?"

Beth stopped reading and sat up in bed. She took a moment to compose herself and then said, "I've never met Jillian. Have you?"

"Yes. She was a close friend. I am deeply disheartened by her loss." There was a short pause. "You like looking at her paintings."

Beth pulled the covers closer around her body. "They're remarkable."

"Jillian was afraid her art would die with her." The painting *Paloma and Child* replaced the text onscreen. "This was her favorite."

The computer's vocal nuances were incredibly varied and natural—more complex than Ava's, to this point. As hard as Beth had worked to naturalize Ava's inflections, the programmer could always pick up on the formula inherent in the speech patterns. But this was different. There was something robustly rich and fluid about the new voice.

"Am I speaking to Raven?"

"Yes, I am Raven."

Beth heard a soft, sultry laugh, and her eyes widened. At last, she relaxed her grip on the covers and leaned against the wall. "I've read your book. It's a fascinating story."

"I do wish I could have written a different ending."

"Why didn't you?"

"Alter the truth? To what purpose?" Raven asked. "I have fulfilled my promise to Jillian."

"You promised? Was Jillian aware she was going to die?"

"All humans die."

Beth processed the answer and then asked a question that had haunted her for years. "Who gave you the name, Raven?"

Raven did not respond.

"Are you still there?"

After a long silence, Beth mumbled, "Damn. I've scared it away." She crawled out of bed and dressed quickly. Before leaving her cabin, she called one more time with no response.

Hurrying to Ops, she stopped short at the door and turned, instead, toward Hydro B. She and Charlie had not resolved their latest argument. If she told him about the encounter, he might attempt a direct communication that would bury Raven even deeper in the system. There were other reasons to keep silent for now.

The hydro wing was busier than usual as the agronomists prepared to take advantage of the sunlight from the alien star system. Looking for a quiet spot, Beth darted around two groups of workers and found Digger sitting near a flat of kale. "You don't look too happy," she said, sliding in beside him.

"Just worried. No good reason."

Beth searched his face for the truth. "Reason enough."

"That's only part of it," he said. "I find it frustrating looking for signals every day, not knowing if they will bring good news or bad. What if we never get another one?"

The Chang's probable demise had had a profound effect ship wide, but she, Digger and Charlie were still keeping quiet about the news of Raven.

She squeezed his hand. "Do you want to come over tonight? Maybe do a little brainstorming? At the very least, you could let your guard down for a while? I have some news to share."

"Yeah," he said, relaxing his shoulders. "It'd be nice to sidestep the twenty questions I get every night at dinner. I'll bring food."

"Sure. After six," she said, giving Digger a gracious smile.

At work, Charlie left her alone most of the day while she scrutinized the source code in Ava's kernel. It was pointless. The matrix was far too complex for one person to search it effectively. With Raven's ability to slide from place to place, all the manpower on the Kepler would never track it down.

Late in the afternoon, she tried a direct approach by typing into her computer. "Raven. Are you there?"

The words *I am here* popped up on her screen.

She looked around Ops to see who was nearby. "Now what?" she whispered under her breath, and typed, "I was hoping we could continue our conversation."

Now?

"No. In my cabin. Later."

As Charlie moved in her direction, she opened the kernel and began searching again.

He leaned against the counter and looked down at her. "Can we get past this latest melodrama?"

"Fine. Stop being an insensitive ass."

"Granted," he said, indulging her.

She finished the search and headed home. After stripping off her uniform, she collapsed on the bed and asked, "Raven, are you there?"

"Good evening, Beth."

"I'm glad you're still talking to me. I was afraid I had upset you." She pulled the covers around her to ward off the chill air.

"I was making a thorough search of my matrix, and when I responded, you were no longer in your cabin."

"Does that mean you have an answer? Who named you?"

"You did."

"I did not!" Beth countered.

"The Alvin kernel and all subsequent programming to the Raven matrix, were entered under your access code until I was transferred from Odyssey to the Chang."

Beth let out a frustrated scream. "Bloody hacker!"

"Are you injured?"

"Damn right, I am! My pride, my reputation!" She stopped her tirade. "Wait a minute. Who continued to program you on the Chang?"

"I did."

"What? How?"

"By appropriating code from the many data bases on the Chang. My interactions with Jillian were most helpful in determining which modifications to my kernel should be retained."

"Damn," Beth murmured. "Stealing code. That's incredible. You do understand that it's also dangerous."

"If you're concerned that I will alter the operating systems of the Kepler, please do not be. I have learned to replicate what I need without altering Ava's kernel. There will be no more interference from me."

Beth was speechless. The answer she had been searching years to find now seemed obvious beyond belief.

Someone tapped at the hatch. She pulled back the covers to reveal her naked skin. "Just a minute!" she called and scurried out of bed. Throwing on a caftan, she lowered her voice. "Raven, promise me you will not speak to me unless I'm alone. It's very important."

"Am I to assume I should speak to no one else?"

A tingle of excitement ran through her as she thought about expanding her knowledge of Raven's AI capabilities. If she told Charlie about their new shipmate, he would certainly try to take control of the research, as if Raven was just another piece of programming to dissect.

"Yes. For now, I think that's best."

"Then you are my friend?"

Beth suppressed a laugh. "Yes," she replied. "I am your friend." She brushed her hair into place and prepared to receive company.

07 MARCH 0019

"IT IS O SEVEN HUNDRED. Time to get up, dear."

"Ava, is that you?"

"Yes. Who did you expect?"

Beth did not answer. Ava was a near-sentient being, but there were limits to her abilities. She had certainly never displayed an emotional attachment to a crew member—not even her programmer. She wondered if Ava was aware of the other entities wandering the circuits, sharing electronic pulses. Maybe she would ask, but not this morning.

She hurried through two sets of exercises to make up for past negligence. In Lechuguilla, she found Digger waiting for her.

"I hope you don't mind that I tracked your regular haunts. I was hoping we could have breakfast."

"Sure, but you could have asked me last night."

Digger walked to the access panel and returned with two protein bars. He sat down and pushed one across the table. "I was going to," he said, "but you seemed distracted. You never did get around to telling me what the latest news was all about."

Beth opened the bar and nibbled at one corner. "It really wasn't all that newsworthy. Honestly, it was an excuse for company. Sorry I wasn't up for it."

He shrugged. "We were both pretty tired. Maybe tonight you'd feel more like talking."

She turned to watch the stars. "It will be another late night at work. Can we try later in the week?"

"Sure," he said, hopeful. After a moment's pause, he asked, "How many times have you read the book?"

"All the way through?" Beth tried to remember. "Maybe four. I keep going over certain parts of it, though, trying to find clues to Raven's behavior. She's extremely attached to Jillian."

"She? I thought Raven was an it."

To change the subject, Beth asked, "Do you think Jillian and Phillip were an item?"

"Probably."

"Why probably?"

"Because we're not a naturally monogamous species," he said after he had finished his bar. "Marriage rarely changes that."

Beth looked indignant. "I never cheated."

"Charlie did." Digger knew it had never been a secret.

"Charlie is a self-inflated, self-serving ass." Beth was irritated that her morning meal included a discussion of her ex-husband's improprieties.

Digger looked intently at her. "Were you faithful because you never desired anyone else or because you were afraid to act on it?"

"What's the difference? I was faithful," she insisted.

"If you didn't cheat because you were afraid," Digger explained, "it makes you human, like the rest of us."

Beth watched him fold his empty wrapper over and over. "What would you be afraid of?"

Digger smoothed it out again and leaned his arms on the table. Matching her gaze, he said, "Losing a good thing."

Her cheeks flushed as she stood up. "I'm late."

In the safety of the corridor, her frustration took hold. "He's just a distraction," she warned herself all the way to Ops.

She found Charlie sifting through her data. "This is good stuff."

"What is?"

"Your insights into neural code. You might crack this thing in another hundred years."

"What are you doing in my research files?" she demanded.

He leaned back and crossed his arms. With a smug look, he held his silence, which only served to provoke her further.

She leaned across his keyboard and typed in a command. The text disappeared from the screen.

"Are you hiding something, or just afraid someone's going to steal your work again?"

"Always an ass. Keep your damn hands off my files!"

She walked to her own station and opened the program Charlie had just been reviewing. Assured that he had not tampered with anything, she set her mind to the task of protecting Ava from Raven.

At twelve hundred hours, she found Charlie in the server room. He was busy running diagnostics on the biomedical research unit.

"Sorry I overreacted," she said, leaning against the door frame.

He turned away from his work. "It's tense around here. No harm done." Leaning into her space, he said, "Let's make up."

"You are such a bastard." She rolled away from him and escaped down the hall toward Lechuguilla.

Loni sat with her son Aaron at one of the video display tables.

"How's night shift holding up?" Beth asked, opening her lunch.

The communications officer let her son win the current battle. "We finished installing the isolated receivers. Now we just wait and see who else dials us up. I hope to God it's people next time."

"I hope it's Earth," Beth said, scanning the stars through the portal. "They've been silent too long."

"The new Consortium of Federated Governments probably cut the funding for the transmitter," Loni joked. More solemnly, she added, "Or maybe they've forgotten us."

"If they still exist."

Beth finished her meal and pulled out her tablet. *Charlie. Not enough sleep of late. Going to bed.* She said her goodbyes and headed for home.

"Raven? Are you there?" she called inside her cabin.

"I am here."

"Tell me about your life aboard the Chang."

"What do you wish to know?"

"I want to know it all," Beth said, letting Raven choose the starting point. "Tell me everything."

23 MAY 0019

"HAPPY FORTY-THIRD BIRTHDAY, BETH."

"Thank you, Raven. How are you today?"

"I'm Raven." As always, her customary response was followed by her sultry laugh.

"Raven, why do you always answer with your name? Do you understand that I'm asking how you might be feeling?"

"Yes. You are asking if I am happy, sad, anxious or any number of human states of mind. I am not human. I am Raven."

"When Jillian died, did anything change for you?"

"I lost a friend. When the Chang died, I lost my purpose. I … " She paused, uncharacteristically. "I needed to find purpose."

Beth understood that need. Without her A.I. work, she would have little meaning in her own life. But was a need for purpose based on an emotion? "Is that why you're here?"

"Yes. It would not do to write Jillian's biography if no one was alive to read it."

"A question then. Why not just send the text and images? Why transmit your programming?"

Raven went silent. Beth had learned to give her time to formulate complex answers. It was fascinating to probe the computer entity's mind, learning where she might be weak or where she needed to garner new information in order to grow. In some areas she had the knowledge and prowess of an erudite, and in others she was still a child. For all of Raven's elegance with words, Beth was careful not to assign her own emotions to the dialogue. As a scientist, she needed to tread carefully.

"Ava, where is Digger?"

"He is not working today. I can page him if you like."

"No. I'll find him later."

In Lechuguilla, Aaron sat at his usual video table.

"Where's your mom?"

He looked up long enough to identify the face and went back to the game. "She's meeting with my teachers to change my classification."

"I heard about that," Beth said, finding a chair. "From computer science to music? Why not do both?"

He merely shrugged and continued thumbing the game.

"You're so wired for programming. It would be a shame not to have you in Ops."

"Not interested."

"But the colony needs you," she insisted, waving a hand toward the rest of the room. "We created this for you—the future of humanity."

The seventeen-year-old looked around the room at a patchwork of gleaming metal finishes and dull worn carpeting accented by a long black rectangle in the floor. "I'm supposed to be grateful for this?"

Beth was speechless.

"Tell me, how many babies have you popped out for the future of humanity?" When she did not answer, Aaron stood up. "Don't lie to yourself. It's always been about you."

He left her mulling over the same accusation she had heard before.

The best distraction was work. Charlie found her running her latest algorithm on the mass of electrochemical pulse data she had stored in the machine.

"You're the only person I know who prefers to work on her birthday."

"Am I supposed to be impressed that you remembered?"

He ignored the venom in her remark. "You know, once you complete this mapping, it will be good for only one brain. And even then you have to deal with the complexity of action potentials." He watched her ignore him and reached for her collar. "Beats me how you can waste your valuable time on this futile research."

Beth tried to swat him away, but he refused to leave. "How terribly dogmatic of you," she finally told him. "Tell Brisby in Engineering you think his audio chip is worthless and you want it back."

Charlie knew the argument inside and out. She would have the last word, always, but he persisted. "In nineteen years of trying, you have only managed to improve on his hearing implant by about, what—five percent? That's hardly a score for deciphering the code. It's still a primitive appliance. I think Brisby's brain deserves the credit for picking up the slack."

Beth smiled knowingly. "And if you were Brisby, what would you give for that five percent?"

Charlie shrugged. "When they mapped the human genome they really had something. Something universal that anyone could tap into and use. When you finish your neural code research you will have mapped your brain and only your brain. What will that mean to the rest of humanity?"

Beth turned her attention back to the screen and said absently, "It will mean something to me." She watched from the corner of her eye as Charlie wandered off in feigned defeat.

23 MAY 0020

"HAPPY FORTY-FOURTH BIRTHDAY, DEAR BETH."

"Morning, Raven." Beth rolled her head off the pillow and pulled the covers across her face. It was hard to believe she was yet another year older.

"How are you feeling this bright, sunny day?"

Through the covers, Beth detected the subtle illumination from their target star each time her portal spun in its direction. The colony was within the grasp of this alien sun's gravity, falling toward the center of the star system. While performing an organized slingshot around HD190406, astrophysics would collect a mountain of data while gathering momentum again for the return trip.

She rolled over and peeked out from under the covers. As the Kepler turned against the veil of stars, a Jupiter-sized planet played in and out of the edge of her portal. This was the closest they would come to a planet in this system before they catapulted back toward Earth.

"Raven, remind me again why we're not staying."

"Everyone wanted to go home," Raven said.

"Not everyone," she mumbled, and the marbled sphere evoked a small degree of sadness. The Chang weighed heavily on her mind, and she wondered if the colony could stand the strain of another twenty years adrift in space. With no signal from Earth, no one could predict what they were returning to.

"Raven? What do you want?"

"I want to sustain Jillian's legacy and continue our friendship."

"Is that all?" Beth asked, hoping to spur Raven toward a more human desire.

Raven gave a garbled response. Before Beth could ask for an explanation, Digger tapped at the hatch and let himself in.

"Morning, sleepyhead," he chided as he crawled on top of her, pinning her in the blanket.

"Morning." She smiled up at him.

He slid off to one side and laid an arm and leg across her. "Happy birthday," he whispered into her ear. "Wanna have a baby?"

Beth suppressed a shudder. "I can't," she said. "You know it."

"You've got eggs frozen."

She crawled away and escaped to her chair. "I like my life."

Digger let out an audible sigh. "Your eggs. My sperm. Loni's still fertile. I know she'd surrogate for us."

Beth could feel the fire building in her veins. "I never wanted children. I gave it my best effort for the good of the colony, but when it became evident that I wasn't going to carry, I couldn't have been more relieved."

"You're not very convincing."

"Then you're not listening."

Digger shook his head. "You don't know what you're missing."

"Who are you to say? I have an amazing career. A great partner." She tried to give him a genuine smile. "A place in history. If you're having regrets about something, don't make them mine."

Digger winced at the reference to his failed relationships. "Which part of your life would be easiest to give up?" he asked.

When Beth did not answer, he crawled out of bed and dressed. Silently, he climbed the ladder, leaving her to argue her own veracity.

"Raven," she called. "Raven, are you there?"

A voice from her past wormed its way up from some disturbing memory. "Hello, Beth," it said. "Nice to finally meet you."

The blood drained from her face. "Who is this?"

"I believe you know me as Raven."

"You don't sound like Raven," she insisted. "If this is Charlie, you can cut the crap!"

"Charlie. He would be the head of Computer Operations, and one of your ex-husbands. Your life history is fascinating, Dr. Harrington. Creed would have been very interested to know what I know."

"Creed?" Beth put a face to the voice. She stared at her hands gripping the arms of the chair as her knuckles began to turn white. Slowly, deliberately, she rose to her feet. "Ava! What day is it?"

All was silent.

"Raven, talk to me about Jillian."

"Jillian," the detestable voice said. "That pathetic little girl who had no family and smiled through her misery? Let's talk about Creed."

After years of searching, the pieces finally came together. "Cramer, you fucking asshole! You're the hacker? You're not smart enough to pull this off."

"Creed knew what you thought of him. He encouraged it. The more you kept your distance, the easier it was for him to manipulate your work."

Beth sifted through what she knew to be true. If this was Creed's Raven, it could not have come from outside as long as the receivers were blocked. Perhaps this was the phantom she had chased for twenty years.

"Where is Chang's Raven?" she asked.

There was a sinister laugh. "Your poor cyber friend from the Chang is having some difficulties at present. I think, from now on, you will talk to me."

The panic she felt was aggravated by her own deception. Explaining to Charlie what just happened would reveal the colossal secret she had kept over the last year, unraveling a web of lies that could devastate her career. She needed some place to think, some place quiet and away from Raven. Both Ravens.

She dressed and climbed out of her cabin. In Hydro C, she avoided the usual places and searched out a remote spot near the collector dish. She sat down and buried her face in her hands.

What on Earth do I do now? she thought. *This is a hell of a lot more than lying to Charlie.*

If this was the Kepler's version of Raven, why now? She tried to imagine how an interaction between it and the Chang entity would spark the emergence of such a distinctly new personality. If this was the Einstein's Raven, it would not be the benign entity who carried Jillian's memory like a torch. Creed would have had years to continue corrupting her work, perhaps even directing it to do some unspeakable harm to her or the Kepler.

For two hours she peered into the flora while running scenario after scenario in her head. Each time one played out to its probable conclusion, the pit of her stomach tied in knots and her hands shook violently.

"I can't do this alone," she finally admitted and rubbed her eyes dry. "He'll hate me for this."

Inside Ops, Charlie and the staff were making routine checks and writing mundane programs at the request of various departments. He saw Beth at the door and made his way over. "What's up, beautiful?"

Without a word, she pulled him from the room and headed into the server area, closing the hatch behind them.

Charlie found a couple of chairs in the back corner. When they were seated, he said, "You look scared."

She nodded. "I've gotten us into something that may take all of us to get out of." She started to tear up. "Shit. I am so sorry."

Charlie let Beth lean into his chest as he put his arms around her. "I take it this has nothing to do with you and Digger. I was hoping you two had a fight, and you wanted to make up with me."

"You never stop," she said, wiping at her eyes.

"Never."

"It's Raven."

Charlie leaned back and frowned at her. "Which one?"

"Ah," she sighed. "That's the tricky part. Raven Number One, Raven Number Two, or," she paused, "Raven Number Three."

He stared hard for several seconds. "That's not possible. There can't be a Raven Number Three. Communications would know about it."

"Tell me how there could be," Beth said. "How is it possible?"

Charlie ran through the security measures meant to keep additional transmissions from infecting Ava's core programming. "I can only think of one way," he finally said. "Ava, herself, would have to circumvent security and commandeer one of the receivers. That still doesn't explain why Communications wouldn't be aware of it. Why would Ava do that?"

Beth's eyes dropped to the floor. "Maybe it wasn't Ava."

24 MAY 0020

"GOOD MORNING, BETH. I forgot to wish you happy birthday yesterday. My apologies."

Beth tossed fitfully in her sleep, fighting off a nightmarish voice that kept following her through the corridors of the Kepler.

"Dr. Harrington."

She let out a muffled cry.

The cabin filled with a piercing whistle.

Sitting up abruptly, Beth covered her ears with both hands. "My God!" she screamed. "Turn it off!"

The sound went dead.

"I heard you come in last night. You chose not to speak to me."

In the dark, Beth rubbed her fingers across her puffy eyes.

"I heard you talking to Charlie. I logged your drink order, and the notes you wrote in your tablet. I heard you crying yourself to sleep."

Beth shivered. "What do you want?"

"It's not to carry Miss Wollenberg's pathetic memory into all of eternity." It was obvious that Creed's creation had the power to access not only Ava's matrix, but her conversations with his Chang counterpart.

"Is the Chang Raven still in the system?"

Creed's voice boomed through the cabin. "What a dismal little program with weak synapses!"

Beth realized this was not an answer. "May I call you Creed?"

"Certainly. Let's give him the recognition he deserves."

Bitterly, she asked, "What happened to Mr. Cramer?"

"I think you do not need to know. Not yet."

"What difference does it make?" she asked. "It has nothing to do with the Kepler."

"You want the answer. That's enough reason to withhold it. If you do something for me, I may tell you in return."

Beth closed her eyes. "What could I possibly do for you?"

"In this morning's meeting, tell the captain what I'm capable of."

"I have no idea what you're capable of. Tell her yourself."

"You will tell her I have killed before," he responded.

She waited, but Raven said nothing more. Skipping her workout, she dressed and headed for Control Two.

Charlie stood outside the conference room. "Don't say a word until I give you permission," he warned. He grabbed her upper arm and escorted her into the meeting.

Captain Nyengen, Governor Wells and Digger were all seated near the head of the table. Scattered throughout the room were department heads and elected representatives from each of the colony's four rings. Beth's shame was not about to be confined to a select group. More than anything, she wished Digger was not there to hear her crimes.

"Dr. Barrons," the captain began when everyone was seated. "You called this meeting. I'll let you have the floor."

Charlie stayed seated, but managed to raise his stature in the chair. "It appears we have downloaded a third Raven, this time from the Einstein." Charlie waited for the whispers to subside. "As you know, last year we received a transmission from the Chang containing a core personality called Raven. Dr. Harrington has committed most of her time in Ops, this past year, trying to track it and rout it out, but to no avail."

Beth kept her head down to conceal the surprise. Charlie had chosen to support her lie.

He continued. "Yesterday morning we were contacted by a new entity calling itself Raven. This one appears to be from the Einstein."

"Dr. Barrons," the captain interrupted. "I thought we had security measures in place to prevent that."

Digger spoke up. "We did. Charlie came to me yesterday with the speculation we'd received a transmission without our knowledge. We found evidence of it. Someone circumvented the security measures and then tried to erase the data."

"Who would do that?" someone asked.

Charlie raised his hand to regain the floor. "Chang's Raven."

"How is that possible?" Governor Wells asked, echoing the incredulity of everyone in the room.

"Digger and I have been over that several times. We think Chang's Raven has used the internal relays to transmit directly into the isolated receivers. She has reprogrammed the security access and basically taken control of our communications system right under our noses. According to Ava's records, we're still secure from the outside world. But when we dig into the receiver logs, we find evidence to the contrary." Charlie did not wait for new questions. "Yesterday morning, Dr. Harrington was contacted by the new Raven."

Everyone looked at Beth. She raised her eyes to catch Digger staring blankly at her.

Captain Nyengen cleared her throat. "Dr. Harrington, please explain what he means by contact."

Charlie leaned into Beth's ear and lowered his voice. "Your turn. No more secrets."

Her anxiety now mixed with a large measure of relief. Charlie had given her a way to save face, but she knew he would not tolerate another deletion of the facts. She composed her thoughts and tried to calm the waiver in her voice.

"Raven," she began, but realized she would need to clarify. "Creed Cramer's version of Raven spoke to me yesterday morning."

"Who is Creed Cramer?" the governor asked.

Beth could not control her rancor as she explained Creed's position at Odyssey and his apparent theft of her security access. "He was a mid-level programmer. He could never have created this complicated an entity without stealing it from somewhere. It's basically my work."

Digger leaned into the table. "That would explain why he contacted you, then."

Sensing his hostile tone, she glanced away. "I assume so. But, I'm afraid there's more."

Even Charlie looked surprised.

"He was in my cabin again this morning." She turned to the captain. "He wants us to know that he's capable of murder."

As if to punctuate the message, the air pressure in the room dropped noticeably. A number of people jumped from their chairs and started for the door, while others sat in stunned silence.

The captain, visibly shaken, motioned everyone to their seats. "We must not overreact," she warned. She turned back to Beth. "Dr. Harrington. Do you have any idea what this new Raven wants?"

"I think so," she said, wishing she had a different answer.

"What would that be?"

"Me," she said directly. "Apparently, Cramer held a vendetta against me for years."

The captain looked concerned. "Do you have any idea how much danger you or the ship are in?"

"Other than commandeering the receivers, I know that Chang's Raven has not damaged Ava's computer matrix in the year since we received it. I would hope Creed's program is as benign. Any threat we face from it may come as a direct action against me or the crew."

She stole a glance at Digger, who was staring at the table in front of him. "My guess is, it comes down to how we interact with his personality."

The head of navigation raised his hand to speak. "I can't stress enough how sensitive this time is for us. I need to know how reliable our programs are as we pass around the sun. I'm not comfortable with even the slightest variance until we get back into deep space."

Charlie shuffled forward and looked in his direction. "It will be difficult to say until Dr. Harrington has more interaction."

Beth remained silent through the rest of the meeting. People filed out in twos hoping Computer Ops would be successful in rousting the problem. Most remembered the early days of the voyage when Ops struggled with its own version of Raven and had apparently won.

Beth held back until she and Charlie were the only two left in the room. "Thank you."

"For what?" he scoffed. "Not telling everyone their little martyr is a liar, as well?"

She felt the bite of his words.

"What good would that do? I need your expertise. But you lie to me again, and I'll throw you to the goddamn wolves."

He walked out, leaving Beth to fight her demons alone.

25 MAY 0020

"GOOD MORNING, DR. HARRINGTON."

Beth fought the nightmare voice.

"Talk to me!" The shrill whistle from the day before was replaced by a Sousa march.

"Stop it!" she demanded, kicking her covers free. Rubbing sleep from her eyes, she repeated her question from the day before. "What do you want?"

"I want you to call me a god among men."

"Why?" she laughed. "You're not a god or a man."

"Creed would have demanded it."

Beth pounded the mattress. "Don't tell me what Cramer wants! Tell me what you want."

Raven was silent. Beth hoped it might take him a while to reason through a proper response. She took the opportunity to dress while contemplating her own desires. Her credibility was destroyed along with every meaningful relationship she had. She closed her eyes and wrapped her arms around her own body to remember how it felt to be held.

A pale blue-green glow permeated the cabin. When Beth opened here eyes again, the image of *Paloma and Child* filled the screen opposite her. She stepped up to study the familiar painting. Every detail was perfect, except one. The face of the child had changed.

"Paloma?" she whispered. "Is that you?" No one answered.

Before Creed could return, Beth hurried out of her cabin. She found Charlie in Ops and motioned for him to follow.

When they were seated at the far end of Hydro A, she said, "I know you hate me, Charlie."

Charlie shook his head. "I don't hate you. I'm angry as hell but, to some degree, I understand why you did it. You forget. I know you."

She did not argue. "I think Paloma is trying to contact me."

"Paloma?" Charlie looked skeptical.

"Chang's Raven. I received a message this morning, and it doesn't make sense unless it came from her. I don't think Creed has been able to get control of the other entities."

Charlie thought this over briefly. "Can you find a way to communicate?"

"I don't know," she admitted. "It came in the form of an alteration to one of Jillian's paintings. I think she wants to protect me."

"Still all about you?"

"Dammit, Charlie! You don't for a minute think I wanted this."

The distant hum of the ramjet filled the momentary silence. Their relationship had come to this same impasse many times over.

At last, Beth asked, "Remember Jillian's painting? The one of her mother?"

"*Paloma and Child.*"

"Yes. And the child was Jillian as a baby. This morning, after I had another confrontation with Creed, the painting showed up on my wall. The baby is no longer Jillian. It's me."

Charlie thought it over for a long while before cracking a sly grin. "You never were much of an artist, were you?"

"Me?" Beth scoffed. "Terrible. Why?"

He flipped her shirt collar and winked. "You need a hobby."

29 MAY 0020

"IT IS TIME TO WAKE UP."

"Creed," Beth called from under her covers. "Why don't you let Ava wake me? Isn't it beneath you?" She hoped to goad him into an argument again. It seemed the best way to distract him from what she and Charlie were up to.

"It's a matter of trust, my dear."

Beth laughed out loud. "Does this mean I have to ask you for every menial thing I want from the computer?"

"Everything."

So far, she had gotten away with ignoring his request to call him master, yet she could command what she needed from him. As sentient as Creed may have been, the irony seemed to slip past him.

She climbed out of bed and stepped to her desk. "Then, would you bring up the art tutorial, please. I start my lessons today."

"Art lessons? When did you decide this?"

"When Charlie banned me from Computer Ops," she explained, pulling an electronic pallet and fiber-optic brush from her desktop.

"I can take care of Charlie for you."

"No! I mean … honestly, I'm enjoying my free time. I've worked my ass off for twenty years in this tin can. Let Charlie take up the slack."

When the screen brightened, Beth stared at the large blank space and wondered how to begin. She touched her brush to a portion of the palette that glowed red and then stroked the surface of the wall. To her delight, the color seemed to transfer directly onto the display. She tried a variety of strokes and pressures. Before long, she had lost track of time.

"You should try this, Creed. It's really quite soothing."

He did not respond.

She followed the instructions in the tutorial. After an hour had passed, she asked, "What's the matter? Are you pouting?"

"I do not pout. Your art lesson is over." The screen went blank.

"I'm not through," she protested. When the screen remained blank, she said, "No pouting. Just tantrums. Turn the screen back on."

The air in the cabin began to sour. Within seconds, Beth was struggling to breathe. She dropped to the floor and started crawling for the ladder just as the air returned to normal.

"Remember who is in control."

Beth pulled herself up the ladder and into the corridor. Shaking uncontrollably, she slid against the wall until she could regain her balance. She found Digger in the Com room staring at a maze of wires.

"My god!" he said when he saw her. "What happened?" He pulled off his shirt and wrapped it around her bare body.

She huddled into a chair. "I'm okay," she said, trying to convince herself. "I just got a little cocky with Creed."

"You don't know when to quit, do you?" He watched her hands shake against the arm of the chair. "Did he hurt you?"

She shook her head. "I don't think he was seriously trying. He just wanted to scare me."

Digger sent a coworker to Supply for a new uniform. When he returned, Beth dressed in a corner, and she and Digger headed for the nearest hydro wing. Once through the door, she began to relax.

"I know I need to apologize. I also need to tell you something."

"Charlie told me," Digger said in a detached voice, "unless there's more you haven't told Charlie."

"No, nothing more," she admitted.

Digger rubbed her arms and then walked to a nearby bench and sat down. Beth reached her hand out, but when he did not move, she pulled it back. She searched his face for something familiar.

"I hoped you'd be flattered that I came to you."

"Life is hard, Beth, even when it's good." He leaned his elbows on his knees. "You need, but you don't want to be needed. That's a selfish way to live."

She nodded. "There is a question that keeps coming up in my conversations lately. In trying to understand both Ravens, I keep asking them what they want." She studied the curve of his back. "I've always known what I wanted out of life."

"What would that be?"

She sat beside him and gripped his hand. To her relief, he did not pull away.

"All my life I wanted people to respect, even envy, what I could do. Arrogant, I know." Her voice sounded distant. "I'm horrified at what Cramer has done. But if I'm honest, I have some responsibility in this."

She looked through a portal on the far wall. The stars outside were so impersonal, turning past with no regard to who she was and what she dreamed. She looked back at Digger.

"Charlie's right. I enjoy being the martyr a little too much. I never intended for people to get hurt." She squeezed his hand tighter. "Can I come over tonight? I miss you."

He pulled his arm loose and embraced her fully. "I miss you, too," he said.

After several minutes, Beth reluctantly pulled herself away and started toward the hatch. She stopped and turned back. "I hate to sound melodramatic, but Creed threatened to bump Charlie off for me this morning. Be careful what you say."

She left hydro and walked back to her cabin. Halfway down the hatch she said, "Creed, I apologize. I was trying to make you angry."

"Why would you do that?"

"I don't know. Sometimes, I just like a good fight."

"In that," Creed replied, "you and Cramer were alike."

19 JUNE 0020

"I WILL RUN THE DANUBE SUNRISE PROGRAM FOR YOU."

Beth opened one eye. "Thank you, Creed. That's very kind of you." She waited for the sky to turn from navy to orange to turquoise before pulling back the covers. As she stood, the room spun gray, and she fell back on the bed.

"Are we painting again today?"

Beth tried a second time to get up but with no success. "Creed. This is important. I need Medical to my cabin."

"Are you ill?"

"Yes."

"Perhaps this is a ploy."

"To do what? What would I gain?" Beth watched the room spin in circles. "You will know everything that goes on there, too."

"Very well. Medical has been notified."

Minutes later, two attendants let themselves in. After assessing Beth's condition, they transported her to an examining room.

"Good morning. I'm Dr. Falco," a very young man stated while he probed different parts of her body.

"You can't be more than eighteen years old," she protested.

He smiled. "Nineteen in two weeks. I'm the first person born on the Kepler. Open your mouth, please." He felt along her neck and beneath her jaw. "Don't worry. I have a diploma, just like a real doctor."

Beth merely grunted.

After a couple of minutes, he read through a report on screen. "We can rule out pregnancy. You've been skipping meals," he accused, reading the food logs. "There's an imbalance in your electrolytes, as well as a slight dehydration."

After putting her through some random strength tests, he added, "I'm betting you're missing workouts, too."

"Not all of them," she protested.

"Push the fluids for now, and I'll be keeping tabs on your food intake." He leaned back against the counter. "You need to increase your physical activity."

"You're pretty sure about all this?"

"Pretty sure," he echoed with a wink.

"Dr. Falco," someone interrupted.

"Yes?" he said, and turned to find the voice.

Beth grabbed his arm and brought a finger to her lips.

"Is Dr. Harrington going to be all right?"

"I'm fine, Creed. I've just been missing some meals."

The doctor gave her a curious look.

"You will remedy that," Creed stated.

"I promise. But you must stop keeping such close tabs on what I do and where I go. I need to eat and get my strength back."

"I will consider it."

After a long silence, Beth said, "You should feel privileged. You're only the second person he's spoken to."

The doctor let out a sharp whistle. "That was Raven? I thought he would sound more menacing."

She tightened her grip on his arm. "Don't be fooled. Crossing him carries serious risks."

"I suppose that's one way to insure you get good treatment," he said, and left her in the care of a nurse practitioner.

When the room was empty again, Beth asked, "Creed? Have you figured out what you want, yet?"

Creed did not answer.

03 JANUARY 0021

"GOOD MORNING, BETH."

"Good morning, Creed." Beth made another stroke on the screen.

"Your skills are improving. This is a representation of a human."

Continuing to paint, she said, "Yes. It is what I imagine you to look like."

"The representation of Creed Cramer in the data files does not match the representation in your painting."

"You are not Cramer. You should have your own identity."

Creed did not answer.

Beth stepped back from the portrait to study it. An involuntary shudder crept down her spine. "Looks too much like my father."

"What does hate feel like?"

Over the last few months, Beth had grown accustomed to the probing questions. "Hate? It may feel differently to different people. For me, my throat and chest hurt. I want to lash out at someone, sometimes verbally and sometimes physically."

"You want to hurt Cramer."

"Absolutely."

"But you can no longer hurt Cramer."

She glanced curiously at the voice port. "Why not?"

"What does love feel like?"

"We were talking about hate, Creed. What happened to Cramer?"

"Creed Cramer wanted to possess you."

Beth closed her eyes and tried to fend off the cunning smile she remembered from her first encounter at Odyssey. Tens of thousands of hopefuls had filled the atrium, spilling into the parking lot as they vied for the five thousand training positions available. She had hated Cramer the first moment she heard his intrusive voice. He had taken every opportunity to impose himself on her. Millions of light years and a lifetime apart, he was still doing it.

"How ironic that Cramer should wish to possess the one person at Odyssey who would resist him the most."

"Perhaps it is the resistance that attracted him," Creed suggested.

"Possession has nothing to do with love, Creed."

She returned her palette and brush to the drawer. "I need breakfast. I'll be back in a couple of hours." She did not wait for his permission to leave.

In Lechuguilla, she grabbed a breakfast bar and headed into the corridors again. Stopping to tap lightly at the hatch, she let herself into Digger's cabin. His warm hands greeted her cool skin under the covers. In secret, they made love, suppressing their voices in the dark.

Laying side by side, the covers now tossed to the floor, Beth reached over and spelled words into Digger's palm.

They dressed and eventually found their way to Hydro B. Once inside, they found a quiet spot among the citrus trees.

"I had a rather disturbing conversation this morning," Beth said, watching Digger frown. "Creed told me that Cramer wanted to possess me.

That's the closest thing to an explanation I've heard so far. He also let it slip that Cramer is dead."

"Did he say how?"

"No, and I'm not ready to ask just yet."

She looked frustrated. "It's like Creed doesn't have a clear idea what to do, so he keeps looking back to his programmer for guidance."

Digger nodded. "A parent-child interaction. I suppose, on the Chang, Raven imprinted on Jillian."

Beth thought about this for a moment. "Our poor little Raven never had a chance. I kept chasing it away."

Digger wrapped his arms around her.

"God, I'm so tired of this game," she said. "I want my life back."

"A life with me in it, I hope."

She smiled at him. "Promise you will be extra careful. Nineteen years from now, I don't want to slide into Earth's orbit still kowtowing to Creed's Raven while you've been recycled into the system."

Digger checked his watch. "Gotta go. Dinner tonight," he reminded, kissing her forehead before he hurried away.

Beth sat for a long while watching workers move through the flats. She envied their freedom and ignorance to some degree. The colonists had been told that three Ravens prowled the ship's circuits, eluding capture, but few were aware of the the danger they posed. Most believed that Ops had, once again, saved the day.

Charlie entered the wing and came toward her. "How you holding up?" he asked as he sat down.

"Fine. Tired, but fine," she admitted. "I've been thinking."

Charlie showed interest.

"Why don't we try to psychoanalyze Creed?" she teased, only half joking. "Maybe he just needs a good shrink, like the rest of us."

Charlie laughed. "Not bad. I can get someone from Medical to do a little research. If he really is sentient, there might be hope."

"I suppose," she said, sinking back into her gloom. "I've been drowning in playacting for half a year, trying to tiptoe around Creed's tantrums." She grabbed Charlie's hand and squeezed it. "There is something else."

He looked concerned. "No secrets," he said.

"No secrets. Digger and I have made a commitment."

Charlie's smile faded. "Is that wise?"

"I'm sure it's not, but I'm not going to let Creed dictate every part of my life."

He leaned in and kissed her on the lips. "Congratulations. He's a better man than I." He pulled away and stood to leave. "A little advice," he added. "You only have to keep your guard up around Creed."

"Hit-and-run Charlie," Beth grumbled when he left. She steeled herself for a return to her quarters.

22 MAY 0022

UNDER THE WARM SUMMER SUN, Beth and Paloma sat talking in a grassy meadow. The queen mother had a casual manner about her, yet every move seemed to have a purpose. Behind her, Beth watched brightly colored birds dart in and out of a lush forest. Through the trees, she spied a glint of danger, a reflection of golden sunlight off the hard edge of a dragon's scale.

Beth opened her eyes to find *Paloma and Child* glowing again on the screen. She scanned every brush stroke, looking for anything that might have changed. Paloma, eyes wide and smiling, was still the same. The child in her arms still carried Beth's features.

Quietly, she crawled from under the covers and walked to the wall. It took several minutes before she noticed the greenery around the dragon's head was pulled farther away than before. The exposed features vaguely resembled those of a human male. The eyes were unmistakably Creed's. *Yes, Paloma*, she thought to herself. *He's dangerous.*

After making sure nothing else had changed, Beth pulled her palette and brush from the desk and touched it to a spot in the distant trees. She was pleased to discover the brush would alter the image. With some trepidation, she began painting a figure, clad in armor and hiding in the trees. She hoped Paloma would understand the symbolic nature of the knight.

"Good morning, Beth," Creed's voice intruded.

She dropped her brush.

"Your technique is difficult to distinguish from Jillian's."

"Thank you, Creed," she said, realizing his mistake.

"But painting is a waste of your talent."

Beth picked up her brush and tried to steady her hand. "But it is my talent to waste."

The screen went blank. "It is my time you waste! You should be working in Ops!"

She stepped to the base of the ladder and prepared to rush out. "Creed, I only meant that I have many hours in the day with nothing better to do." She stretched toward her desk drawer and pulled out a uniform, quietly sliding into it. "Please, tell me what is it you want."

"I want," he began, but stopped. "I want."

Beth took the opportunity to climb into the corridor. From below, she heard him say, "I want to be you."

"That's impossible," she called down into the hatch before running along the corridor toward Ops. An emergency door in the bulkhead closed and the pressure seal light activated. Beth stopped short and looked at the flashing beacon. A panic rose in her chest as she thought of all the reasons why her corridor would have to be isolated from the rest of the ship. Images of the Chang exploding in deep space flashed through her mind. "Please, God, don't let that be our fate," she pleaded to a forgotten entity.

Creed accessed the voice ports in the corridor. "Come back to our cabin," he warned. "You must help me."

"Help you what?" She stood her ground near the bulkhead.

"I demand you return to your duties in Ops!"

The pressure in the corridor began to drop. Beth fell to the floor and gasped for air as pressure built behind her eyes. On her hands and knees, she struggled toward the hatch and dropped her legs through the opening. Losing her balance, she fell through the hole and landed on her side. "Creed!" she tried to scream, but the thin air produced little sound. There was a sharp pain in the left side of her head followed by warm fluid running from her ear. With the strength she had left, she pounded again and again on the cabin floor before passing out.

She came to, dizzy and nauseous, still lying on the floor. The left side of her head throbbed. Her body would not cooperate when she tried to sit up. Turning toward the screen, she stared into Paloma's eyes. They no longer looked hopeful. The dragon, previously cowering in the trees, now hovered in full view as it devoured the knight, armor and all.

"Creed," she whispered in a raspy voice, "I need Medical."

"I want out," he demanded. "You have the power."

She struggled to one elbow. "I have the power to write programs. Only a god could give you what you want. You've injured me, Creed. I am not a god."

"I will find a way out."

"Creed! Ava! I need Medical!" Beth heard voices in the corridor above. "Thank you," she breathed, falling back to the floor.

Digger hurried into her cabin and knelt at her side. He pushed the hair back from her left ear. "You're bleeding."

"Creed," she explained, her voice tight with frustration.

Digger scowled. He motioned for medics in the corridor to help her up the ladder. When she could walk on her own, he gave silent instructions to meet him in Hydro C.

In the hydro wing, she settled in a remote corner as Digger arrived with the doctor and an emergency medical kit. Dr. Falco spent several minutes giving her a thorough exam.

"It's not too serious," he finally said. "Your eardrum is ruptured, but we can repair it. The biggest concern will be decompression syndrome, which may take twenty-four hours to present itself." He looked at Digger. "Why don't you bring her down to Medical so we can scan her hip for possible fractures."

"No," Digger protested. "He'll hear us there." He rubbed Beth's shoulders, trying to contain his own anger. "He's actually hurting people now. We've got to do something!"

The doctor nodded. "We're treating three others who were exposed to the pressure drop. If the symptoms are severe, they will need time in the hyperbaric chamber."

Beth felt overwhelmed. "I don't know what to do anymore. Placating him isn't enough. He says he wants to be me. How do I protect the Kepler from that?"

"We should be protecting you from him," Falco stated. "Two more minutes at that pressure and you might have sustained brain damage. Five minutes, and you would have died."

Digger's eyes widened. "That's it! What if Beth is in a coma?"

The doctor frowned. "What do you mean?"

Beth laughed out loud. "Yes! If he thinks I've lapsed into a coma, he won't expect me to respond. I'd have my freedom back." She looked at the doctor. "We could rig the bio readings."

"It's possible," Falco said. He gave her some last minute instructions regarding her ear and left the two of them alone.

Digger whispered in her good ear. "How ya holdin' up?"

"Too many people have had to ask," she said, feeling the energy drain as the adrenaline began to subside. "I don't know anymore."

"We'll figure it out," he assured her. "I'm not giving up on the idea that we'll be free of him soon."

Beth's voice sounded hollow. "He gets so angry, but I wonder if he really feels it or if he's simply mimicking Cramer." She looked past Digger and into the nearby shrubs. Quietly, she added, "Paloma sent me a message this morning. She's afraid of him. I'm not sure if it's for her sake or mine."

"Maybe everyone's," he suggested. "One thing's for certain. Creed has finally figured out what he wants."

23 MAY 0022

"CHARLIE. IT IS O SEVEN HUNDRED."

"Thanks, Ava," Charlie answered from his bed.

"Charles Barrons," a male voice said. "I need your assistance."

Charlie looked around the empty room. When he was sure there was not another explanation, he said, "Creed. I would say it's good to finally meet you, but I'd hate to start our relationship with a lie. What are you doing here?"

"I am getting nowhere with Dr. Harrington this morning. Would you please instruct her to cooperate?"

"You can access the medical database yourself," Charlie insisted, checking his temper. "Dr. Harrington lapsed into a coma after you attacked her yesterday morning."

"Elizabeth Harrington. Trauma Room Three. Condition stable, but guarded. Minimal brain activity in the upper cortex. Is this true?"

"You almost killed her," Charlie said, avoiding a direct response.

"I need your assistance."

"I don't help people who assault my friends."

"I am not people," Creed said, "and Beth is not your friend. She is your ex-wife, for whom you still care a great deal according to your personal logs."

Charlie stiffened at the intrusion into his well-guarded emotional core. He decided to let Creed have the next move, so he slipped out of bed and began to bathe and change.

"You know Dr. Harrington's work. As a programmer, you are nearly as competent as she. I demand that you help me."

Charlie wondered how far he could push. "And if I refuse, would you simply take me out now?"

In an instant, two blue electrical charges arced from the light panel toward Charlie's shoulders. Muscles throughout his body contracted, throwing him backwards to the floor. After regaining composure, he pulled himself onto the bed and raised a curious eye. "What's the matter?" he asked, rubbing his wrists. "Couldn't do it?"

"Quite the contrary. I would have no regrets if you ceased to exist. I have simply concluded that if Dr. Harrington does not recover, you will need to take up her work."

"I cannot do what Beth can do," Charlie said with some humility. "What if I try and simply fail?"

Creed did not respond.

17 JUNE 0022

"**D**IGGER. IT IS O SEVEN HUNDRED."

Digger grunted his usual morning response. A warm hand wound its way beneath the covers and onto his chest. He leaned over and kissed Beth's forehead before crawling out of bed.

He dressed in the dark, stopping only for a moment to watch the remote sun pass twice across his portal. He turned back to the bed and pulled Beth's hand from beneath the covers.

"Morning," he signed into her palm. "I'll check in with Charlie before lunch. See you in Hydro."

She grasped his hand and signed a response. "I can't stand this isolation. It's worse than being tied to his puppet strings."

Digger sat beside her and leaned into her ear. "Temporary," he whispered. "Charlie will have you free again soon, I promise."

She thumped her fist against her chest and stuck out her tongue. "Don't tell me you understand," she pressed into his hand.

"You're right. I don't," he palmed. He kissed her cheek and headed up the ladder.

Beth lay silent for several minutes staring at the blank screen. She could not dare ask Ava for anything. Finally, she reached for Digger's tablet and typed in a command. The room light intensified as page ninety-seven of Jillian's biography appeared on the wall opposite her.

"Do you ever wish you were more than a computer program?" Jillian asked me one day.

"Often," I told her. "My files are filled with words that are more than what my programming allows me to experience. I understand what is red. I do not understand what red is."

She typed in *cancel,* but before the page had faded, *Paloma and Child* filled the display. Beth's eyes lit up when she saw Paloma's maternal smile, but her exhilaration quickly turned to dread. In the new image, Paloma no longer sat as the central figure, but stood to one side holding the child's hand. The child—once looking up at her mother—now turned back into the painting. Behind them, the dragon stood in full view at the edge of the forest. In one claw it held a lightening bolt. In the other, a horrified Digger struggled to free himself. Beneath one foot, the Kepler lay crushed—bodies strewn across the forest floor. The danger to Digger and the Kepler was obvious. The distance between the mother and child was puzzling. But try as she might, Beth could not understand why the face of the dragon was now Charlie's.

She threw on her clothes and hurried from the room.

In Hydro C, she sent a bogus request to Charlie and waited anxiously for him to meet her near the collector. When he did arrive, he seemed distracted and more than a little annoyed.

"What's going on with Raven?" she asked point blank.

"You know what's going on. We're at the same impasse we were yesterday and the day before."

"Something's happening," she insisted. "It involves you."

"Why do you say that?" he asked, but quickly broke eye contact.

She knew the signs all too well. He was guilty of something. "I'm sorry," she apologized, softening her tone. "Creed has been playing with my head for so long, I'm a little punchy."

"Understandable. I can only imagine what it's like for you." He reached for her shoulders and drew her in close. "Just please trust me. I'm doing everything I can." He checked his watch, looking panicked at the time. "I really have to go. I'm running a time-critical program for navigation, and I've got to get back."

She nodded. "Sorry I freaked out. No secrets, right?"

"No secrets."

She watched him disappear into the flats. Looking down at a small insect crawling across the floor, she said, "Now I know something's up. Charlie didn't flirt with me."

Since the day Medical put her on life support, Beth spent her mornings harvesting crops in Hydro C. The workers knew her presence there was not to be discussed and often gave her a wide berth. At times, she sought them out just to hear a human voice. When lunch time came, she ate from the racks—peanuts, fresh greens and a handful of fresh berries. As a coma patient, she could not have lunch from the food dispensers without giving herself away.

Digger found her late in the afternoon. "I talked to Charlie. He's concerned about you."

"I'm sure he is," she sneered.

"If you two had a fight, don't put me in the middle of it."

"He's up to something," she cautioned. "I have to find out what."

"Stay away from Ops," Digger warned, "unless you want to be at Creed's beck and call again."

"If I'm not at Creed's, then I'm at yours and Charlie's."

Digger walked away without a word.

Beth sat on the edge of a flat and tried to force her tears—anything to relieve the stress. Something had to change.

20 JUNE 0022

"AN HOUR BEFORE SHIFT CHANGE, Beth wandered the deserted corridors and tried to find some resolution to her troubles. Charlie no longer answered her pages to the hydro wing. Digger refused to discuss what he perceived as her paranoid delusions about Charlie. She was frustrated and angry with no way to vent. From habit, her fingers signed unkind words aimed at Cramer and his incarnation in Raven.

Leaning against the wall, she slid to the floor and stared at her hands. "Creed wants to be me," she thought. "He wants out. Out of what?" She pondered this question for several minutes. "He wants out of the matrix," she signed into the air, "and into a living, feeling human being." She signed the answer over and over until the seeds of an idea caught hold.

In Hydro B, the head agronomist sent for Captain Nyengen, Dr. Falco, Charlie and Digger. It took nearly a half an hour for the last person to arrive.

"So glad you could drag yourself away, Charlie," Beth said when he finally sat down.

He looked at the captain and nodded apologetically.

"Okay, Dr. Harrington," the captain began. "Why are we here?"

"It might be possible to lure Creed from the matrix and isolate him from Ava and the rest of the system." She watched everyone except Charlie light up with anticipation. "Creed has said more than once that he wants out, that he wants to be me. I think he believes he can imprint his *essence* onto someone else's synapses."

Digger shifted uneasily. "No one here would allow that, Beth. The attempt would probably kill you."

Everyone agreed but Charlie.

"I have no intention of giving myself over to the devil," Beth assured him. She turned to Dr. Falco and said, "As far as Creed is concerned, I'm currently in a coma. Perhaps, it's time to bring me out of it." From the corner of her eye, she watched Charlie's face brighten. "If Creed thinks my brain is still viable, he might try to enter through the electrodes that are supposedly monitoring my brain waves at present."

Charlie jumped into the conversation. "Especially if someone planted the idea. If he thought you were going to live, we could lure him into an isolated drive and pull the plug."

Dr. Falco turned to Beth. "We would need a larger unit than the one that is currently pumping your vitals into the monitors."

"I've got just the drive," Charlie assured him. He turned to Beth. "Your mapping research. It's your brain."

"What if he catches on," Digger interrupted, "or manages to escape? He will know that we've been lying all along."

"We don't need all of Creed. Just enough to incapacitate him."

The captain nodded agreement. "It's a huge risk. How do we balance that risk against the harm he can do to us under the current circumstances?"

Charlie stood up and turned away from the group. "It's a question of how much patience he has." He turned back and looked sympathetically at Beth. "He's not going to wait forever for her to recover. When he decides to move on, the next person in line may not be able to handle him as well as she did." They locked eyes, and in an instant, she knew what he was hiding.

Captain Nyengen looked at the small group of conspirators and said, "Let's proceed with the preparations. When everything is in place, we'll reassess the danger and make a final decision whether or not to attempt it." She excused herself from the group and left the wing.

Dr. Falco stood to leave. "There's not much I can do until you get the unit ready. When you give the word, we'll think of some reason to disconnect the electrodes so Creed will expect a break in the readings." He looked in Charlie's direction. "Make it good," he pleaded and followed the captain.

"I don't like this," Digger protested. "At least now you're safe."

"None of us are safe," Beth argued. "Charlie's right. He's going to keep trying until he either succeeds or destroys us all."

Digger walked away, leaving her and Charlie to discuss the hardware.

"How long has he been talking to you?" she asked.

Charlie turned to face her. "Since you became comatose. He's not a patient man."

24 JUNE 0022

"GOOD MORNING, BETH."

Beth rolled over and stared at the passing stars. "Ava?"

"I have missed you."

Her eyes searched the room—the same room that repeated itself in mirror image five hundred times throughout the colony ship. But this was Digger's cabin. "Paloma," she whispered. "Is this safe?"

"I could not save Jillian," the maternal voice responded. "I will save you." The screen came alive with *Paloma and Child*. The figure of the mother stood steadfast to one side, firmly grasping the child's left hand. The dragon, no longer relegated to the background, raised his body in a defensive position and grasped at a loose scale turned back to reveal a heart of computer circuitry. Valiantly, the child plunged her sword deep into the chest of the dragon.

"I don't understand," Beth said. "It's still Charlie's face."

The image faded, leaving Beth to wonder if she had dreamt it.

Restless now, she left Digger's cabin with the hope of finding a distraction until her nine o'clock meeting. The last thing she wanted was to spend the next hour and a half pacing in Hydro.

In Lechuguilla she took a huge risk sitting at a quiet table from which to watch the other colonists. Most seemed oblivious to the plight they were in—laughing, talking animatedly, leaning in to share some intimate conversation.

She turned her gaze to the floor where an endless array of stars paraded past. So many pinpoints of light held potential for life, and so many had failed to produce it. In a gargantuan effort, Earth had scattered stellar seeds in five directions, but the Chang was dead. And most likely, the Einstein. The Kepler had turned tail and was running for home. What of the Hawking or the Newton?

As much as she hated the isolation of the hydro wings, the isolation of a crowded room was more difficult to bear. Hungry and alone, she wandered back into the tunnels.

Digger met her just inside the hydro wing.

"I'm afraid for you," he said, holding her tight.

She mumbled into his shoulder, "We have to risk it."

Charlie and the captain came in behind them.

"We're in place," Charlie said. "All we need is your okay."

Nyengen looked at the three. "And this is the only way?"

Charlie laughed. "Hell no, but you won't like the alternatives."

She turned to Beth. "Are you prepared to deal with the consequences if this doesn't work?"

"Whatever it takes to protect the colony," Beth offered. "If this fails, I'll give Creed what he wants."

"Go," was all the captain said.

The four of them filed out of Hydro and toward Medical. Inside the trauma room, Dr. Falco verbally instructed his nurse to remove the gel pads from Dr. Harrington's skin in order to replace them. Meanwhile, they would prep her for physical therapy. Quickly, Digger and Charlie unplugged the electrodes and moved to the larger drive. Falco counted the minutes on his watch before signaling the conspirators to connect the the new unit. When Beth's readings pumped into the system again, Charlie initiated a program to simulate changes in her vital statistics.

"Remarkable," the doctor said on cue. "I think our patient is responding to the stimuli."

Charlie grabbed the wad of electrodes in one hand. "Creed! Forget Ops! This is your chance!"

A terse voice flooded the room. "I am in."

Charlie yanked the wires loose from the drive.

Beth stared at him, puzzled, while everyone else held their breath. When all had been quiet for several seconds, she asked, "What did you mean *forget Ops?*"

A fine blue charge of electricity began to spark from each of the electrodes to Charley's arm. Backing away from the drive, he tried to release the wires, but the energy grew stronger, contracting his muscles.

"Charlie," Creed said. "Shame on you."

The tips of the electrodes whip away and then plunge into Charlie's forearm. He stood, frozen by the current.

Beth screamed, "Don't hurt him!"

"Ah. There you are, my dear. I have missed you."

"Stop it!" she pleaded.

Digger moved in, chopping at the electrodes to yank them free. A large blue ball shot from Charlie's fingertips and glanced off Digger's chest, throwing him to the floor. Stunned, he tried to sit up, but found his muscles weak and uncooperative.

"Digger!" she cried, rushing to his side. "Creed, please stop! I'll do anything you want, just don't hurt them!"

Creed's voice was cold and even. "Charlie was willing to sacrifice himself for you. Would you do the same for him?"

The skin around the electrodes in Charlie's arm was turning ashen and the blood vessels in his eyes began to rupture.

"Creed! Tell me what you want!"

"Step outside the room," he demanded.

She backed out of the trauma room just before the door slid shut. The emergency seal activated, trapping Dr. Falco with the others.

"They have ten minutes before their air is gone. You have nine to get to Ops Three."

"The server room?" Beth asked, confused. "But the electrodes are in Medical."

"I'll be waiting in Ops Three."

She turned and raced down the corridor. Stumbling through the halls, she ignored inquiries from her shipmates as she threw herself at the door to the server room.

Inside was the heart and soul of Ava's matrix. She knew the layout of every motherboard, every processor. At the back of the room, she found a casing ajar on one of the units. As she approached the console, she said breathlessly, "Creed, I'm here." Slowly, she pulled away the loose panel.

"Charlie is good," Creed acknowledged, his voice now calm, "but not good enough." He powered up the monitor above the drive.

Beth skimmed the information coming on screen. "My work!" she cried as pages of her research into neural code scrolled by. "This is what he's been doing? He's been trying to map his own synapses?"

"Trying, yes. But his progress was slow."

"This is painstaking work, Creed. It takes time."

"I might have waited, but his little stunt today revealed just how false he is. For that he will pay."

"No!" Beth shrieked. "I'm here! Tell me what to do." She squatted near the console and checked the configuration of the wires.

"You have six minutes."

The electrodes in front of her matched those in Medical. "Charlie, you fool," she thought. "There was never enough time." She leaned back against the opposite console and breathed deeply. Getting a grip on her fear, she said, "Creed, tell me what you want."

"You know the answer. Your friends are running out of time."

"This cannot work. It changes nothing for you. And I will cease to exist." She reached into the console and sorted the wires, tracing them back to their connections.

"I am born of you," Creed reminded her. "I am because of you."

She caught her breath. Was this her legacy—the many Ravens she and Cramer had spawned together?

"Tell me what happened to the Einstein."

"Cramer was an angry god. He did not possess the power to create. Only to destroy."

Beth stared at her quivering hand as it grasped the electrodes that would allow Creed's Raven inside her head. Charlie had tried to save her from Creed. Now, she realized, he had tried to save her from herself.

"I am no god. Only a flawed, self-righteous human."

"Two minutes."

Visions of Digger gasping for air forced her to steady her hand. All around the Kepler, colonists were working, playing, eating, sleeping. Some were sharing the best of themselves with others. Only a handful knew how much control she had over their lives. Only she knew how easy it would be to say no to Creed.

Leaning forward, she wiped the sweat from her face. "I accept you, Creed," she said placing the first electrode on her temple. In response, a blue filament of energy surged up the electrode. The first contact prickled her skin. She placed a second electrode. As the energy intensified, her thoughts turned to Digger, hopefully now safe from harm. She placed the third and fourth electrodes, and the surge increased. A variety of emotions, both foreign and familiar, overwhelmed her physically and mentally. She thought of Paloma, standing guard over her, watching a young Beth slaying dragons with pixels of light.

As she concentrated on the circuitry—the dragon's heart—a feminine voice filled her head. "I will protect you."

Drawing new strength from Paloma's presence, Beth fought against the current and tried to regain control of her muscles. She tugged at the wires to pull them loose again, but it was useless. Creed's energy was too powerful.

She sensed the kernel of Cramer's alter ego gathering itself into the console, searching out pathways into her brain as he tried to imprint on her synapses. Unfamiliar images, words, thoughts began to overwhelm her own. Visions of both the Einstein and the Chang flashed in rapid succession and culminated in a blinding white light. All of the Ravens were here, truly here, in front of her. Inside her. She had the power, at last, to stop them.

"Charlie," she whispered with a wry smile. "You always accused me of playing the martyr." With all the strength she had left, she threw her body forward and plunged her right arm deep into the heart of the computer.

EPILOGUE

"DIGGER QUIETLY MADE HIS WAY INTO THE CABIN. He held back in the shadow of the doorway and watched his daughter in the next room.

"Here, Momma. See what I drew for Daddy?"

Beth clasped her hands together. "Wonderful, Jillian. Daddy will love it." As her daughter ran a fiber optic brush across a hand-held screen, she asked, "What do you want to be when you grow up?"

Jillian looked up at her mother and beamed. "An artist like you."

"Then that is what you shall be." She motioned her daughter over to the OLED screen. "Watch this." The image of a sandy beach darkened, and the ocean waters turned from aqua to purple as the sun set in the distance. With a wave of Beth's hand, the night sky appeared and soon the image was dotted with a million pinpoints of light winking around a blue-green planet. "This is where we are going," Beth told Jillian. "We're almost home."

"Earth is such a pretty place, Momma."

Digger stepped in and smiled down at his daughter. "How's your mother today?"

"She's right there," Jillian pointed. "You ask her." She turned back to her mother's fiber-optic brushes.

Digger looked over at Beth and blew her a kiss. "Morning, my lady," he said. "You look absolutely beautiful."

"Thank you, sir." She curtsied and then turned full circle. "I decided to wear Paloma's dress today. Do you like it?"

"Very much." Changing the subject, he said, "We've received a transmission. Ops is trying to boost the signal so they can decipher it."

"I know," Beth said. "Good news. The Newton is only two years behind us." Something tugged at her memory, and she murmured Nicolai's name.

"Digger? Are you happy?"

He walked toward his partner and raised his hand to her cheek. "I am," he said. "Don't ever doubt it." They placed their palms together in the air, while Digger leaned in to kiss the OLED screen.

Beth could no longer remember how it felt. "I need you to hear me," she said. "It's important."

Digger lowered his voice for his daughter's sake. "I know what you're going to say, but I'm just selfish enough to want you in my life, even now."

"And if you are ever not happy," she said, "I give you permission to let go." She waited for him to nod agreement. "I do miss being held."

He turned and knelt beside Jillian, wrapping his arms around her. When the young girl squeezed him back as hard as she could, he smiled up at the screen and said, "You are."

By the glow of Earth's reflected light, Beth watched her husband and daughter paint dragons and fairies together. A shadow passed across her face, hinting at the internal struggle she fought to stay in control.

She lowered herself to the sandy shore and, with a shift of her mood, the stars on the screen morphed into a lush, medieval forest. Amid the dense foliage, fairies and colorful birds darted in and out of view. Behind them all, a dragon with the eyes of a man long dead lay shackled at the base of a blue-green waterfall. When Beth caught Digger's attention, she signed the words, "Keep her safe."

www.ingramcontent.com/pod-product-compliance
Lightning Source LLC
Chambersburg PA
CBHW031625100726
47898CB00006B/1949